mine to lose

mine to lose

a mine to love novel by

T.K. Rapp

mine to lose

by T.K. Rapp

© Copyright Notice

This book is a work of fiction. Names, characters, places and incidents are either product of the author's imagination or are used fictiously. Any resemblance to actual events, places or persons, living or dead, is entirely coincidental.

All rights reserved. This book contains material protected under International and Federal Copyright Laws and Treaties. Any unauthorized reprint or use of this material is prohibited. No part of this book may be reproduced or transmitted in any form or by any means, electronic or mechanical, including photocopying, recording, or by any information storage and retrieval system without express written permission from the author, T.K. Rapp.

Cover Design by Amy Queau - Q Designs

Copyright © 2013 T.K. Rapp

All rights reserved.

ISBN-13: 978-1494909406
ISBN-10: 1494909405

mine to lose

dedication

For my Dixie, the best friend a girl could ask for. I'll miss you sweet pup.

"You don't know who is important to you until you actually lose them."

~Mahatma Gandhi

mine to lose

chapter 1

"I have to go." His voice spikes up in frustration.

"No, Ryan." I spin to face him. "You don't have to do anything, you *want* to go."

"Is that what you really believe?" He sounds shocked by my words, but continues, "I have no choice."

"You have a choice." I throw my hands in the air in exasperation. "We *all* have a choice! You've been looking for any reason to get the hell out of here."

"Last I checked, Em, we have bills to pay, and we aren't exactly in a position for me to walk away from a decent paying job. Besides, this will set me up to get a promotion sooner than if I stayed around here."

When I look at my fiancé, floored at the words that come out of his mouth, the disappointment that I feel in this moment is crushing. Of course, we rely on his income to make ends meet, but to say that he *needs* to leave for work makes me feel as if I don't matter. I can't believe we're in the middle of planning a wedding, and we are already having a huge crisis in our relationship. What does this mean for our marriage? Maybe I'm being dramatic, but it feels like he's bailing on me.

"Ryan, do you understand what this could do to us? Look at us." I wave my hands wildly between us. "This isn't normal. We've only been here nine months; I packed up and followed *you* to Denver. You know how hard it was for me to find a job out here, but I found one, and I love it. It ripped my heart out to leave my mom and my sister behind, but I have finally started to make friends out here and now you want us to pack up our lives and move, again?"

"*Want*? No, I don't *want* to leave." He runs his hand through his hair and tugs before finishing. "But in order to get ahead, I have to move. We have no kids, it's the perfect time to take these chances; I'm doing this for us."

"You're not doing this for us," I scoff in annoyance. "And what about me and my career? Am I supposed to follow you? Are you trying to tell me that my career isn't as important as yours?"

His body rears back, as though I physically slapped him, his brow furrowing at my words. I know that I've hurt him, but I am too upset to care. How did we get here? How did my fiancé, the person I trust most in the world, become a virtual stranger? We've both been so busy at our jobs that I guess we missed the signs. I figured we would have time to sort things out, but the way this conversation is going, I'm not sure there's a way out.

"When they told me about this position I knew you wouldn't be happy with moving, so I looked for other jobs, but there's nothing out there. This economy is shit, and if I walk away now, it could be months before I find something else. I'm not asking you to do anything but understand what I have to do." He walks toward me. "I can't turn this down; it's just another stepping stone to prove to them that this is where I want to be."

"Well, while you're proving to them where you want to be, you're showing me where you *don't* want to be. Here--with me."

"Damn it, Em, stop it!"

"Stop what? Questioning you? What you're doing to us? I'm sorry, I thought that this was *our* relationship!" I can't help the rise in my voice. "This is *our* life you are messing with; do you get that?"

"God! Why are you making this about us? This is for my career," he counters, defeat evident in his voice.

"If you don't realize that this is about us, then this whole thing is far worse than I ever imagined." My eyes sting with unshed tears, but I refuse to let them escape.

Ryan reaches out for me, but I shake my head and step away from him. "Stop. Just leave me alone. Believe it or not, I understand where you're coming from. But the fact that *I* don't even factor into your decision says more than you'll ever know." I choke out my thoughts past the lump in my throat. He's ripping out my heart, and I don't care to try to hide it. As much as I want to give him the benefit of the doubt, *doubt* is all I seem to have in me.

"You know you are the most important thing to me." He tries desperately to explain, reaching out for me again, but I don't want to hear it.

"There was a time that I wouldn't have ever questioned that, but that was before you started putting your career first. You took the job without even talking to me. What am I supposed to think?" I constantly move around the small living room to avoid looking at him.

"So what are you trying to say?"

"I'm not saying anything, Ryan. You have said everything there is to say, haven't you?" I let my eyes meet his and gaze upon him with a blank stare. It's a look I have mastered in the last couple of months. "I think you need to go."

He shakes his head in disbelief. "What? Are you serious right now?" His annoyed glare lands on mine. "Where am I supposed to go, *Emogen*? This is our home."

"If you're not leaving, then I will," I say flatly. I make a show of heading to our room with every intention of grabbing my things. I don't know where I'll go, and I sound immature, but my heart aches at what's taking place right now. He heads to our room and blocks my path, preventing me from leaving.

The silence is palpable as we stand, staring each other down. I'm not sure which of us just won this argument, but I'm pretty sure that it was neither. He waits for me to crack, like I always do, but after a minute, he scoffs before stepping aside. "Fine, I'll call Dean."

I walk to the couch and throw myself into my usual spot in a huff before grabbing one of the throw pillows. He's going to Dean's place, and as much as I like his friend, the guy's a ladies man, always partying and bringing home different women.

I rest my chin on my hand that hugs the pillow and try to think of something to say. *Do I want to take back everything I've said?* Not really, because it feels as if he's putting me last. *But do I want him to leave?* Of course not. This is Ryan, the man I love, and the man I plan to marry. And as much as I don't want him living the bachelor life with Dean tonight, I don't want him here either.

The lump in my throat grows larger when he emerges from the room with a duffle bag in hand. Tears continue to form in my eyes and my nose burns as I try to fight the emotions that want to be set free. Seeing him, still so handsome but determined to win, almost destroys me. It would be easy to give in to him, but if I give in now, I'll be giving in for the rest of my life. I'm too stubborn to stand and stop him or to even say goodbye.

He walks over and stands near me, but I stare at a small clump of lint on the wood floor under the entertainment center. I hold my gaze to it, as if it alone can save me. If I look at him, I'll cry; if I speak, my voice will give me away. I hear him sigh heavily before he leans down to kiss my cheek. Apparently that's when my body decides to react. I pull away, just as I feel his breath near. His sharp intake of air lets me know that he's hurt. I feel a silent delight knowing that I've hurt him, because he's just ripped my heart out.

"I'll see you later, Em," he says while walking to the door. I hear him stop, and I can only assume he looks back at me. "This isn't what I want."

When I turn my head to look at him, all I see is the door closing behind him, and then the tears spill out. I stay glued to the couch for at least an hour, trying to determine if I will ever get up.

* * *

I cried all night, so I doubt that I look my normal, put-together self. I think I finally fell asleep sometime after three in the morning, which means I only got two hours of sleep before my alarm woke me up. When I look at my appearance in the mirror, all I can see are the bags under my eyes. I shouldn't have those at twenty-two, at least I assume I shouldn't. When I get to the office, I fill my mug with coffee before retreating to my desk to hide away in my work for the day.

"Hey," Cam exclaims from her desk nearby, "we still on for lunch today?"

Crap! I forgot we're supposed to go out; I don't feel like putting on a happy face for anyone. "Cam, can we do it another day? I'm not really up for it," I say, moving papers around my desk to act swamped with work.

I've only been working for six months, but in the short time I've been here, I've come to consider Cam a good friend. Good enough to read me better than most people who've known me my whole life. She walks over to me and without skipping a beat replies, "No, we're going today. But I think you need to vent." She looks at me with wide eyes, waiting for a response. "M'Kay?"

I smile, thankful that she is willing to put up with me, and even though I don't want to go, it might be exactly what I need. "Yeah Cam, sounds good."

When eleven thirty rolls around, Cam's almost too eager to get me out, no doubt because she wants to know what's going on. She practically packs my office up for me to get me out quicker. "C'mon, we only have forty-five minutes, and something tells me we'll need every second of that."

"You have no idea," I mutter under my breath.

Lucky for me, Cam picks the deli down the road and finds an empty table in the back. She heads to the counter to order our usual and I sit, numb and disinterested in anything else around me. When she takes her seat across from me, she stares at me in silence, and I appreciate that she doesn't push me to talk. At least not before I'm ready.

"Ryan left," I finally admit, once the silence has gone on too long. The moment the words come out, I bury my face in my hands and start crying all over again. Saying the words out loud causes a stabbing pain in my heart, which only makes me cry harder.

"He what?" I look up to see her face stunned by my confession.

"Left," I answer. "My fiancé left."

"Hold on." She puts her hands on top of mine. "What happened?"

"Ryan was offered a position in California for the next year, and he accepted without so much as a conversation about it with me. So I told him he needed to leave."

"But why? What's going on?"

I start from the beginning and tell her that he has a job opportunity that he says he needs to take for his career. I explain that we had a huge fight because he accepted and expects me to follow. When I finish talking, Cam leans back in her chair and looks as exhausted as I feel. I don't know why I unloaded everything on her, but since I moved from my family in Utah, I don't have anyone close by to talk to besides my best friend, Joss.

Cam remains quiet for a while, picking at her paper napkin on the table, and I'm not sure what she's going to say. I do know when someone stays silent for this long it's usually because they don't know how you're going to take what they say.

"I've never met Ryan." She raises her eyebrows, asking for some leeway before continuing. "And it doesn't sound like he really wanted to 'leave,'" she says with air quotes. "But it seems to me that you two are on different paths. You're getting married in, what, a year?" I nod before she finishes. "Did you two talk about what you wanted? Long-term?"

I try to think back, but I don't know that we did talk about these things. However, my embarrassment keeps me from admitting that truth. "Of course we talked. But things change, I guess."

"Does that happen often? Things changing?" I know that she sees through my lie, and I look down at my hands that are clasped between my knees.

I shake my head before making eye contact with my friend. "No." I'm barely able to whisper.

She leans over and reaches for my hand, so I release it from my own before giving it to her. "What do you want, Em?" I hear the sympathy in her voice and my heart swells.

"I want Ryan," I answer simply.

"But why? Why do you want Ryan? Is it him? Or the idea of him?"

"It's all the same thing, isn't it?"

She shakes her head. "No. It isn't. So maybe you need to figure out why you fell for him in the first place."

We sit in silence for what seems an eternity when the waitress brings our orders. She sets the plates on the table and leaves me mulling over Cam's question. *Why did I fall for Ryan?*

Before I can answer, she hits me with another question. "How did you and Ryan even meet?"

I don't even try to contain the smile that creeps onto my face. Three years ago, the first time I laid eyes on Ryan, I fell in lust.

chapter 2 ~ *3 years ago*

It was early fall and I had arrived at campus early for a nine a.m. class. I had seen him in passing on more than one occasion, but never had the chance to talk to him. That's probably because I was scared easily. As I sat in my car, I began to read over the notes for my next class. I was trying to study for my exam but I had to admit he was nice a distraction. He was sitting in a dirty red Jeep with the windows down, and he looked to be sleeping, or maybe he was just listening to the music. I couldn't tell because of the sunglasses he was wearing.

I took the chance to ogle what I could of his handsome face, noting his chiseled jaw and full lips. He had the seat leaned back and his arms were crossed over his chest. He was relaxed and sexy and I wanted to know him. What color were his eyes? What did he do for fun? Did he have a girlfriend?

Was he smirking?

His messy brown hair ruffled slightly and he turned his head in my direction and flashed a crooked smile. I couldn't tear my eyes away fast enough as I tried so hard to play it off, looking around for a ghost of sorts, but failed. He knew I was looking at him, and maybe he knew the whole time, but I couldn't tell through the sunglasses.

I turned my radio up and tried to ignore what had just happened, but every time I thought about it, my cheeks would burn again.

"Stupid!" I muttered to myself. "What were you thinking?"

I grabbed my cell phone off the console in my car and dialed a number, any number, as fast as I could.

"Hello?" my roommate answered, and it was clear that I had woken her up.

"Hey, Joss. Sorry to wake you." I felt bad for calling, but I knew she'd understand. "I just made an ass outta myself, and the guy is still nearby. I just need to look busy." As I finished telling her, I peeked in his direction, only to see that he was no longer sitting in his car. I closed my eyes in relief, my embarrassment quelled.

"So he was hot?" she asked, and I was so glad to have her back me up.

"Yeah. Very hot," I buzzed, "but he's gone now. I'm sorry I woke you up; go back to sleep."

"Hot guy?" She paused for a moment and laughed. "You can wake me up anytime."

I looked at the clock on my radio and realized I only had thirty minutes to get to class. I started gathering my things together, but all I could picture was the handsome guy, resting in his Jeep. He had scruff on his chiseled jaw, as if he hadn't shaved that morning. It was sexy. His brown hair was messy, but I couldn't help think that it was all well planned. The only thing I didn't get to see were his eyes, because they were hidden behind his sunglasses. But by the way the rest of him looked, I was sure he had to have gorgeous eyes. I felt a sudden urgency not to let the opportunity slip away, so I pulled out a sheet of paper from my bag and scrawled a note.

I was the girl in the black Acura. Sorry I stared, but I thought you were sexy. Just wanted to tell you.

I folded the note and grabbed the rest of my things before getting out of the car. I looked around to make sure he wasn't nearby, and when I didn't see him, I wedged the note in his car door and headed to class.

That afternoon, after spending all day on campus, I was more than ready to get home, relax, and catch up on some of my shows. I had already forgotten the earlier incident in the parking lot, so when I opened my door and a note fell to the ground, a smile broke out.

I thought you were cute, too. Call me sometime. 435-555-8383.

~Ryan (guy in the Jeep)

I didn't even think to leave my name or number, the only thought I had was, *there is a guy, he's hot, and I'm going to tell him*. Yet, there I stood with a note in my hand from said guy, realizing he had placed the ball in my court. I looked around to see if he was still there somewhere, but he wasn't, and butterflies instantly filled my stomach. The huge grin that spread across my face could not be contained and all I could think about was how I was going to proceed. *Do I call him? When do I call him? Does he really want me to call him?*

I spent the afternoon mulling over my next step, and I decided to talk to Joss to get her opinion. Of course, she informed me that I *needed* to wait the obligatory three days before calling him so that I didn't appear too eager. However, I *was* eager. I tucked the number away somewhere safe so I wouldn't slip up and call. School kept me distracted and soon assignments and studying had me so busy that three days turned to four. Before I knew it, a week had passed and I had lost his number. I turned my room inside out trying to find it, with no luck. I could have kicked my own ass. *Why didn't I leave it somewhere obvious?* I had finally gotten up the nerve to approach a really hot guy, and I no longer had any way to contact him.

I realized there must be some reason I had lost his number, so I just had to suck it up and stop worrying about it. Even though I told myself that, I would still get butterflies when I saw him walking across campus.

It wasn't often, but when I did, I would notice the confident strides he took as he walked toward wherever he was going.

He never walked with anyone, especially any girls, so I held out hope that maybe he was still single. Something about him drew me in every time, and I would just stare until he was no longer visible. Joss caught me gawking one day. "Creeper."

"Where?" I asked, snapped out of my daze. I started looking around to see whom she was talking about.

"Next to me," she whispered conspiratorially. I tried looking past her, and she widened her eyes until it clicked that she was referring to me. I gave her a playful shove and she laughed at me. "Why don't you just go talk to him? Tell him you lost his number."

"Yeah, and why don't I look pathetic in the process," I said under my breath.

"You don't think you look pathetic right now?" she pointed out with a teasing laugh, as only Joss would do.

"I'm late, I gotta get to class." I grabbed my bag from the ground and headed off before my best friend could say any more about it.

* * *

It wasn't until two weeks later, when Joss was dragging me to some kegger at her boyfriend's frat house that I got my chance to see him again. I didn't want to go, but she begged, and I could never turn her down.

"What am I supposed to wear?" I asked.

"Just wear jeans. It's nothing special. We're just gonna hang out and drink all night." She smiled mischievously.

With her instructions in mind, I grabbed my worn out jeans that were faded and ripped at the ankles. They were a little long on my five foot seven frame, but they fit perfect everywhere else. I figured a t-shirt would be more than fitting for an outside thing, so I pulled on a concert tee from the previous year, pulled my wavy blonde hair into a loose bun and told her I was ready to go. When we got out to the field, the crisp night breeze and the smell of smoke in the distance from the tiny fire filled the air and I was glad I brought a sweatshirt.

Joss went to go find her boyfriend, Mason, and left me to fend for myself. I knew most of the people there, anyway, so I wasn't uncomfortable. I made the rounds saying hello to everyone, and that's when I spotted Ryan, in his Jeep, *again*. He looked like he would rather be any place but that field and I was strangely offended by that idea. I laughed to myself because, even though I didn't know the guy, I *wanted* to know him. That was enough to propel me to do the second craziest thing I had ever done.

Since I was the designated driver that night, I didn't get a shot of liquid courage to help me out. It had been two weeks since I left that note on his Jeep, and I still thought about him. I knew that I would regret it if I didn't take advantage of him being alone, so I hopped into Joss' pickup to check my makeup in the visor. I gave myself a mental pep talk and when I had myself fooled, walked toward him. I radiated confidence, which I really didn't have, and looked directly at him as I approached.

I watched him playing with his phone, the screen making his face glow when he glanced up for a moment. I was unsure if he had noticed me walking to him, and I was okay with that. I strode to the driver's side of his truck and took a deep breath before speaking.

"You gonna sit in there all night?"

He seemed startled by my presence, I guess he really didn't see me coming. "I'm sorry?"

I smiled and repeated my question before adding, "Do you want some company?"

"Oh, yeah, sorry. I was just getting ready to head out."

My ego was deflated. All of that prep and determination to finally talk to him went up in smoke. I nodded and turned my back to rejoin the party when he continued. "Want a ride?"

I turned back to face him and he was wearing a playful grin as I heard the door click to unlock. I tried to act unaffected as I shrugged my shoulders, "Okay."

Disappointment hit when I remembered that I was the one responsible for Joss that night, but I still wanted to go with him. I sent her a quick text to let her know I was leaving.

Me: Hey. I'm going somewhere with Ryan. Eek! Ok?

Joss: Np. Call if you need anything.

Me: You ok to get home?

Joss: I'll call a cab if I need a ride.

I tucked my phone in my back pocket and started to walk around his Jeep, taking my time. He was opening his door when I looked over at him and must have had a confused look on my face. He shrugged. "Thought I'd open the door for ya." I was taken aback, not even my previous boyfriend that I dated for six months ever opened a door for me. I wasn't looking for chivalry, but he was offering, so I smiled in appreciation.

As I followed behind him, I took the opportunity to look him over. He towered over my small frame; I assumed he was easily six feet tall. He was wearing worn out jeans that were ripped at the bottom--just like mine, and a frat t-shirt, but I didn't know which one. I liked the casual appearance he pulled off, which was of the *I don't give a fuck* variety. When he opened the door, as I walked around him, I could smell his cologne that smelled of musk and mint, and when mixed with the night air, was perfect.

I suddenly realized that we had never actually met, even though it was apparent that we had some mutual friends. I couldn't help but wonder how many times we had both been to one of these things and had never bumped into each other before. "Emogen," I said as I stuck my hand out in greeting.

"Ryan," he returned, his hand swallowing mine. It was strong and warm and caused tingles in the pit of my stomach.

"Yeah." I nodded as I climbed in to the passenger seat. "I remember from your note." I smiled.

He looked at me bemused before it clicked. "You never called me."

"I lost your number."

He smiled and closed the door. When he got into the driver's seat he raised his brows in question. "Where to?"

"I don't have anywhere to be," I started, when I realized he might have other plans. "Unless you just wanted to be alone."

"Nah, I've been alone long enough. You hungry?"

"I could eat," I offered.

"Don't tell me you're one of those girls who doesn't really eat anything but salads," he teased, squinting his eyes as if judging me.

I pursed my lips and pretended to think for a moment. "No, it costs a little more to feed me. I'm a burgers and steak kind of girl."

"Great! Buckle up," he ordered as he started the engine. He looked over at me. "I know the perfect place."

The drive to the Shack was short, so it was easy to find things to talk about. "So what frat are you in?"

"What fra-?" He looked down at his shirt and threw his head back with a light laugh. "This isn't mine. It's hard to find clean clothes when you live with two other guys, so I grabbed the first shirt in the laundry room that smelled clean." I let out a relieved sigh and he jumped on that. "What was that? You don't have a problem with frat guys do you?"

"Not really." I covered my face with my hands, embarrassed that he caught me. "I just tend to think most of them are assy."

He turned a curious look at me and gave the most breathtaking grin. "Assy, huh?"

"Yeah, at least according to my friends."

He didn't push any further because we finally arrived at the hamburger joint. I had never been there before, and I could see why. It was a tiny hole-in-the-wall that looked pretty sketchy, but it was packed, so I figured it must be okay. Ryan came around to the passenger side to open the door for me again. He must have seen the look on my face because he leaned down and whispered in my ear, "Try it before you make any assumptions." His breath against my ear caused the hair on my arms to rise, and I knew then that I was putty in his hands.

He closed the door behind me when I climbed out and placed his hand on the small of my back, guiding me to the front door. The action wasn't territorial, or even sexual in nature, but it was strong and comforting. He held the door open and the rustic interior was only overshadowed by the scary exterior. We found a table in the back and sat down across from each other. Ryan handed me a menu, and we sat in comfortable silence as we decided what to order. I had never felt so at ease with a guy before, but he felt familiar, even though we had just met.

We placed our orders and started talking about the obligatory 'what's your major, where are you from' questions. From that short conversation I learned that Ryan was in his first year of grad school and was originally from the East Coast, where his family still lived. I was barely twenty, and there he was, almost twenty-three with an undergrad degree and working on his master's. Needless to say, the guy was even better once I got to know him. He was easy to talk to, until he wasn't.

"So I guess, since you're here with me, you're not seeing anyone." It wasn't a question, more of an observation that made him appear a bit too cocky for my liking.

"Seeing multiple someones," I lied. He nodded, impressed with my response. "And what about you?" I continued, "I could assume the same."

"Just ended something a few weeks ago." He shrugged. I could tell that whoever it was, and however it had ended, hurt him, or at least kept him from being open to something else.

"Sorry to hear that." I don't know where my next words came from, but I think they shocked him as much as they did me. "Well, sorry for you, but kinda happy for me."

A burst of laughter erupted and he shook his head in disbelief. "You're a little surprising, Em."

I returned his smile, loving that he just gave me a nickname. Granted, it wasn't anything I hadn't been called before, but Ryan calling me Em felt right.

The rest of the night flowed and was relaxed, filled with easy conversation and witty banter. I didn't ask about his ex because I really didn't care. All that mattered to me was that he was smart, single, funny and very sexy. We talked for what seemed hours about everything and yet, I still wanted to know more. But when a yawn escaped me, he paid our tab and we walked back out to his Jeep where he opened the car door.

Right before shutting the door, he furrowed his brow like he was gauging his next sentence, and cocked his head to the side. Finally, he flashed a crooked grin. "I'd like to take you out again sometime."

I was doing a happy dance inside, bells and whistles were going off in my head, but I kept my composure and played it cool. After all, I was the one who approached him with confidence earlier. I returned his smile with my own coy version. "We'll see."

I was surprised when we drove back out to the place where our friends were still hanging out. We both got out of his Jeep and met at the front, standing there with his headlights shining on the bonfire in the middle of the field. There was music blaring from someone's radio as laughter filled the air, and it felt like anything was possible. Ryan reached his hand out for mine, and of course I gave it to him. He pulled me close and started two stepping to whatever song was playing, and I followed, happy to be in his arms. I didn't care that I might look like a lovesick girl with my arm draped over his shoulder, his hand around my waist and his other hand holding mine close to his heart. It was perfection. I closed my eyes and did everything I could to seal the moment in my memory. I knew then that the real Ryan was so much better than the Ryan I created in my head weeks ago.

After that night, we were inseparable. We were together every night, either to study or to go out on a date. I fell hard and fast for Ryan Tate, but he owned my heart the moment he called me Em.

chapter 3

I've never understood how people can go through so much crap in their personal lives, but check it all at the door when it comes to work. I understand it now, because that's what I've had to do since our fight last night, and I'm not sure how much longer I can keep up appearances.

"Cam," I call over to her desk. "I'm meeting Joss later for dinner. You up for it?"

"Any word from Ryan," she asks, but I shrug as if I don't care. "Have you called him?"

As if on cue, my phone rings next to me, and without looking, I know it's him. I can tell by the ringtone that I made just for him from *our* song. I flip the phone to silent, intent on ignoring the call. I feel my cheeks flame when I look up to see Cam looking at me with raised eyebrows because she heard it too. She shakes her head, silently reprimanding me, as she looks down at whatever she was working on before I interrupted her. I do feel guilty for not answering, but I've already brought enough drama from home with me. I refuse to leave today in tears.

Elle, the owner of Elle E. Grant Events, is a great boss, and I've been able to make a name for myself rather fast under her instruction. If I start letting personal crap invade my work, I'm just asking for problems. Between Elle and Cam, this place is my dream job, hence why I'm so intent on staying for a while.

Cam's been here for about a year, and she was tasked with showing me around the office and filling me in on client protocol when I started work here six months ago. Before I got this job, I had never worked in an office setting, and I figured it was going to be cutthroat, but it's not. I'm so glad I have Cam, except when she gives me *that* look.

"I'll call him in a little while," I say somewhat defensively as I silence the phone and shove it in my drawer. "I promise."

She doesn't say anything, but her silence speaks volumes. I get back to working on the T.M. Enterprise event so I don't have to feel guilty. I've done a ton of research on what this corporation does, as well as what their past events have been like. The last few nights, work has come home with me while I sit at my computer to find out more. This is the first client that Elle has let me take on alone. It's not her biggest client, but like she says, 'there are no small clients.' Unfortunately, for the last few days, my point of contact has been a little hard to get a hold of, and I've decided that I might just have to go to the owner. It's not something that Elle encourages, but when there is a job to do, and deadlines that need to be met, you do what you have to do.

I hit print on some forms that I need and I'm about to ask Cam for the owner's contact information, but when I swivel in my chair, she is standing right next to me with a sympathetic look. "I'm not trying to give you a hard time about Ryan. It's none of my business."

"It's fine." I give her a fleeting smile. "I appreciate your concern."

I'm not the hugging type, so as I push myself out of my chair to go to get my copies from the printer, I'm surprised when she throws her arms around my neck.

I don't want to cry, but this small gesture causes me to choke back a sob.

"It's gonna be okay," she whispers so no one can hear. I nod in agreement, and the tears sting my eyes. I exhale a controlled breath, hoping that the tears dissipate before anyone notices.

"See?" I swipe my eyes with the tips of my fingers to dispel any evidence of emotion. "This is why I need to go out."

"I can't go tonight, but promise me that you'll call if you need anything?"

"I promise." I put my hand up to swear. Desperate to divert the attention off of me, I get back to the matter at hand. "Before I leave, I need to get the contact info for Mr. Miller at T.M. Enterprises. Do you happen to have that? Sandy isn't returning my calls or emails, and there are some decisions that need to be made soon."

Cam goes to her desk and pulls up the information. "His name is Trey Miller; I'm emailing his contact information to you now." I give her my best smile and get back to finishing up my day.

My desk is in order, and I've gotten everything together that I need to take home. I'll have to work from home this weekend, because there is so much that still needs to be done. I'm not sure *what* I'll get done, but hopefully I can at least send an email to Mr. Miller before I go out with Joss tonight. I stop by Cam's desk one last time to see if she can join us, but she says she has plans, so I let it go. I don't think she has plans, but at the same time, I think she would rather be alone than be anywhere near me and my crazy.

The entire drive home I think about what I want to say to Ryan, but I can't formulate a single coherent thought. All along it's been me who has taken the steps to keep us together, and I'm tired of it. I want to scream and yell, I want to cry and hit something. But all of the rational parts of me remind me that there is only one way to handle this. *Take a stand.* I start to give myself a pep talk that I'm not going to be pushed around and what I might say once I see him. When I get to our apartment parking space, I notice that Ryan isn't home, and I breathe a sigh of relief. Our fight will wait until later.

When I walk in the door, I expect to find it as I left it this morning but something feels off, out of place. When I close the door behind me, I drop my bag on the couch and go to our bedroom to change into some comfortable clothes. I slip my dress off and pull on a tank and yoga pants before going to the bathroom to wash the makeup off my face. As I dab my face dry with the hand towel on my side of the vanity, I notice it. It's small, but it's missing. *Ryan's razor is gone.*

I start to look around to see what else is out of place. His side of the closet has less clothes, so I look for the other duffle bag that he reserves for his camping trips, only to discover that it's gone, too.

"What's going on?" I start talking to myself, realizing I'm about to have a full-blown panic attack. I walk to his side of the bed and the book he is reading is still there, but his phone charger is gone. My purse is on the couch, so I walk out there to grab my cell phone to call him, but I'm stopped in my tracks when I see an envelope sitting on the counter. I creep to the letter and eye it as if it has the ability to attack me. *'Emogen,'* is written on it, in Ryan's handwriting, and I find it hard to bring myself to open it.

I smack the letter against my hand, trying to prepare myself for the contents. "A letter?" I ask of no one, since I'm alone. The couch is my favorite spot in the apartment, so I sit at the edge and imagine what his words say. *I'm leaving you. I don't love you anymore. I made a mistake.* I could sit here all night and conjure up the worst, but I have the words already in my hands.

Em,

Don't freak out but I came by earlier and packed some things up. I'm staying at Dean's place because I think we need some space. I tried to call you earlier, but you never answered. You said you need time to think.

I'm not sure what that means, but it makes me think that I need to do the same. You are making this a bigger deal than it needs to be. But at some point, we do need to talk, so call me when you're ready.

Ry

Ry? He just signed his name? No, *"love Ry,"* nothing? Just his name. I am so angry I can't see straight. I won't give him the satisfaction of a phone call - not now, maybe not ever. He has the nerve to write me a damn note to say he's gone.

I slide my finger across my phone screen and immediately find the number, among my favorites, that I want to call.

"Hello?"

"Joss, it's me," I say in a rushed tone.

"Of course it's you," she grumbles. "I see your name. What's up? Still want to get something to eat?"

"No, I need to go out, I need to drink."

"What's going on?" Her voice goes from fun to concern. I haven't gotten to tell her about our fight yet, which is why we are going out for dinner, so we can talk.

"Ryan left," I say in a low monotone. It's not even the truth; at least it's not the truth, *yet*.

"Be there in ten." She doesn't say goodbye because she knows I mean business. I should feel bad for not telling her the whole story and letting her worry, but he did just leave me a *note*.

I'm so angry and I don't think that my typically modest attire will suffice. I hurry to my closet and search for the skimpiest dress in my possession. When I find what I'm looking for, it's so far in the back I'm afraid if I blow on it, dust might actually fly off of it. I change out of my comfy cloths and slip into the sexy purple off the shoulder dress that I haven't worn since college. It is one of Ryan's favorites; maybe someone else will like it, too.

I'm looking for trouble.

I look down at my hand and eye the ring, a promise that we made to each other. The hurt I feel is greater than my desire to wear something that I'm not sure represents the original promise. The ring has taken up residence on my finger for over a year, so when I take it off, the white line shows the remnants of what once was. There's a light knock at the door that startles me out of my ring-induced trance, so I finish touching up my makeup before answering.

I am expecting Joss, so seeing Ryan standing in the threshold surprises me. The look on his face goes from neutral to shock-filled in less than a second, and I beam inside, knowing that he might be pissed.

"What are you doing here?" I ask, annoyed.

"I thought we could talk." Confusion laces his tone.

"I think you said everything you needed to say in your *note*," I bite out. "Besides, you told me to call when I'm ready, and well, I guess I'm *not* ready. In fact, I have plans." Before I can elaborate, Joss walks in, sees the two of us in a standoff, and starts to back away.

"Hey, Joss." I call to her, from around Ryan in a chipper tone. "I'll be ready in five." She nods her head, but looks as though she might not be around in five minutes because she wants to bolt.

"Em," he says my name in a warning tone. "We need to talk."

"You're right, we do, but I guess this is how things will work now. We just do whatever the fuck we want without consulting each other." I grab my purse and walk past him, but stop at the still opened door. "And like I said, I have plans." I turn to leave and shut the door behind me, but the moment I'm outside, I feel my legs tremble. I worry that I just made a big mistake.

Joss turns to me as I catch up to her on the stairs. "Care to tell me what that was about?"

"Just get in the car. I don't care where we go, I'll tell you about it when we get there."

* * *

After going to her apartment and filling Joss in on everything that has happened in the last twenty-four hours, she agrees that I need to get out and unwind. I haven't been to a club in a while, and the last time I went, Ryan was with me.

Ryan.

I try to turn off all thoughts of Ryan and enjoy the night, but I know that's not going to be an easy thing to do.

We get to the club and with every drink I have, my moves become looser and I become less inhibited. And with every drink, I know that tomorrow I'm going to regret tonight. Joss and I remain on the dance floor for what seems like hours, dancing to song after song. I find myself missing my engagement ring, if for no other reason than to keep the guys at bay. They're bringing us drinks, and we accept with a smile before turning our backs and ignoring them for the rest of the night. Most of the guys seem to take it in stride, but there are a few who are insistent on dancing with us. I politely turn them down, and eventually they walk away. Some leave with a *"Bitch"* remark, while others give us dirty looks before finding someone else.

Joss yells to me, over the blaring music, that she is heading to the restroom. I nod, opting to remain on the dance floor. I'm swaying to the music, enjoying the energy, when a pair of hands find the sides of my rib cage and graze their way down my side and stop at my hips. The motion is swift, seductive, and unwelcome. I spin, in a hurry, on my heels to push the groper way. When I do, I look up to see my fiancé with a serious look on his face waiting for a reaction.

"What in the hell are you doing here?" I yell over the music.

"So you just let guys touch you?" The disappointment in his question tugs at my heart, but his question doesn't deserve an explanation. I shove past him and walk away. Of course he's not one to let it go, and I know he is stalking behind me. I get to the table and set my clutch on the top so I can try to get the attention of a bartender.

"You won't talk to me, but you'll go to a club and dance with strangers?" He glares at me, and I counter with my own annoyed stare, but he continues, "I don't get you."

I'm normally very good at giving the cold shoulder, but the cocktails that I've had have me loose lipped. "Ryan, you left."

"You told me to leave! Hell, you said if I didn't go, you were. All we've done this week is fight."

"So you run away?" I ask. My voice is raised, only so he can hear me over the music.

He opens his mouth to respond but stops short when he looks over my shoulder. His look is murderous, so I turn to follow his stare to see a man standing behind me. *Walk away*, I think to myself.

The guy looks down at me, never making eye contact with Ryan, "You okay?"

"She's fine," Ryan answers for me and I turn to him. "My *wife* and I were just leaving."

I smirk at Ryan and his use of the term "wife" before turning to see my would-be hero. He's attractive. In fact, he looks like Joss' type, but I'm not looking for someone to save me.

Hero-guy narrows his eyes, assessing me, as if making mental notes about my condition and I feel self-conscious under his stare. He pulls his eyes away from mine and looks directly at Ryan. "I don't care if she's your wife, you need back off. I was talking to her." His voice is calm and strong, like he's someone who doesn't take shit from anyone.

I blink in shock over his words to Ryan, who looks like he's about to blow up. I give hero-guy a tight smile and nod that I am okay, but he doesn't look completely convinced. He cocks his head and drops it a fraction lower, silently questioning before he walks away. Part of me is grateful to see Ryan act out of sorts. But the other part of me is annoyed, because being the jealous guy isn't his thing and now is the wrong time to start displaying his tough-guy act.

"Ryan, I am not leaving with you. I'm here with Joss," I inform him, but I realize that Joss hasn't returned from the restroom. I start turning my head in that direction to see if I can spot her.

"She called me," he states, answering my unasked question, clearly annoyed. "That's why I'm here. She told me where y'all were, along with some other slurred things I couldn't make out, but they sounded mean as hell."

My best friend drunk-dialed my boyfriend, who I am not speaking to at the moment? I'm irritated and the room is spinning, but I need to find Joss. "Where is she?"

"I saw her near the front and told her to wait for me." He grabs my clutch and reaches for my hand, which I impulsively pull away. "Let's go."

"Fine," I answer tersely.

I don't let him put his arm around me. I don't let him hold my hand. In fact, I don't let him walk behind me. I will not give him the satisfaction of controlling this situation. I follow him out of the bar and out to his car that's parked in the side lot. I guess we'll just come back for Joss' car tomorrow. My friend looks in too bad of shape for me to be angry with her, so I quietly climb into the passenger side of his Jeep.

The entire ride to Joss' place, I stare out the window and look at the buildings we pass along the way. I know I'm drunk, but the gravity of what's happening in our relationship has me sobering up. I don't bother to look at Ryan because either I will speak first and say something stupid, or *he* won't say anything at all. This is one fight I don't want to lose, but if I'm not receptive to a conversation, the only thing I'm going to lose is the love of my life.

We arrive in front of her building and Ryan gets out to help her inside. Joss clambers out from behind me, and as she turns to shut the door she gives me an apologetic smile that is easy for me to return. I love my best friend, and although I don't know what her motives for calling him are, I know it wasn't malicious.

"Call you tomorrow," I tell her as she walks to the entrance of the building. She looks over her shoulder when she gets to the door and offers a sloppy wave before shutting the door behind her. Ryan gets in and starts off for home without another word.

The ride home is silent except for the ringing in my ears from the loud music in the club. I don't feel the urge to bother with conversation and I guess Ryan doesn't either, because he turns up the volume on the radio and never takes his eyes off the road. When we finally get to our place, I just about bolt out of the Jeep and head to the entrance, with my key in hand. I hear him behind me, but I increase my pace until I am at the door. I push the key into the lock, open the door and toss my clutch onto the counter before flinging the door shut. But it never shuts because Ryan catches it before it has a chance.

"Ryan." I turn to face him to question his presence, but I don't get the chance as he grabs me and his lips land on mine. My hands instinctively move around his neck as he continues to kiss me. But as reality hits, I struggle in his grasp before I finally pull my face back from his. "You need to go," I plead as the room spins and I'm not sure if it's the kiss, or the numerous drinks I've downed. I'm breathless and not at all sincere when I push him away. His movements are slow and gentle as he kisses a trail from my cheek down to the base of my neck. I could get lost in this moment- in him. I want this and the simplicity of the moment. But then I recall his note, and it's the cold shower I need. "You need to go," I repeat.

"No," he says, as he finally loosens his grip on my waist. "You told me to leave last night, and I did. I don't think we are better for it."

"Well, I'm not the one who packed a bag today," I remind him.

"We have some things to talk about," he says. "Like, what was tha-"

"Hold that thought," I interrupt, rushing to get to the bathroom, fighting a sudden wave of nausea.

I empty the contents of my stomach not once, but three times, before finally passing out. I wish the night had ended differently; perhaps with me making love to my fiancé, who will soon be leaving for another state.

chapter 4

After Ryan left the other night, I had nothing but time on my hands to think. Sometimes, when you say something before you can stop yourself, all you have is regret. I didn't really want him to leave, but I was so pissed, and letting him see how upset I was went against everything inside of me.

Waking up, not sure where Ryan was, I am shocked to find him on the couch. It leaves me feeling uncomfortable. I know that I acted like an ass last night, but in my inebriated state, I really didn't care. In the light of day, I cringe. I know he will be expecting for us to talk, but I'd rather sleep off my hangover.

I finally get up to the smell of coffee brewing and clattering coming from the kitchen. When I move to sit up, I realize that I'm still wearing my black bra and panties from last night. Ryan's watch is on his side of the bed and for a moment, I feel like everything is normal. I wish this feeling could stay forever. *Minus* the raging hangover. A buzzing noise sounds from somewhere in the room and I begin searching for the source. Feeling around and listening to the buzz, I drop to my knees to find my phone hidden beneath my bed. I can only imagine how it ended up there. When I look at the screen, there are a few texts from Joss and Cam.

Joss: Are you pissed at me?

Cam: What the hell happened? Why did you call me at 2 am?

I feel guilty for bothering Cam. I'm not sure why I called her last night, but since Ryan is here, I'm pretty sure I can guess. I send them both texts to let them know I'll call later before tossing my phone aside. I gather the strength to get to my feet and go to the bathroom to wash my face, only to gasp at my train-wreck appearance. My dark blonde hair that was styled so cute last night is a frizzy mess, and my black eyeliner looks hooker-chic, smeared all over my eyes. *Very sexy.* I wince when the slightest movement of my head elicits a pain so sharp, I believe lying in bed all day might remedy the unfortunate position I've put myself in. I move as fast as I can to clean myself up before pulling on a T-shirt and joining Ryan in the kitchen. At least you look a little better, I mutter to my reflection.

When I walk out, I have to stifle a gasp because he looks pretty sexy for someone I'm pretty sure I'm still furious with. His disheveled brown hair and morning scruff are two things I love seeing on the weekends. Today, he's taken it a step further, moving around the kitchen shirtless. I compose myself, walk to the barstool and take a seat without saying a word. Ryan finally looks in my direction and in his eyes I see a flash of amusement, and I know it's because I'm walking around in nothing but a T-shirt and underwear.

I hold back a smile, making eye contact with him, both of us playing a game of chicken. *I will not flinch.* He grabs a mug from the cabinet and pours a cup of coffee before setting it in front of me. My lips turn up in a small smile as I pull the mug to my lips, grateful for the silence. Well, aside from the pounding in my head that I'm surprised he can't hear. I lift my gaze to meet his and he just gawks at me, as though he's never seen me before.

"How ya feeling today?" he finally asks. My hand goes straight to my head, signaling that I have a massive headache. "You need to eat something. How 'bout some cereal?"

I have to fight the urge to vomit at the mere thought of cereal. "I'm good," I say in a rush, hoping he doesn't suggest anything else. "Thanks for the coffee."

The silence stretches between us and I feel that so much is being said in the stillness. I'm always the first one to cave when it comes to what Ryan wants. When it comes to the little things, like what we eat, whether or not we go out, apartments to live in, or even where we get married, I tend to let Ryan have the final say. I have done everything he's wanted, up to now. But I have to stand my ground this time, because this *is* a big deal, even if he doesn't think so.

"Look-"

"We-" he starts to say at the same time as me. "Go 'head."

The tight smile I give in appreciation makes me feel worlds away from this man who knows me all too well. "I was just going to say I'm sorry about last night. I mean, if I said anything…" I can't seem to find the words to tell him anything.

"I -" He seems frustrated, searching for something to say. "Shit, Em, this isn't us. We don't fight like this, and we don't walk away."

"Funny," a scoff escapes, "I thought the same thing, yet there you went."

"You told me to leave," he counters with annoyance, reminding me of my part in that action.

"And you went," I finish as I stand up from the barstool. Fortunately, since the apartment is small, I can reach over and put my cup in the sink before walking away.

"I wasn't walking out on us; I was walking out on a fight. A fight that clearly isn't over, and it's not like you were being rational."

"So I'm the irrational one, is that right?" My hands go to my hips and I fix my glare on him. "It's irrational that I want to be with my boyfriend, the guy I'm about to marry, and that I expect him to put me first? It's irrational that I get pissed when he does the complete opposite?

Do I have that right? Well, let me tell you something, *Ryan*, I think that you are being a complete jerk."

I barely get two steps into storming off when he is suddenly at my side, grasping my wrist and pulling me to him. I push at his chest, trying to get away, but his other hand finds my waist as he pulls me close.

"Em." I'm trying to turn my face away from him, but he places a gentle touch to my chin, urging me to look at him. "We can't keep this up."

I stop resisting and my arms fall limp at my side. Ryan *is* the most rational person I know, and maybe that's the problem. Where did his passion for me go? I feel like I'm fighting for us, and he's fighting for his career. I can't do the fighting for the both of us. This realization cuts deep inside of me, and I feel my heart physically ache.

"You're right," I admit past the lump in my throat. "We can't."

"So what's our solution?"

"I think we both need some space, Ryan." His body goes rigid at those words, and my face that is nuzzled into his chest lends me the ability to hear his heartbeat. I hurry to elaborate. "I love you, you know that. I just don't want to fight anymore, it's getting us nowhere."

"We have to talk it out." He holds my hand in his, pulling me to the couch. I try to resist, but he only squeezes tighter. "I'm sorry about the way I told you. I really didn't think-"

"No, you didn't think." I turn a fierce glare on him.

He stares at me for a second before raising his eyebrows in question, "Are you going to let me finish, or would you rather have this argument alone?"

Adequately put in my place, I shut my mouth and let him finish. "I didn't mean to dump it on you like that. I really thought you'd be happy with the opportunity. I know you're pissed and you don't want me here."

I finally turn to look at him, only to give him a knowing look. He doesn't give into my tantrum and continues his lecture. "Ok, well, I thought maybe I'd get some resistance with that one, but whatever. Point is, clearly I was wrong and this is something that we need to discuss."

"Fine, talk."

He closes his eyes and shakes his head, and I know I'm irritating the shit out of him. "Are you going to be like this the whole time?"

"Um, yeah." I nod. "Most likely."

"You are being ridiculous, you know that, right?"

I roll my eyes, because I'm not in the mood to listen to him, let alone stay in the same place with him. I stand from the couch and head to the bedroom to change my clothes to make my point. He watches as I walk from the room, standing to follow after. I try to shut the door, but he catches it before I can stop him.

"I already told you, we're not going anywhere until we've sorted this out."

"What are you gonna do? Lock me in the apartment?"

"Maybe." He shrugs. "The way I figure, if you leave, you're only going to go see Joss or call that girl from work, and tell them what you're pissed about. So you might as well stay here and tell me."

I'm not about to cave and talk because he's ready; I need time. "I have some work to do," I say as I move past him and head to the computer. "So, your plan backfired." I pull out the documents containing everything for the T.M. event and set about getting my work done, hopeful he'll leave me alone.

I *think* he's impressed with my stance because there's a flash of shock in his eyes. "That's fine, Em. You work, I'll be here when you're finished." He makes a show of moving to the couch and grabbing the remote to turn on a movie. The volume is turned up to an annoying level, but I know he's trying to get a rise out of me so I choose to ignore it.

The stubbornness both of us are displaying is fast becoming a game to see who can top the other. I still won't say a word to him and opt instead to up the ante by turning up the volume on my computer so I can hear my playlist better. To make it a little more maddening, I select a band that I know he hates and sing along, way off key and missing words. At this point, I know I'm not really getting any work done, not that I was going to get much done anyway, but I'm finding this charade increasingly entertaining.

Ryan gets up from his seat on the couch and I'm sure that I've won, until he goes to the kitchen and turns on the faucet. I don't have to look to know that he's not washing anything; he just knows how much I hate water going to waste. I contemplate my next move, now that it's my turn to make him squirm, so I do the only thing I can think of. I stand up and start walking to our bedroom and just before I get through the door, I take my shirt off, toss it to the couch and pause for only a moment to take off my bra and when I look back at him, the shock on his face tells me I just won. I rush into the room as I see him start to head in my direction and lock the door behind me.

I slide down the door until I'm sitting and reach for my t-shirt that's lying on the floor. No doubt it's dirty, but I'm too tired and hung-over to care. With my head resting on my knees, I try to relax and gather my thoughts. Sparring with Ryan is daunting, but being more stubborn than usual is making this day a little more tolerable. In the solace of our room, I use the time to reorganize my drawers, shuffling things around, even though it makes no sense. Every so often, Ryan knocks and asks if he can come in, which I respond to by turning the radio up a little louder.

"Mature, Em," I hear him huff on the other side.

He's right; there's nothing mature about the way I'm acting and yet, he's still here. He wants to talk and I guess I need to be open to the conversation. I turn the music down and unlock the door before taking a seat at the edge of the bed. When he comes into the room he sits down next to me and offers his hand and I give him mine.

"I won't go," he says in a hush, looking down at the floor.

That's what I want more than anything, for him to choose me, but from what he's told me that's not a realistic choice.

"What would happen if you turned it down?" I have to ask the question, because he hasn't even mentioned this.

"Turn it down?" He repeats with sarcasm, as if he hadn't thought of it. "It's not like they'll fire me tomorrow, but I certainly won't be up for any promotions anytime soon. They'll think I'm not a team player."

I shake my head when I realize that he might really turn it down if I ask him to, but is that something I want to do?

"I love you, Em. There's nothing that I wouldn't do for you, and despite what you think, I am thinking of us. This position is temporary; you and me, we're forever."

"Ryan, I know how hard you've worked for a chance like this. I really am proud of you- I don't want you to go, but I get it."

He walks toward me and hugs me tight. "Come with me."

"I can't," I repeat the words I've already told him. "Things are starting to pick up for my career, too. I'm not going to beg you to stay, I know this is a great opportunity for you, but I can't go with you."

"I know," he whispers into my ear before kissing my head.

"Besides, a year isn't so bad."

He pulls away and looks down at me as if no stranger words have ever been spoken, especially by me. "It is a long time, and you know it."

"We'll be okay." I try to convince him, as much as I try to convince myself. "This is just a nasty hurdle we have to make over, and once we do, it will be a small blip on an otherwise calm journey."

"You know you're a terrible liar, right?"

"I'm just tired of fighting," I admit. "And I really think that everything will be okay. Don't get me wrong, it's gonna suck and it'll be hard, but we can do this, right?" I need reassurance from him. He's always been the logical one, but right now, I need him to be the one that tells me what I need to hear. If he sells it, maybe he'll believe it, and if he believes it, maybe I'll start to as well.

"You're right." He stands up and takes my hands to help me up. He pulls me close and brushes my hair out of my face before looking down at me. "We can do this, Em," I nod, turn my head into his chest and breathe him in as though it's the last time. When we finally break apart, I decide to shower, and properly fix myself up.

"Wanna grab something to eat?" He questions when I turn to leave the room. The mere suggestion elicits a loud growl from my stomach.

I smile the first genuine smile I've given him since our blow up the other night. "Yeah, just let me take a shower, and I'll be ready to get out of here." I start walking to our bedroom and stop when I feel him just behind me. "What are you doing?"

"I'm going with you to take a shower," he explains, as if it makes complete sense.

"I don't recall inviting you," I counter, with a raised brow.

"Well, actually, your little tease did earlier. So yeah, I'm taking a shower with you." He looks at me and gives me the same gorgeous smile I fell in love with. "You started it." He throws his hands up signaling there is no choice, so I turn my back to him and continue walking. As soon as I get to the bathroom door, I remove the t-shirt I had put back on and concede defeat with a grin.

chapter 5

The rest of the weekend flowed and in the end, Ryan and I seemed to be in a better place. Are things perfect? Of course not. Do I still have my concerns about him leaving? I wish I could say no, but a year is going to be so hard. Part of me wishes I could pack up and follow him, but it doesn't seem realistic.

Despite the weekend shenanigans, I was able to shoot out a few emails and finally got a hold of Mr. Miller about his corporate event. He responded and informed me that my contact, Sandy, was no longer employed with them. Until he finds a replacement, I'll have to send everything to him, but he seems pretty agreeable to everything I've sent so far. I'm happy that I can show up to work this morning and report to Elle that everything is going smooth with the client.

"How did your weekend go?" Cam asks when she passes my desk.

"Started out shitty," I say looking at my screen before facing her. "But it ended up pretty good."

"So you finally talked to him?"

"Yeah," I admit. "We had a good talk. We haven't figured everything out yet, but at least we're both trying."

"Good," she says as she takes a seat. "So what did you call so late for?"

"Shit," I chastise myself, "I'm so sorry. I meant to call you Saturday and tell you about it. But Ryan was there, and it was a little hard to talk. Long story short?" It's rhetorical, so I continue. "Went home, Ryan was there; we left. Went with Joss to a club- got drunk, danced, Ryan showed up and took us home."

"How did he know you were there?"

"Sometime that night, Joss either called or texted and told him where we were." I shrug because I still haven't talked to her to find out what happened, but she probably doesn't remember anyway.

Cam laughs as I recount the evening but seems more satisfied that Ryan and I are communicating. She hasn't met him yet, but I think she might be our biggest fan. "Are you two better now?"

"Getting there," I add. "He wants me to fly out to San Diego with him this weekend to help him find an apartment." The thought of him leaving physically hurts me.

"Of course you're going, right?"

"Yeah, we'll head out on Friday. We spent yesterday looking at some places online, so he's narrowed it down to a few."

Cam is quiet when she returns back to her work and I can only imagine what she's thinking. At twenty-six, she's already been married and divorced; I don't know the circumstances under which her marriage ended. As I'm about to start making some phone calls, she speaks up. "Em, I really hope that you and Ryan do everything you can to make it work. If you try and fail, at least you know you did everything you could. There's nothing worse than living with the fact that you know you gave up too easily." And just like that, she dives headfirst into work.

I'm stunned into silence, because I know there is more to that statement than she's saying. Maybe someday she'll trust me enough to share, but I won't push her. I have work to distract me from my fears and concerns, and for that, I am grateful. The phone rings just in time to snap me back to reality.

"Elle E. Grant Events, this is Emogen. How can I help you?"

"Just who I was looking for," the strong voice announces on the other end of line. "This is Trey Miller. We've emailed a few times over the weekend."

"Hello, Mr. Miller," I respond, frazzled as I try to pull his file out of my bag. "I was just going to call you about some of the venues I have found for your event."

"That's great." His voice is muffled as he speaks, as though he's covering up the receiver. I assume that he's talking to someone near him, which gives me enough time to open the file so I'm prepared. When he speaks again, his voice is clear as he turns his attention to me. "Listen, Emogen, I have a couple more that I'd like to take a look at. I'll be out of town this week, but can you meet with me next Thursday?"

Without even a quick glance at my calendar, I know that I'm not free, that's my last day with Ryan before he leaves for good, and I've already taken the day off. "I'm sorry, I'll be out of the office. How about the following Monday?"

"That'll be fine." He sounds irritated to be put off, but I already told Ryan I'd make the trip to San Diego with him to help him move in.

"I can do it next Wednesday afternoon, if that works better?" I add, trying to accommodate him.

"No, Monday will be fine," he reassures me, this time seeming less annoyed. "Ten good for you?"

"Yes sir," I reply quickly adding, "I'll meet you at your office."

I have so much left to do and local businesses to meet with. I'm sure Mr. Miller will find these vendors to be acceptable.

* * *

Driving to pick Ryan up from work so we can head to the airport gives me time to think about the last few days. Ryan and I have been together every evening this week. There is a desperate need to cling to each other whenever possible, and I do nothing to change the heaviness of that feeling. This afternoon we are flying out to California to look at the places that we found online that he thinks will work best for him. I don't want to go with him, because the reality of everything will set in, but at the same time I need to be with him. He booked our flight and said we would make a weekend of it, but this isn't the vacation I had in mind. Before I went to work this morning, I had everything packed up and ready in the back of my car.

I wish the drive had taken longer, because I'm not ready for this next part. But I arrive at the ARK Consulting offices to see Ryan standing outside waiting for me. He looks so different from the man I've been spending my evenings with lately. He appears polished and sure of himself, whereas the guy I've been with is unkempt and laid back, two things I love about our time alone. This man I'm looking at right now seems so sure of himself, and this move away is killing me. I just wish he were as torn up about this whole thing as I am.

"Hey babe," he says, before leaning over to kiss me, as he closes the car door.

"Hey," is all I'm able to say back.

"Everything okay?" He asks as he furrows his brow.

"Yeah, everything's fine," I lie. "It's been a long day and I'm just really tired."

"Em." He shakes his head. "You realize I know when you're lying, right?"

When I look at him, the grin on his face is enough to melt me on the spot, but I cover well. "I'm not lying."

"Alright. Whatever you say."

The ride to the airport is thick with things still unsaid and he seems as morose as I am. This should be a weekend for us to find some common ground and expectations about what the next year will mean to us. Instead, fear is keeping me from saying everything I want to. The drive to the airport is short and after parking the car, Ryan dutifully gets out and grabs our bags while I lock up. Walking side by side through the airport, neither of us says a word, except the occasional "here you go" while dealing with TSA or the ticketing agents.

I could kick myself, because up until today things have been good. I suppose it's the reality of what's coming that is making me act this way. It's not fair to Ryan, especially when he wants to know what I'm thinking. "I don't like this, Ryan." I look down at my hand that's twirling my engagement ring around my finger. "We're going away to find you a new home. Does that even register as strange to you?"

He shakes his head and scoffs audibly, "Yeah, it's weird. But it won't be home. Home is our place. Together. This is just a temporary arrangement." He reaches for my chin to look into my eyes. "Can we just try to think of it like that? Enjoy this weekend together? I have a few things planned."

Surprise takes over my bad attitude and I try to play along. "What do you have planned?"

He reaches for my hand, brings it to his lips before kissing it, and gives me a quick wink. "You'll see."

During the two-hour flight, Ryan and I don't talk much about his impending move, choosing instead for a lighthearted conversation about my sister, Langley. She met some guy last month and every time I talk to her, she does nothing but gush about how great he is. I'm so glad that she found someone, because it annoyed her that her little sister was settling down before her.

With everything that's been going on between Ryan and me, I have been a poor excuse for a sister, something she pointed out numerous times. I'm not sure where they met, but she said that on their first date, he kept making her laugh and complimenting her. But her favorite part was when he reached out and held her hand; I think she used the word *fireworks*. I doubt she's getting ready to make any big moves with this guy, but it's nice to hear her so happy. Lang and Ryan had an instant bond and he agrees that hearing her so fired up over this new guy is entertaining.

"Maybe he's *the one*," he says with air quotes while laughing.

When I feel the conversation is about to return to talk of us, I opt to focus on the past, not the looming future. I rest my head on his shoulder before I speak. "Do you remember that night we went to see Mumford and Sons?"

"Which time?" he asks nudging his shoulder, clearly teasing me.

"Last year. When it rained."

"Yeah," he says, wrapping his arm around me. "How could I forget? We were drenched and you were freezing."

I let out a small laugh, snuggling closer to him. "Yes, but I'm talking about after."

"Oh, you mean when you made me stay there well after the show ended so you could try to see the band?"

"Hey!" I sit up objecting. "It could have happened. They had to leave at some point."

"True. But you forgot there were multiple exits. Figures you chose the one they wouldn't use," he teases as he hugs my body next to his.

I sigh and close my eyes, feeling as though I could drift to sleep. "Well, that was the night I knew I wanted to marry you. I thought, anyone who would do that, even though he doesn't like the band himself, has to be a keeper."

"Still feel that way?" When he asks, I swear there is a hint of worry in his voice for what my answer might be.

"I'll always feel that way." No other words are spoken, he kisses me and I relax, dreaming of a world where Ryan isn't leaving and there are no unspoken words.

* * *

As we land in San Diego, I feel as though I have the weight of the world on my shoulders. Ryan has a rental car waiting for us, and the drive to the hotel shouldn't take too long. I try my best to keep a positive attitude and not worry about tomorrow or even a week from now when he leaves. The apartments we're looking at all have vacancies, so it's just a matter of seeing which one he likes the best. By the time we fly out on Sunday, Ryan will have a new home. *Without me. In California.* The area is familiar to him because he summered here growing up, but to me, it's another world.

"Are you hungry?" he asks, breaking through my sad thoughts.

"No, I'm good, but if you want to stop, that's fine."

"I talked to the agents this morning, two of them said they could see us at four o'clock. Is that okay with you?" I nod in agreement. Pull the Band-Aid off, I think to myself. Without another word, he turns out of the car rental facility and hops onto the freeway, heading to parts unknown.

The drive to the first complex is only twenty minutes, but he doesn't even bother to stop because the place looks pretty rundown. It looks nothing like the pictures online and I can tell he's disappointed because if the next one is as bad as this, we'll have to start from the bottom. Fortunately, the next apartment is down the road and when we pull up to the leasing office, I can tell he already likes this place. The complex appears to be older, but it has been maintained really well.

The leasing agent greets us when we walk in and extends her hand to Ryan. "Mr. Tate, I presume?"

"You must be Reese," he greets her warmly.

She smiles and picks up a phone that begins ringing nearby. "I'll be right with you."

While she's taking care of that, we walk around the leasing office and check out a few of the amenities. I can tell Ryan is happy with what he's seen so far.

"Would you like me to show you the unit, or would you rather look at it alone?" Reese asks as we walk toward her.

"I think we're good." He looks at me and I nod in agreement. "Just point us in the right direction."

Hand in hand, we walk down the sidewalk to the apartment, and I'm surprised at how much larger this one is compared to our place back home. I've always heard rent in California is expensive and the places are small, but then again, his company is paying for this place. It appears to have been renovated recently, because the updated faux wood floors and granite countertops look new. The cabinets, carpet and paint are all muted brown hues and the place screams 'bachelor pad.' There's a twinge of jealousy, or maybe insecurity, seeing where my soon-to-be husband will live alone for the next year.

I remain rooted near the kitchen area while he explores the rest of the apartment. I resist the urge to look around since I'm finding it hard not to get upset. If I were moving out here with him, this is exactly where I would want to be. He emerges from the bedroom and shrugs his shoulders. "I guess this is my home away from home." His sigh is heavy, and I know that he's just trying to make the best of the situation.

I turn away and walk to the window to distract myself from the reality of this moment. This *will* be his home, and I'll be in Colorado without him. I wipe the tear that sneaks out before responding to his statement.

"Have fun."

chapter 6

I didn't expect Ryan to pick the second place that he looked at, but then again, he's pretty laid back. Had the first complex not looked scary, he may have chosen *it* on the spot. I guess it's good that we got the hard part out of the way, because now we'll be able to spend the rest of the weekend exploring the city and spending our last bits of time together. I've never been to California, so I am excited to see the beaches.

There's no way to treat this like a vacation or anything other than what it is. The relocation and the move are ever looming over our heads. Ryan checks us into the hotel and I remain uncharacteristically quiet as I follow him to the room. He swipes the room card in the door and holds it open for me to enter, and as I do, I toss my purse on the dresser. Before I can do anything else, he pulls me to him and catches me off guard with a passionate kiss that he plants on my lips.

"What was that for?" I ask, touching my lips, eyeing him.

"I know this is hard for you, but you're here with me." The look in his eyes is loving and I feel like I melt into him when he holds me.

"Ryan is this weird?" I mumble into his chest. "We're about to be married, but I've just helped you pick a home away from me. I feel like everything is changing and not for the better."

"Don't think of it that way," he starts as he pushes me back so he can look at my eyes. "Think of it as the temporary arrangement it is. *You are my home*; this is just the place where I'll be staying. A place you will be visiting. Often. I hope."

Wrapping my arms around him, I try to push any negativity out and focus on Ryan. The man I love. "I'll come out as often as I can."

I'm sure the reality of that statement isn't lost on him. Working for one of the most well known event planners in town, with a growing clientele, is a dream. But it also keeps me quite busy. During the week I'm scheduling, consulting and monitoring events, and as of late, my weekends are filled with weddings and other corporate events. The chances that over the next few months I'll be able to fly out on the weekends are slim to none, but I can't say that to Ryan because he will assume I'm trying to be difficult.

He grabs my luggage and lightly tosses it on the chair near the window before looking at me. "I'm gonna grab a shower, wanna join me?"

I shake my head and smile. "I'm good, Lang called earlier so I need to call her back."

The way Ryan looks at me, I know he's trying to figure out how he's going to respond. "Alright then, I won't be long." He takes his shirt off and throws it at me and grins. "Tell her I said hi."

Once the water starts, I pull my phone from my purse to call Langley and of course she answers on the first ring. "Hey, sis. Nice of you to finally call me back."

"Did you forget that I'm in San Diego with Ryan for the weekend?"

"Nope. That's why I called. I knew you were probably moping and whining and being an overall bitch, so I wanted to snap you out of it. Was I right?"

I am quiet for a moment before answering. I could lie, but my sister knows me better than anyone. "Yeah, you're right," I respond begrudgingly.

"Right. So then, what are you gonna do about it?"

"There's nothing I can do, Lang. He's moving out here. He already signed the lease for his new place and-"

"That's not what I mean, I know he's moving. What I'm asking is, are you going to let this ruin your weekend and your time with Ryan? Speaking of, where is he, anyway?"

"He's taking a shower," I acknowledge, hearing the shower still running.

"And you're on the phone with me, why?" I know what she's getting at, but I try to ignore it.

"I had to call you back," I start to remind her, but she doesn't let me finish my explanation.

"Go. Now. Be with Ryan. And, Em," I can tell I'm about to get a warning from my big sister and I smile when she doesn't wait for me to answer. "Stop sulking, it ages you, and you don't want me to look like the younger sister."

"Yeah, yeah." I smile a genuine smile. "I gotta go. Love you."

"Love you, too," she answers and just like that, we're disconnected.

Our conversation was only a few minutes, and I can still hear Ryan in the shower, so I get up and head over to join him. Opening the door reveals my handsome fiancé. He's standing in the bathroom in his boxer with that killer grin on his face. "Damn, girl! It took you long enough."

"How did you know I was coming in here?" I ask, puzzled. I want to snap at him for letting the water run, but this is about me and him, not another argument.

He looks at me and shrugs his shoulders. "I didn't. Just hoped."

It takes only a second to realize that he's as unsure of all of this as I am. He doesn't know how things are going to turn out, but he's trying to make the best of it, and I need to meet him halfway. So I do.

I start to remove my jeans and I feel his eyes gaze upon me while I make a show of doing it slow and exaggerated. I shimmy out of them, leaving my panties on before I start to remove my blouse. He looks like he's trying to remain composed, standing only a short distance away. "I can help you with that," he offers with a sexy, controlled tone.

When I look up, Ryan is leaning against the counter with his arms crossed over his chest. I walk toward him and smile. "I *think* I could use some help with the shirt."

He brushes his knuckles along the side my face and tucks my hair behind my ear before kissing me. He trails his kisses from my jaw to my ear and then whispers, "I have something planned. You up for it?"

"What do you have in mind?" I ask, in a voice that sounds too needy to be mine. But Ryan, kissing me and holding me, is exactly what I want.

"Right now? All I want is this," he says before his lips land on mine once again. It has to be one of the most passionate and sexy kisses I have ever been on the receiving end of and it's easy for me to get lost in.

I don't care that my shirt hasn't been completely removed, or that my bra and panties are about to get drenched. All I know is that as Ryan backs us toward the shower door, I only want to be here, in his arms. I laugh as he drags us both under the running water and he resumes kissing me again, separating only to pull the shirt over my head. He brings my body close to his and I hold on to him for dear life.

* * *

My eyelids feel heavy, but I can tell from the light that seeps in through the curtains that it's still daylight. Between the shower, and what happened after the shower, I could quite possibly sleep for days. Ryan rolls over and places his arm over my waist and squeezes me to his chest. I rest my hand over his and entwine our fingers, feeling that here in his arms is where I belong.

He raises himself up and rests on his arm so he can look down at me. "You tired?"

"Depends," I start. "What do you have planned?"

He leans down and kisses my nose. "I know you've never seen the beach, so I figured we could drive out to PB and maybe grab some dinner."

I can't contain my smile; this is one perk to this little trip I've looked forward to. "What's PB?" I ask, my smile fading in confusion.

"Sorry, Pacific Beach," he smiles. "I forget you've never been out here before. Why don't I take you to see some of my favorite places out here?"

"That sounds great," I admit, turning to fully face him. "I really love you, you know that, right?"

"I love you, too," he says, between kisses, the final one becoming slow and sensual.

* * *

When we finally get out of bed Ryan, true to his word, takes me all over the city, showing me the beaches, malls, and military base. There is so much to take in, but I have to admit, I really do like it out here.

We continue driving, and since I have no clue where I am, I figure we are heading to eat, but he slows the car in an old neighborhood. He parks on the side of the street and turns the car off to show me a small home where he spent countless summers. In the years that we've been together, he's not returned to San Diego, and though I can see this is hard for him, he fits here.

He used to tell me about the times he would come out here to visit his grandparents for a few weeks every year. Both of Ryan's parents worked, and I guess he was a bit of a handful, so they would pawn him off on the retired pair. Only, they didn't realize how much he loved it.

When he was a kid, he said that they would take him to the zoo at least once each visit. However, as he got older, he would go to the beach and rent a surfboard and spend all day trying to learn to stay up on the board. His grandmother surprised him one year with his own surfboard, which he said was the best gift he'd ever gotten.

"See that garage, right there?" he asks, pointing to a tiny shack in the back. "Grams had Pa clear his 'junk' out of it, as she called it, and said I could do whatever I wanted with it."

"So what did ya do?" I turned smiling at him.

"Not much really," he admits. "I tried to turn it into a bungalow because I had this idea that when I got out of high school, I'd come out here and just be a beach bum, living with them."

I look at my fiancé, loving there are still things about him I don't know. "So what happened? Why didn't you come out here?"

"I did," he responds. My jaw opens slightly to question, but he continues, "for the summer. I told Grams I wanted to move out here. I said I didn't want to go to college, but she said that if I didn't go, she would disown me."

"And, what? Just like that, she was able to convince you?" Ryan is very headstrong, and when he makes his mind up to do something, it's hard to sway him.

"Nah, we spent a lot of time going back and forth. Every time I had a reason to stay, she'd give me three to go."

"Such as?"

"Grandpa didn't go," he offers with a grin. I figure that must have been his favorite thing to point out. "She would raise her eyebrows in that 'don't fuck with me' way and start in on how times were different back then and he had a family to support."

"She sounds tough." I smile, thinking of my own grandmother.

"Yeah, she was. Eventually, she resorted to cheap blackmail telling me I would break her heart if I didn't go."

"I'm glad she got to see you walk across the stage," I remind him.

"Me, too. She was really bad off by then. I was afraid the flight out would kill her, but she was determined to see it happen." He looks like he's in another world, thinking about her.

"I wish I could have met her. She sounds a lot like my Gamee," I say past the lump in my throat. Ryan was with me when I got word that she passed away last year. My heart broke because there was so much I wanted to tell her and never got the chance to. I shared everything with her and when I introduced her to Ryan, I told her that he was the one, even before he proposed.

"She would have loved you." He wraps his arm around my shoulder, both of us missing the women we held in such high esteem. "Did I ever tell you what she told me when she saw me after I graduated?"

"I don't think so."

"She told me to go back and get my master's. She said that I needed to have my life in order because I was going to meet someone who was going to turn my world upside down, in the best way. 'She's out there, Ryan, and hopefully, if you don't find her, she'll find you.' Six months later, I met you."

I'm speechless. There are no words that I can say in response to that beautiful story. I have heard numerous tales about his grandparents, but I know that this is one that he has never shared with me.

After she died, his mom and her sister moved his grandfather to a home near them in Charleston. When he died last year, I went with Ryan to the funeral, and he was devastated. He told me the best part of his grandfather died when she died, but moving him away from all that the two shared was harder on him than anything else.

mine to lose

I think Ryan really believes that his grandpa died of a broken heart.

chapter 7

It must be self-preservation, because I find myself doing anything and everything to make this transition easier. Trying to find the silver lining in any of this is hard, but maybe the time apart will push us to communicate with each other better. Maybe distance does make the heart grow fonder and we'll defy the odds and make it through this next year stronger than ever. No matter what I tell myself, I know it's going to hurt like hell when he's gone. In four days, Ryan will be in California for the next year, and I will be here. *Alone.*

My whole day has been shitty. Elle decided that since I won't be in the office on Thursday or Friday, I need to come in early and stay late to make sure I'm ready for my meeting with Mr. Miller next Monday. I left this morning before Ryan woke up with a note that I would pick something up for dinner on my way home. After our weekend away, things have been less strained, so I've been looking forward to our time together. That is, until he texted around noon to say that he would be home late and not to worry about getting him dinner. Apparently his boss has some things they need to get together for a client that he's turning over to someone else. Regardless, I'm annoyed, because I'm busting ass to get done so I can spend his last two days with him, but he's making no concessions whatsoever. Part of me wants to tell Elle that I'll be out all week, but deep down I know I'd never do that.

I ignored his text.

Add to my day that Mr. Miller has sent numerous emails instructing me to have a list of suggested menu items, as well as potential caterers, for our meeting on Monday. He has yet to nail down whether it will be a Friday or Saturday event, but considering it's less than five months away, I need a date. I need to make sure these vendors are available. Now I'm a frazzled mess, and I want nothing more than to vent about it to Ryan.

Me: I'm heading home

Ryan: I'm still at work

Me: How much longer?

Ryan: Not sure. I'll call

I look at my computer and groan, because it's almost six thirty. I'm drained, annoyed and now pissed at Ryan. He's still here, and already I feel alone. I didn't move out here and agree to marry him, just to wind up by myself. This day has dragged, but most likely it feels that way because I am eager to get home.

Me: Don't bother

Why am I being such a bitch?

I clean up my desk and grab a stack of things to take home with me before shutting everything down. Just as I walk out of the office my phone rings and I look to see it's Ryan and roll my eyes.

"Yeah?"

"Hey," he stumbles over his words. "Everything okay?"

"No, Ryan," I snap back, "I'm not. You leave in four days but you have to work late."

"Don't you think I'd rather be home with you?"

"I don't know what to think. We just picked out your new home for the next year, you're closing up things at work, and I'm busy. I'm just not sure when we'll get to spend any time together before you leave. Before you know it, Friday will be here and we'll have missed out."

"Em-"

"No. You know what? Don't worry about it. I'll just see you when you get home." I don't wait for him to say anything else. I hang up and stuff my phone into my purse and storm out to my car to head home.

The entire drive home, I go between sniffling like a child to getting fired up over Ryan leaving. By the time I pull into my parking spot, I'm finally calm and feel like maybe I'll just go to sleep and put a nail in this day. To my surprise, those ideas are put on hold because when I open the door to let myself in, Ryan is leaning against the back of the couch, staring at me.

I'm trying too hard to keep my composure, so I walk to the counter and place my purse on one of the two barstools and turn to face him. I'm unsure whether to walk over and hug him or to stand back and wait for him. But before I can decide one way or the other, Ryan pushes to his feet and walks over to me and wraps his arms around my waist, pulling me close. I bury my head in his chest and I am crumbling all over again. The pain of him leaving consumes me and I begin crying inconsolably. I wrap my arms around him, holding tight, as though my grasp alone can keep him here.

"I'm sorry, baby," he whispers into my hair.

"I'm morry, moo," I answer muffled into his chest between sobs. He chuckles and loosens his grip.

"What?"

I look up at his face, take a deep breath and clarify, "I said, 'I'm sorry, too.'"

He runs his thumb across my cheek, wiping a stray tear and leans down to kiss me. This single act has the tears escaping all over again, so he takes my hand and urges me to sit on the couch with him, "I already ordered from the Chinese restaurant you like, it should be here in a bit. So we have time to talk."

I look at him with a questioning eye. "You think all of our problems are going to be solved in twenty minutes, Ry?"

"No, but we can at least start. Unless you want to do something else with those twenty minutes," he teases.

"You give yourself too much credit," I joke, and the laugh he releases causes a smile to finally appear on my face. He leans into the cushions, pulls my back to his chest and holds me close. I hear him breathing and the silence between us stretches, but I know that we both have thoughts running through our heads. Thoughts that we have been putting off far too long.

"Em, you know I want you to come with me-" I start to sit up, but he pulls me back, shushing me. "But I know you have your job here."

"I know this is a huge opportunity for you, but I can't just quit and follow you for a year." I look down at our fingers that are entwined as I try to share my thoughts with him. "Ryan, I'm scared. We're on shaky ground right now. Can't you see? I'm not sure we'll make it."

"Wow." His arms fall away from me, but I grasp his fingers tighter. "What the hell is that supposed to mean, Em?"

"I didn't mean it like that," I rush to clarify my bad word choice.

"Then how did you mean it? Because first, you can't come with me, or won't. And then you're saying that a year is gonna break us. I don't know about you, but that says a lot about what you think of our relationship, don't you?"

I turn to face him, ready to have the second biggest fight of our short time here. "Don't put words in my mouth, besides, you're the one trying to uproot us for *your* career."

When he looks at me, confusion is etched on his face, "Yes, I need to take this job for *my* career, as you point out, but it's not like I have a ton of options out there. Last I checked, *we* need for me to have this job to make ends meet."

I'm not going to yell. I take a steadying breath and turn to look at the frame on the end table next to me because I cannot look at him. *One. Two. Three. Exhale.*

My voice is steady when I counter his argument. "*We* came out here, because *you* said this was the best place for us, and I followed, because I love you. It took me months to line up this job with Elle, when I had one already waiting for me back home. But again, I did it for you. And as far as making ends me, you are *not* the breadwinner here, Ryan. *We* are a team, but this is one move that I will not do for you."

"Em!" he starts to yell, but I know that he's trying to remain calm. "I already said, *I don't expect you to come with me.* Do I want you to? Yes, but not if you don't want to. You're making it sound like I'm choosing work over you, but I'm not."

"It sure feels like it," I counter.

"Well, I could say the same thing back to you." He looks at me, knowing that he has a point.

We're in a standoff, neither of us willing to back down, and I feel both of us are wrong. The silence is deafening, but I'm afraid if I speak, I'll cave. Ryan is the first to make a move when he takes a seat at the kitchen counter, and exhales a frustrated breath. I follow by sitting back down on the couch waiting to see how this will play out.

A loud knock on the door breaks through the silence and Ryan gets up to answer it. He pays the delivery guy, sets the food in the kitchen, and starts to pull out plates from the cabinet. The conversation could be over, but I'm not ready to let this one die. "How's this really going to work, Ryan?" My question is barely a whisper, but I know that he's thinking the same thing.

"I'm not sure."

"I know people go through far worse things than being temporarily apart, but all I can see is us, and what effect this could have. I'm really scared." When the words are finally out there, I give in to my pain and fears. Ryan sets down whatever he was holding and joins me on the couch. He reaches over, entwining his fingers with mine and for once, this small gesture makes me feel even lonelier. "What are you thinking?"

"I'm thinking that this is gonna suck ass," he starts. "But we'll see each other as much as we can on the weekends. You are amazing and the fuckin' strongest woman I know. I don't want you sitting around here moping while I'm gone. That's not fair, so go on about your normal day. Go out with friends, work, and do whatever else. I may be gone, but it's not like we're breaking up or anything. And until I leave, we are spending as much time together as we can. Okay?"

I let his words filter through and try to think of any other solution that might help us out of this place. Maybe I should just go with him. But I would resent him, and if I beg him to stay, he would, but he would resent me. "Alright," I say in defeat.

"Alright," he parrots. "Unless you don't want to spend time with me," he asks teasing, because it's obvious from my attitude that I want nothing more than to be with him as much as possible. I move closer to him on the couch to straddle his waist and take his face in my hands before answering him. I could get lost in his beautiful brown eyes if I stare too long, so I kiss him briefly. "Alright."

He wraps his arms securely around me and pours so much passion into his kiss. He stands with me still in his arms, never removing his lips from mine, and I know that our dinner is going to be cold when we

finally get around to eating it.

chapter 8

The alarm screaming next to me is the only thing that pulls me out of bed to get up for work. It's going to be a long day, starting my new weekly routine sans Ryan. That thought alone is enough to tempt me to crawl back under the sheets and call in sick. But an alert on my phone reminds me that I'm supposed to meet with Mr. Miller, so I have to be on my game.

I spent the entire weekend curled up in bed crying my eyes out. Mom called to check on me, I ignored it. Joss and Cam both texted me, but I only sent them a short response that I was okay. My sister was relentless, calling at least five times, but I sent every single one to voicemail. The only call I did take was from Ryan. I tried my best to sound upbeat, but of course he could hear my sadness, and the concern was evident in his voice. I just did my best to push through and feigned interest in whatever it was he was telling me. The evenings felt so lonely without him; they still do. But I know it's only been a couple of days.

Fortunately, when I look at my reflection in the mirror, I see that my eyes aren't too puffy from crying although my nose is a little red from the constant wiping. Nothing that a bit of concealer can't fix. I'm young, but everything about me just looks worn and old today. I draw my blonde hair into a messy ponytail so I can clean my face, hoping to wash away the tired appearance as well.

I make my way through our room to the kitchen to make a cup of coffee and I notice that our tiny apartment feels huge without him here. His side of the sink is noticeably vacant, I'm not tripping over his dirty laundry piled in the corner of the small bathroom, and I don't have to put the toilet seat down. Not that the toilet seat is a space issue, but it *is* a convenience issue.

I examine my face in the mirror while I run the shower to get the water warm, but as I'm about to step in, my phone rings. My stomach drops when I see his name flash on the screen. I wrap a towel around me and shut off the water before answering.

"Hey," I answer, my voice tired and sad.

"Hey," he manages back. I'm lifted slightly hearing that he sounds as miserable as me. "How'd ya sleep?"

"Not too good," I admit. "The first night I could pretend you were gone for the weekend, but now reality is setting in. I'll be waking up every morning without you. How did you sleep?"

"Not so good," he pauses and takes a deep breath. "Shitty."

I smile, knowing that he misses me, too. "I have a big meeting with Mr. Miller, today."

"Okay, I don't want to keep you, I just wanted to tell you I love you, Em."

My voice comes out as a whisper. "I love you, too."

I stay on the line and listen for him to hang up, and when he does I take a deep breath and exhale dramatically, keeping myself in check.

Why can't things just be easy?

Why can't *I love yous* be enough?

And why can't time stop, because now I'm running late for work.

* * *

"Excuse me, Elle," I say, knocking on her office door. "Do you have a second? I'm getting ready to meet with Mr. Miller and wanted to go over a few things."

"C'mon in, Emogen," she says, motioning to the seat across from her desk. Elle is a well-put together specimen of a career woman. Before I met Ryan, she's the type of woman I aspired to. Her tall, thin frame and strong facial features make her appear intimidating, but when you get to know her, she's a kind woman and a great boss. "I needed to talk to you about this meeting anyway."

"Is there a problem?"

"No, nothing like that. I just wanted to check the status since this is the first account you've handled on your own. Is everything going okay?"

"I believe so," I say, pulling out his client form. "The budget for T.M. is fifty thousand dollars, and with everything Mr. Miller has requested, I believe it's likely we'll come in under budget. I need to know if that's how you want to go with this, or do you want me to up-sell so we maximize profit?"

Elle sits back in her desk chair with an impressed smile on her face before she shakes her head. She points a finger in my direction. "You're good, Emogen. *Very* good. That's what I like to hear. If our client has a set budget, I do like to stick within their constraints, however, if we are able to offer additional things they didn't consider, that's how I like to do things."

"Great," I say, as I stand up and straighten my skirt. "I'm going to head out then and meet with him. I'll be back to formalize all of the arrangements and see where things stand after today."

When I leave her office, I ask Callie, our secretary, to give me direction to T.M. Enterprises. Even though we've lived in Denver for the last nine months, I still don't know my way around too well. Callie has lived here all her life and knows the back roads, so I have enough time to make it to the meeting with no issues. I've managed to avoid being cornered by Cam so far. I know that she wants to make sure I'm okay, but the question alone is likely to leave me in tears, so I keep moving.

Until she catches me.

I knew she had a meeting of her own today, so I figured I would see her this afternoon. However, she breezes through the front doors and heads straight for my desk. "Got a second?"

Glancing at my watch, I still have more than enough time, and I curse how everything is in slow motion today. "Yeah, I have to leave in about twenty minutes. What's up?"

"What's up?" she repeats in annoyance. "You're boyfriend just moved away, I called all weekend to check on you, and you didn't pick up once. That's what's up."

Now that I have been well chastised, I cock my head trying to assess how I should respond. She crosses her arms over her chest and rests her weight against the edge of my desk, letting me know she means business. There's no way I'm getting out of this. Exasperation takes over and I do my best to relax before answering. "It sucks. No, it fucking sucks. I slept like hell, I look like hell, and I have to leave to handle my first solo client." I stand up and gather everything I need for the meeting before finishing. "I don't want to talk about this at all, but," I pause and look at her, "come over for dinner tonight and I will talk. Joss is coming over; I got the same lecture from her. Besides, it's time you two met each other, then you can both rip me apart for being an asshole."

Cam steps aside and ushers me to the entrance. "What time?"

"Six?"

"M'kay." She nods. "I'll see you then. What can I bring?"

"I'm ordering in. We'll just pick when you get there."

Once I'm safely away, I can't help but be thankful for the few friends I have out here. Moving away from everyone and everything I knew was tough, but when Joss came out here three months ago, it was as if something in my life finally went my way. And meeting Cam was just icing. I really hope these two like each other.

* * *

T.M. Enterprises is nestled on the third floor of an impressive building in the middle of downtown. The company is a relatively new start up that handles public relations for some of the smaller businesses in the area. My understanding is that the owner, Mr. Miller, worked for one of the larger firms in town. He noticed how often the others were overlooked because they weren't Fortune 500 companies, so he branched out on his own about two years ago, and now runs one of the trendier, sought out firms.

Their office space is quite similar to Elle E. Grant, informal but professional. Looking around the office, most of the staff appears to be young, and the interior design is modern. Any research I've done on T.M. Enterprises, up to this point, seems to be inaccurate. However, despite my growing nerves and concerns about my lack of knowledge, I'm determined to push past and prove that I have what it takes to pull off the corporate event Mr. Miller is looking for. I finally make eye contact with the receptionist when it appears she must have asked a question.

"I'm sorry," I respond, finally looking at her. "Emogen Tate to see Mr. Miller."

She nods and pushes a button on the phone before speaking. "Yes, sir. She's here. Okay." When she looks back at me she instructs me to take a seat. "He'll be out in just a minute."

I have a seat in one of the chairs, trying to relax, but it's hard when you're getting ready to pretend like you know what you're talking about. Up to this point, I have only shadowed other planners, like Cam, and while it's been helpful, it's different when you're going it alone. I try to appear confident, but I'm intimidated by thinking he's going to see right through me. I glance at the phone in my hand to check my email and I have a few, one of which is from Ryan. I instantly smile, even without knowing what it says.

"Emogen." I look up, startled, to see the man behind the voice, which I have heard numerous times. "Trey Miller." He extends a hand. "Nice to meet you." I stand up, take his hand and return the greeting. There's something familiar about this man, although there's no way I've met him before. He seems to have the same reaction but covers it well. "Why don't we talk about what you've come up with before we drive all over the city?"

I gather my things and follow him to a spacious office down the hall.

"I'm sorry I wasn't able to meet you last week, Mr. Miller," I start before he interrupts.

"Trey," he insists, "no one here calls me Mr. Miller."

I nod before continuing. "Trey." Referring to him as Mr. Miller, having now seen the man, seems strange, but I prefer professional titles at times like this. He's not much older than me, I'd guess maybe in his late twenties or early thirties, and what he's been able to accomplish at such a young age is impressive. I spread everything out on his large conference table before explaining to him what I envision for their corporate event. "As you can see, we have a few options, and depending on which location you choose, we might be able to add some extra-"

"Where do I know you from?" I look up and he's studying my face with his eyes scrunched, trying to place me.

"I'm sorry. But I'm pretty sure we've never met before."

"Did you grow up around here?"

"No?" I say, caught off guard by his question. "I've only been here for about nine months."

He still isn't convinced. "I'm certain of it. I don't forget a face."

"I assure you, Trey." My eyes widen when I say his name because it feels much too informal. "We have never met before. Perhaps I've worked an event you've attended or maybe I just have one of those generic faces."

He gives me a look that says he's not quite convinced by my explanation, but gestures for me to proceed with my presentation. I continue explaining my vision and he seems impressed with what I have laid out for his event. There are two locations that I plan to show him, along with the two he mentioned to me before, but I feel that my selections will likely be the best fit. When I have finished showing him what the plan is, he leans back in his chair and appears to be mulling it over while nodding his head.

"Well," he states, pushing back his chair, "are you ready to take a look at these places?"

"Yes, sir."

"Why don't we take my car, you can give me the address." I'm more than grateful he insists on driving, because I'm still not confident in knowing where I'm going all of the time.

"That sounds great." I stand and walk toward the office door. "Let me get my other bag from the car and I'll meet you out front."

Business must be going pretty well, because I'm ushered to a silver Infinity IPL G, which is apparently new since it still has the temporary license plates. He tells me more about how his company started, a story I find interesting. The company began small two years ago with five clients; but since then, it has grown to over a hundred. He hopes that this party will introduce him to potential clients who will eventually choose to sign with his company.

When we pull into the parking lot for Ivy Glen, the old building that is situated on the back end of the lot oozes character. It's a two-story building that was once a bank but sold to a private businessman in the eighties when the financier merged with another. The intricate design of the deep reddish-brown brick and mortar, still original from when it was built in the fifties, makes this place look more like a church than a reception facility.

I hurry to get out ahead of him to meet my contact, Lisa, while he takes a call. I've talked to her a few times and she has been patient and guided me as I try to navigate the world of event planning.

By her voice, I pictured a young, thin, bubbly woman with red hair. The only part of that description that was correct is the bubbly personality. Lisa is probably in her early forties, tall with striking green eyes, dark brown hair, curvy figure, and a quirky sense of style. From my conversations with her, she's been in the Denver area for over twenty years, so I assume she moved here after finishing up school.

"Lisa," I greet her, extending my hand. "It's so nice to meet you finally. My client should join us in just a minute." She glances past me and nods, acknowledging his presence.

Lisa's warm smile turns devilish when she takes in Trey, and I internally roll my eyes. "It's nice to meet you, Emogen." She makes eye contact with Trey. "Mr. Miller." He doesn't correct her, and that strikes me as odd, but she shows us in to her office. As I pass her, she whispers, "Well done."

I peek at her and smirk before shaking my head. She gives me a quick wink as she rounds the table and opens up an album. I laugh at her insinuation. While he looks over her portfolio of past events, I sneak a glance at Trey to see what it is that Lisa seems so impressed with. Perhaps it's his tall stature, or chiseled jaw, but neither of those are enough to elicit the reaction she had when we walked in. *At least, not in my opinion.* To me, his rugged appearance seems out of place for an office setting, but then again, when you own your own business, I guess you can make whatever rules seem to fit. He *is* attractive, but if I compare him to Ryan, there's no contest. I shrug off her obvious attraction to him and try to turn my focus back to the album in front of us. Only when I do, Trey looks up and catches me looking at him, smirking as he returns to his conversation with Lisa.

I'm instantly embarrassed because I'm sure he thinks I was checking him out, and my bright red cheeks will only solidify that thought more. I sigh and resign my thoughts to the business at hand, the T.M. Enterprises event. "Excuse me, Lisa," I interrupt as she describes the most recent corporate even she hosted. "How many did you say this facility holds?"

She looks through her folder and hands me a sheet of paper. "The room just across from us holds three hundred, and the smaller room holds about one hundred and fifty. If you wanted the entire place, we can accommodate approximately six hundred."

Trey is pleased with her numbers, as well as her presentation. I had a feeling he would like Ivy Glen, which is why I wanted to bring him here first; now all the others will have to meet these standards, at a minimum. He gives me an appreciative nod and I wrap up our meeting with Lisa, letting her know that I'll be in touch soon. Walking out of the Ivy, I feel even more confident that I will be able to provide everything that is needed for this event.

"So how's your husband?" Trey asks as we approach his car.

Bemused, I look at him, and then down to my hand, fidgeting with my engagement ring. "I'm not married. Why do you ask?"

"Whoever he was looked ready to kick my ass the other night," he answers, as he continues walking, leaving me standing in place, realizing where I know him from.

Fuck.

chapter 9

To say the ride back to his office was uncomfortable is an understatement. Awkward? Yes. Hell on earth? Absolutely.

I would be lying if I said that I didn't find Trey attractive, because he is. Riding in a car with Mr. Miller, my client was professional. *Easy.* But riding with Trey Miller, the handsome stranger that wanted to save me not too long ago, I felt vulnerable. For some reason, learning that he was the guy from the other night made me feel exposed. There was a need in me to find something about him to connect the would-be-hero to my client.

I tried to keep my gaze from falling anywhere, except on him, but it was hard to ignore his presence. I was aware of his arm between us and watched as his strong hand flexed when shifting gears. He had taken his jacket off before getting into the car, so his white fitted dress shirt left very little to the imagination.

He clears his throat and speaks with an apologetic tone. "I didn't mean to make you uncomfortable."

"I'm not uncomfortable," I lie. "It's fine."

"I told you I knew you from somewhere," he says. When I look at him, an amused smile crosses his lips. *Is he flirting with me?*

"Yes." I return his smile and nod. "You did say that. Guess I should have listened. I have to admit, I'm a little embarrassed now, knowing that was you." I can feel my cheeks turning hot. "I don't drink in front of my clients."

"Well, lucky for you, I wasn't a client that night." His eyes remain fixed on the road ahead. "Just a guy who wanted to help a girl out," he finishes, causing my pulse to quicken.

Neither one of us says anything else for a few minutes, but then he glances at me, and speaks up again. "So if you're not married, why did he call you his wife?"

My body tenses and my throat feels tight as I try to give a light response. "Actually, we're engaged, and you know how territorial men can be."

"Is he going to be okay with you coordinating this event?" he asks, with a genuine concern that I appreciate.

"Ryan? He'll be fine, not that he's around right now anyway," I answer. *Why did I say that?*

"What do you mean he's not around?" he asks, baffled by my response.

I huff an annoyed breath, "He just moved to California this weekend for work."

"And you didn't go with him?"

"Obviously I didn't," I retort forgetting for the moment that this is a client, allowing my anger to seep through. Not that I owe *Mr. Miller* an explanation, and yet I can't seem to stop revealing too much of my personal shit.

"It's none of my business," he admits. "I apologize for prying."

I nod and give Trey a tight smile, trying my best to change the mood.

A short time later, he pulls into the T.M. parking lot and I try to remain cool as I exit the car. I grab my belongings and notice that he's waiting at the front of his parking space for me. I gather what's left of my pride and I walk over to shake his hand. "It was nice meeting you."

He reaches his hand to take mine and holds it gently, sending tingles throughout my body. "I agree. I hope I didn't make things awkward."

The only thing that's uncomfortable are the butterflies that decide to take up residence in the pit of my stomach at this very moment. I do my best to cover any signs that he's affecting me so I can focus on the task at hand.

"Lisa said she would email me the different table layouts they have used in the past, as well as some caterers that they have worked well with," I say in a rush, trying to allow myself to make a somewhat graceful exit. "I'll also contact the other facilities you mentioned to get an idea of their capacity."

"Okay, well, we can work on that next," he counters, his gaze boring into me.

"Trey?"

"Yeah?"

"I need my hand back," I inform him when I feel my fingers becoming increasingly clammy.

He lets go and shrugs. "Sorry 'bout that. Just let me know when you have that information and we'll set up another meeting."

You know that feeling you get when you know someone is watching you? That's the feeling I have right now, and I can't help but feel self-conscious thinking he's checking out my ass. My suspicions are confirmed when I chance a look back and his eyes snap up to meet mine. He flashes a bright smile, unapologetically checking me out.

Driving back to the office, I keep reminding myself it's not the end of the world. Then again, my fiancé only snapped at my first and only solo client, not that I'm mad at him, he didn't know.

* * *

Since I have been away for most of the day, my desk is empty when I set my files down. I pull out my notes so that I can type everything up to add to the client information sheet when Cam comes by my desk to see how the meeting went. She knows how nervous I was to handle this one on my own. When I look at her, she can tell something's up. "How did it go?"

"It was great. Have you been to their offices before?" I'm slightly over-exaggerating my excitement, and I hope she doesn't question why.

"I haven't, but I heard they're pretty nice,"

"Yeah, very impressive." I start unloading my bag before I sit down. "Mr. Miller wanted me to show him some other places, but we stayed at Ivy Glen so long, we didn't get a chance," I huff, leaning back in my chair.

"Does he want to see the other places?"

"I'm not sure," I start; debating on sharing with her the apprehension I feel after what just took place.

"Well, he either does want to see them, or he doesn't. Did you ask him?"

"Not exactly," I say, avoiding her stare.

"What's going on?" she demands. "Please tell me you didn't blow this?"

The sting of her accusation causes my defenses to go up and my voice becomes very controlled. "No, Cam. I didn't blow it, but thanks for believing in me."

"What am I supposed to think? You won't give me a straight answer, so what's the deal?"

Resigned to sharing with her my experience with Trey, I sit back and wait for her to do the same. "Remember that night I got wasted and drunk-dialed you?" I don't wait for her to acknowledge, because she still teases me about that night. "Trey- I mean, Mr. Miller- is the guy who Ryan got all pissy with."

"What?"

"I didn't even know who he was. I mean, he seemed familiar, but you know how many people we see at the weddings and corporate events we coordinate, I just figured maybe I'd seen him at one of those," I explain to her. "It wasn't until he asked about my *husband* that I knew who he was, even though he pretty much had to tell me."

"Did he-" Cam starts, but is cut off by Elle.

"Emogen." She summons me from her office. "Can you come in here a sec?"

Without so much as another word on the matter, I leave my desk, files in hand, for Elle's office. When I get to her door, she waves me in while leaving a message for someone. She hangs up and folds her arms over her chest, appearing very stern. "I was just talking to Mr. Miller on the phone," she explains.

"Elle, I can explain…" I try to beat her to the punch. "I really appreciate you letting me take this on, but I don't think I'm ready to go it alone yet. Perhaps you could put someone else on this account?"

Her face contorts into confusion as she leans forward, placing her arms on her desk. "Why would I give the T.M. event to someone else?"

"I just think someone with more experience should handle it," I admit half-heartedly.

"I'm sorry, but that's not going to happen, not after the phone call I just had with Mr. Miller," she says. "He just increased the budget by another ten grand. With the stipulation that you continue to handle everything."

"He did what?" I ask, astounded. "Why would he do that? He hasn't even seen the other venues; we didn't get to talk about catering or entertainment, whether they would need a valet service-" Elle throws a hand up in the air, halting my ramblings.

"There is plenty of time for all of that. You will need to set up a time to meet with him to visit the other places, and go over all of the other stuff you just mentioned." With another wave of her hand, she dismisses me. I stand to leave her office, baffled by everything that just happened. "Whatever you're doing, Emogen..." I look back to see her staring at her computer screen. "Keep doing it."

Cam sees me approaching my desk and meets me there, curiosity all over her face. "What was that all about?"

When I don't answer, she tries again to get my attention. "Hello?"

"I'm sorry, what?" I ask, still processing what Elle just told me.

"I asked what happened."

When I finally look at her, I shake away the confusion that has settled over me. "I'll tell you about it when we meet at my place later."

* * *

Joss had things to take care of at work, so she called and said she would be over later, which was fine with me. All I wanted to do was get home, change my clothes, and forget about today. The apartment is still a mess from when Ryan left. I haven't had the motivation to clean up after myself; something about the disaster area lets me feel like I'm not alone. Although I'm sure if Ryan were here, the mess would be ten times worse. We've had a routine since moving out here that Friday night is our cleanup time; after our busy week, straightening up leaves us able to relax for the rest of the weekend.

But right now, staring at the kitchen counter, the couch and whatever is left of the floor, Friday is today, because my friends are coming over, and this mess will just alarm them. I make quick time of rinsing the dishes and loading the dishwasher before picking all the laundry off the floor. The knock on the door tells me one, or both, of the girls are here, so I grab the last of the clothes and toss them into my room, shutting the door behind me.

"Coming," I yell, looking around once more for any evidence of the last few sloppy days. When I open the door, Joss pushes past me, a bottle of wine in hand. "By all means, come on in," I say, following behind her.

"Bitchy, much?"

"I'm not bitchy," I argue, grabbing two glasses from the cabinet. "It's been a long day. But what's up with you?"

She hasn't been still for a second, only makes a show of tossing her stuff on the table so she has both hands to open the wine. "Remember that guy I told you about at work?"

"Would this be 'Evil Bastard' or 'Sleazy Bastard'?"

She stops mid-pour and smiles, touching her heart. "Aw, you do listen to me." I laugh, and encourage her to continue. "Evil Bastard," she explains, "and I have been working on a huge project. We are in the middle of setting up several contracts that will allow the company license to work in the larger cities, which is great. We've been working day and night." She turns to face me. "Look at these." She points to her eyes. "I don't do baggy eyes."

"Shut up, Joss." I grab my glass and head to the couch. "You look great and you know it."

"That's beside the point," she brushes me off to finish her story. "So, Evil Bastard tells me, 'hey, we're almost done with this, let's call it a night and pick up tomorrow.'"

"That was nice."

She glares at me. "Not. Finished." I throw my hands up

apologetically and she continues, "Fucker shows up this morning, early, and goes to the project manager and shows him the completed project. And takes all the credit!"

"He didn't!"

"Yes he did, asshole!" She takes a large gulp of wine and lets out a heavy sigh.

The silence stretches and I huff out a relieved breath. "Wow, and I was going to complain about *my* day."

Joss sits up and turns to face me. "What happened to you today?"

"Do you remember the guy from the club? Oh, no, of course you don't, you were too busy hiding from me because you called Ryan to tell on me." She doesn't even try to argue, because I have let her off the hook, up to this point. "I told you some guy tried to be all 'white-knight' on me that night in front of Ryan, right?"

"Vaguely," she admits, raising her half-empty glass at me. *Yep, this is familiar.*

"Yeah, well, I don't remember much about what he looked like, since I was no better off than you. But apparently, he remembers me."

"What in the *hell* are you talking about? How do you know he remembers you?"

"It figures, Elle lets me take on my first project alone and my client contact there gets fired."

"So?"

"So, now I have to deal with the owner. The owner who just happens to be the guy from the club." When I finish, I grab my glass of wine, raising it to Joss and lean back, exhausted.

"Are you shitting me?"

"I shit you not," I respond, causing us both to laugh. The sudden knock on the door tells me that my two friends are finally going to meet and I just hope they hit it off.

My phone ringing, somewhere, halts me mid-step, and I turn to Joss asking her to get the door while I answer my phone. When I finally locate it, I'm happy to see that it's Ryan. As Joss gets the door I look over at them. "Cam, Joss. Joss, Cam." I nod to Joss. "Fill her in, I'll be right back." I head into my room and shut the door behind me so I can talk privately.

"Hey babe," I answer, with the first genuine smile I've had today.

"How's it goin'?"

"Not too bad." The emptiness of him being gone hits me like a brick. "Awful. I miss you so much."

"I know, baby, I miss you, too." When he speaks those words, I know he means them.

"How was your day?"

"It wasn't too bad. Alex and I had to stay late to finish up some paperwork, so I'm exhausted," he admits, "but I wish I was there with you."

"Me too," I admit, sinking into my bed. If sadness were tangible, it would be my entire being.

"So how did your meeting go today?"

"It was good. Great, actually." My excitement is short-lived. "I mean, I still have to gather more information, and show more places, but the good thing is that they increased their budget, so Elle was very happy."

"That's awesome, Em. I'm so proud of you." I can tell he's smiling that smile that I love, which makes mine show through on my end. "So, you get along with the lady alright?"

"Actually," I pause to figure out what I'm going to tell him, so I leave out details. "I met with the owner. He had to fire Sandy, not sure why, so I'll have to meet with him for the planning."

"What did Elle say about that?" He knows how controlling she can be.

"She was great, insisted that this is my project, even with the increase in budget." I don't tell him that a stipulation was that I handle it myself, red flags would be going up all over the place.

"That's good that she's letting you run with it. You excited?"

"I am, there is so much I can do, and I'm just happy I get the chance to prove what I'm capable of."

"Damn, babe, I really wish I were there to show you how proud I am of you. You deserve it."

And just like that, my mood takes a dive, and this is where he gets off. "I wish you were here, too."

"We'll see each other soon, I promise. Okay?" He doesn't wait for a response, he knows me too well, and knows I'll probably start to argue. "I love you."

"I love you, too, Ry." There is a lump in my throat that I feel is suffocating me, but I try my best to finish, even if it's just with a whispered, "Goodnight."

Looking down at the phone in my hand, I want to cry, and my bed looks like the perfect place to mope. The sudden laugher and talking from the living room pulls me out of my lonely thoughts, so I follow the noise, standing in the doorway, watching my friends get to know each other. They see me standing there, and almost in unison, jump on me. "So?"

"What?" I head to the couch under their intense stares. "It was just Ryan."

"Yeah, we figured that much," Cam teases. "Did you tell him about who you're working with?"

"I did." Not quite the truth, but I told him, so I'm not lying when I say this.

"Did you tell him that the guy whose ass he wanted to kick at the club is the same guy you're having to work with?" Joss rephrases.

Damn it! She knows me too well.

"No. Okay? I didn't spell it out. I mean, what good would that do anyway?"

Joss and Cam both look at me, and then away, like they know I know better. Joss is the first to speak up. "If it's not a big deal, then why are you making it seem like it is?"

"You know how Ryan gets. And it's *not* a big deal, this is my career we're talking about, okay?"

Joss looks over at Cam, a silent conversation taking place between them and I feel like they are teaming up against me. Cam nods her head, prompting Joss to speak up.

"How, exactly, does Ryan get? Because, as long as I've known him, I've never seen him overreact or go all Neanderthal."

"That's not what I mean. There's nothing to tell, and if I make it a point to say mention it, he's going to *think* something's up."

Cam shakes her head at Joss and looks back to me. "Em, Trey is damn sexy."

"So what's your point?"

"See?" Joss goads with a huge grin, "You think so, too."

"You two are jerks! I leave the room for five minutes and you've already discussed my relationship and now you're turning on me. Not cool."

Joss laughs, "Look, since you seem to be drowning in sexy men, both available and unavailable, don't you think it's only fair you let someone else have some fun?"

"Bitch," I say, narrowing my eyes at her with a smile. "You're just lucky I love you."

chapter 10

After the girls left last night, I started to rethink my objections to their concerns. Trey, I mean, *Mr. Miller*, is a client. And while I do think he's attractive, I have Ryan, who I love more than anything, and a job to do.

This is just a job, I remind myself, and I can handle whatever comes my way. With that in mind, I send him an email detailing the information I gathered from our meeting, as well as what I'll be working on before we meet again. However, I didn't count on such a swift response.

> Trey Miller
> August 13, 2013 9:08 AM
> To: Kane, Emogen
> Re: Venue Notes - Ivy Glen
>
> Emogen,
>
> Thank you for the information from yesterday. I am concerned with the location, as many of my clients are downtown. I would like to see a few more locations before making my decision, so if you could set something up, I would appreciate it.
>
> I also need to discuss the entertainment you suggested, because I feel it would be best to have something that

appeals to the entire audience, not just the younger crowd.

Regards,
Trey Miller
T.M. Enterprises

There is no hint of the tension from the day before, and I exhale a breath in relief. The girls were wrong to get on my case for the way I handled things, there's nothing to handle. I send him a response to let him know we are on the same page.

>
> Emogen Kane
> August 13, 2013 9:24 AM
> To: Miller, Trey
> Re: Re: Venue Notes - Ivy Glen

Mr. Miller,

I agree about other locations, and I am contacting the other places to see what they have available. Please let me know when you have some time so I can show you a few of the places I have in mind. I agree that Ivy Glen is out of the way, but I believe it may be our best option for space, and that is one of the few places that allow you to bring your own vendors. I will check to see what other locations, central to the downtown area, will allow this as well.

Regards,
Emogen Kane
Event Planner

Elle E. Grant Events

I press send and start looking for the venues that have proven to be sure things in the past. Elle tends to go for the popular locations, but I believe there is an untapped market when going to the outskirts of town. As someone who has only lived here a short time, I tend to gravitate to the places that I hear about from other people. These people don't live, work and play in the downtown area; they're transplants, like me.

Since Tuesday mornings at work are pretty low-key, we spend most of our time on the phone confirming dates and times, or sending emails to clients about what we need to proceed. The most hectic day is definitely Thursday, because, as planners, we run all over the place to pick up any last-minute items to make sure the events run smooth. I'm at an advantage because I have one client to focus on, where Cam, Elle and the others have the experience to handle multiple clients at once. I guess that's a backhanded advantage, because Elle is still testing me to see what I'm capable of.

I pick up my phone to call The Parlor, another venue I think will appeal to T.M. Enterprise's clientele, but I don't have a chance to make that call. I can hear someone on the other end. "Hello? I mean, Elle E. Grant Events, this is Emogen Kane."

"Emogen," a male voice repeats, and I know that it's *Mr*. Miller. "This is Trey."

"Good morning," I respond. "What can I do for you?"

"I just got your email, and I wanted to see if you could meet for lunch. I have a few questions about the venues you have in mind, but I'm running to a meeting in a few minutes."

"If you'd like, I can email you the places I have along with some details. I know you're busy," I acknowledge, hoping that I don't have to have lunch with Trey, *Mr. Miller*.

"No, that's okay," he sounds distracted. "Just bring it with you. I'll pick you up at eleven thirty. Will that be okay?"

I glance at my calendar, hoping there is something to keep me from being alone with him again. But there is nothing, and I hope the defeat I feel isn't evident in my tone. "No, that will be fine, Mr. Miller."

"Okay, I'll see you then," he says. "And Emogen? It's Trey."

He hangs up, leaving me feeling as though I may have just fucked up. He sounded more irritated than pissed, but then again, he probably hates being called 'mister' as much as I hate someone my age responding with a 'yes ma'am' to me.

For the next two hours, I gather as much information as possible to share with Trey. I have choices for vendors, caterers, entertainers and florists to discuss with him, so there won't be a lull in our meeting. I should have insisted on meeting him someplace, yet here I am, waiting at my desk like a sixteen-year-old waiting for her date to show up.

Callie, our receptionist, buzzes me. "Emogen, Mr. Miller is here for you."

"Thank you, Callie. I'll be right there." I let go of the button and grab my files to stuff them into my oversized leather bag.

When I make my way to the front desk and see Trey, all of my senses go out the window. Ryan who? No, I shake my head. I love Ryan. I love Ryan. I repeat this with every step I take toward a grinning Trey Miller.

"I'm sorry I'm early," he says, reaching for my bag. I pull the strap a little closer to my body, as if it has the ability to save me from my wayward thoughts.

"I've got it," I say, referring to my bag. "My mom always said 'If you're on time, you're late,' so I guess you're just fine."

Why did I just quote my mom? And why did she ever use that line; she's never been early a day in her life. I shake off my thoughts with a laugh and try to refocus.

He smiles and I look back to Callie, who seems to be picking up on my awkwardness. "Can you let Cam know I'll be back in a little?" Trey walks off ahead of me, and Callie's gaze follow him. "Callie?"

"Oh yeah, not a problem," she says looking at me. Then she, not so subtly mouths, "Damn! He's hot!"

* * *

During the drive to the restaurant, I wrestle with what to say, if anything, but fortunately for me Trey makes light conversation that was easy to reciprocate. By the time we make it to Café Cellar, I have become comfortable with his presence. The maître d shows us a table in the back and I immediately begin to pull out the file containing the information I wished to discuss with him.

"Relax, Emogen," he says. "Let's order and then you can open that oversized bag of tricks."

I laugh at his description of my briefcase and exhale, hoping he doesn't hear. We order our drinks and food and it's then that I start running my mouth, as though I have never heard of a filter. "I've told Ryan I wanted to try this place, but we just haven't had time since we're both so busy."

"I've been here a few times, the food is great. I think you'll like it," he says with an easy smile.

"Ryan can be a food snob sometimes, so unless they serve the 'best burger ever,' we haven't tried it."

"That doesn't sound like a snob, sounds like he just knows what he wants," he counters. "Not that I blame him." When I look up he's eyeing me, with a beautiful grin, as if we are more than colleagues.

I feel my face flush and I begin to stammer like an idiot. "Well, Ryan and I haven't lived here for long, so we still have lots to check out," I say, trying to ignore his last comment. "Hopefully we can check them out when he comes to town."

"Emogen," he leans forward, placing his hand over mine. He lowers his voice and waits for my eyes to meet his. "I think *Ryan* is lucky to have you."

My head is swimming in confusion. His words say one thing, but the way he looks at me says something completely different. I feel like he's trying to convince me that he's not interested, so perhaps he should refrain from looking at me the way he is right now. Maybe he's like this with everyone, and I can't help the twinge of disappointment I feel at the notion that maybe I'm reading more into the gestures than he means. It's not like I *want* Trey to be interested in me, but the moment he assures me he's not, I will want it.

"No," I bite out a little harsher than I intend. "I'm the lucky one." I rush to make a mental list of the reasons why I'm so lucky to have Ryan in my life, but Trey interrupts my thoughts.

"So what do you have to show me?"

I pull out his file and begin my presentation for his event. He seems impressed with the rough layout I have created based on Lisa's floor plan. When I give him the options of a theme, he is quick to eliminate a few of them, which makes my job a little easier.

"Mr. Miller." I rush to correct myself, "Trey. Can I ask why you increased your budget?"

He doesn't hesitate when he responds, "Emogen- I'm sorry, can I call you, Em? Emogen seems a little too formal."

Thrown off guard by that question, I nod, unsure what defenses I have just let down. "Yeah, that's fine. *Ryan* calls me that all the time."

He huffs a short laugh and shakes his head. "The thing is, I have many clients, but there are others with my competition that I would like to acquire. So that being said, I want to increase my guest list. But more importantly, I believe you are very capable. You have great ideas and you listen to what I want for the evening. That's why I insisted to Elle that this be your event. Unless you are uncomfortable for some reason."

When he finishes his mini-speech, I exhale and the biggest grin creeps on to my face. "I really do appreciate your confidence in me."

"I have no reason to believe otherwise."

Sitting in front of him, I feel exposed and vulnerable. I know nothing about Trey, where he comes from, what motivates him or what he wants out of life, but he intimidates the hell out of me. The way he looks at me isn't lust, but it still feels intimate. That's a word that should not ever enter my mind when thinking about a client. *Hell, I shouldn't even be thinking about a client at all.*

The food comes out at the perfect moment and it looks amazing. We are both fiddling with our plates and silverware. I place my napkin in my lap and pick up my fork, ready to dive in, when I look up to say, "Thank you, Trey."

He looks up at me and his next words cause my cheeks to flame. "Em? Ryan *is* a lucky man." And then disappointment sets in. "He has nothing to be worried about."

Why do his words bother me so much?

chapter 11 ~ *3 weeks later*

"Babe," he whispers, kissing my cheek, as I lay sleeping. "C'mon, we need to get up."

"Five more minutes," I answer, rolling over as I pull the comforter over my head.

When he peels the comforter back, he brushes my hair away from my face and plants a kiss to the crook of my neck that sends a shiver through my body, but I keep my eyes closed, just loving his touch. His hand rests on my hip for a moment before it begins a slow movement from my waist to my chest. "I can think of other things to do if you're not ready to wake up yet," he says suggestively. The mere suggestion of early morning extracurriculars leaves me restless, but he doesn't yield his teasing.

"We can't," I whine, but only halfheartedly. "Just lie here and hold me."

His hand is splayed across my stomach and he pulls me to lay on my back, and because I'm so tired, I follow his movements lazily. Before I can register his action, his mouth is meshed with mine and my hands thread through his hair, holding him to me. The feeling of him beside me one second and over me the next leaves me aching for more and slowly giving in.

"Changing your mind?" he asks, as he grins against my lips.

"You always change my mind," I tell him between kisses.

Being in these arms and feeling him pressed against me is where I want to be. Screw work and getting up, my world is perfect; *he* is perfect.

"Trey-" My voice sounds needy, even to me.

The moment his name escapes, my arms flail and I am jolted upright as I look around the room trying to figure out what's going on. Something inside finally clicks and I rub my eyes furiously as they burn with the light creeping through the window. My heart rate is accelerated and I realize that I'm in my bed. *Alone*.

"Not again," I groan, throwing myself back onto my pillow. I have woken up from the early stages of a dream. *A bad, bad dream*. Guilt and embarrassment wash over me when I realize I was about to have another sex dream about Trey, Mr. Miller - my client. My client who is *not* my fiancé. The same client that has made it clear that he has no interest in me. I have to chalk these dreams up to spending so much time with him while planning his party.

It all started when he made a point to tell me that he was no threat to Ryan. I never considered him a threat, but when he put it out there, it seems that's all I've been able to focus on. Of course he's not a threat, I love Ryan, and we are in the middle of planning our wedding. Some of the details which we plan on taking care of this weekend when he visits.

The cell phone is charging next to my side of the bed and it begins buzzing, snapping me out of mentally chastising myself. At first I think it's my alarm, but I quickly discover that it's actually ringing. A surge of excitement runs through me when I see that it's Ryan, but my excitement fades when I remember I just woke up from a sex dream. About Trey.

It was just a dream, I try to remind myself, but I don't think my brain is getting the message.

"Hello?" I answer, clearing my suddenly dry throat.

"Hey babe." His tired voice filters through the phone. "You up?"

"Yeah, just got up. You never called last night. Everything okay?" I ask, looking at the time on my clock.

"Sorry about that?" he says in a tired voice. "I had a late night; stayed behind to help Alex get this package together to send out in the morning. We still didn't finish, so we have to go in early today, just to check it all and make sure it's put together right."

"That sucks," I respond, still distracted from my dream.

"Everything okay? You sound like you're getting sick." I smile because he's concerned about me, so I go along with it.

"Yeah, I might be coming down with something," I start, "and it doesn't help that I got a crap night's sleep last night."

He laughs lightly, and I can picture his face when he speaks. "Sometimes you say the weirdest things."

"It's not weird," I argue back, teasing him. "It makes perfect sense to me."

"Alright. If you say so. You have a busy day ahead?"

"I have several meetings, and I have to take my client to see a few florists today." The moment I mention my "client," my cheeks burn, my neck feels hot and I start to look around like I've just been caught, which is ridiculous since Ryan isn't even here.

"Okay, then, I don't wanna keep you," he starts. "I was just thinking about you, wanted to make sure we're all set for tomorrow."

"I made sure to let Elle know that I'm only working a half-day, so I'm all yours after that."

"You're always all mine," he counters quickly, leaving me grinning like some sort of idiot.

"Always," I agree.

"I better let you go, I just wanted to hear your voice before I started my day."

"It's a great start now." I smile, because it's true.

"I love you, Em." His voice grows painfully quiet and I wish he were here holding me. "Call me later?"

He sounds so sad with that question and my heart clenches. "Of course I will, and Ryan?"

"Yeah?"

"I love you, too."

Our goodbyes late at night and early in the morning seem to be the most intimate, the most real. There's a pain to them, something so raw. Every time we say it, I remember again how much I love him, and why I'm doing my damnedest to make this work. Hanging up the phone, I try to relax, when my dream comes blazing through my memory again.

"Shit!"

I take a quick glance at my watch and I have just enough time to call Langley and see what she has to say. My sister always gives the best advice, even if I don't always listen to it. I hope that I don't catch her and her man, Reid, at an awkward time. Just thinking about it, I want to hang up the phone and call later, but then she answers.

"Hey Emmy." Her use of my childhood nickname makes me smile. "Why are you calling so early?"

"I'm sorry, I was just about to hang up. I know you probably have a busy day," I admit, but only because I really don't want to talk now.

"I'm up now, what's going on?"

"It's nothing, really," I say, trying to come up with another reason for my call. But when I can't come up with anything, I go with the truth. "It's just, I had a dream this morning. It was starting to get pretty hot when I woke up."

"Nothing wrong with that," she teases. "Besides, Ryan will be there tomorrow and you can take care of that."

"Well," I pause, unsure how she'll take the rest of it. "That's the thing, it wasn't about Ryan."

"Trey?" she asks clearing her throat. I hear her shuffle, I assume, to make sure she's alert for my answer.

"Yeah?" I wince on my end, because saying it out loud makes me feel really weird.

"This guy must be pretty damn good looking if you dream about him."

"Lang," I groan from embarrassment, "this wasn't the first dream. I've had similar ones for a few nights now."

"You're overthinking this, okay. Ryan has been gone for what, a month now? You miss him, you don't see him every day like you used to, but you do see your client rather frequently. It makes sense that you would have dreams about him, but it doesn't mean anything. You'll get to see Ry tomorrow, and I imagine when he leaves, you'll be having all sorts of dreams about what you want to do to him. It's not a big deal."

"Are you sure?"

"Do you want the dreams to mean something?"

"Of course not," I protest, offended by her question.

"If you say so," she says in that condescending tone that only Lang can get away with.

"Why do you have to go there? I wasn't implying I want there to be something more, I know there's nothing more. I just needed you to help me sort through it. Hell, you're the damn psych major, I thought maybe you'd have some insight that didn't come with a side of morning bitch," I snap in a snarky tone.

"Feel better?"

"Yes!" I huff before I start laughing. "Thanks, I needed that. I gotta go; I'm already running a few minutes behind. I'll call you this weekend."

"You better not call me!" Her voice is playful. "I expect you to be tied up with Ryan all weekend, and I really don't want to hear any of the details. So just call me when you're sitting on the couch, curled in your little ball with your blankey and a box of tissues after he leaves. Then I'll remind you, again, why this will all be fine." The way she delivers this monologue implies she is familiar with getting my attitude in check, although the blankey part is a stretch.

"I love that you have so much faith in my falling apart," I quip.

"If you didn't fall apart, you wouldn't need me," she snaps back, but she knows that's a lie.

"Fine. You're right, I'll call when I fall apart on Sunday, five o'clock work for you?" I ask joking.

"Yep, got you penciled in." She pauses. "Love you Emmy, it'll be okay."

"Thanks and again, I'm sorry I called so early."

When I hang up, I feel much better. Even if the dream does come to mind, it doesn't cause me to have guilty feelings or even blush, so that's a step in the right direction. I make quick time of getting ready, which is a little easier since I had already pulled out my burgundy knee-length flowing dress to wear with my favorite cowboy boots. I wash my face and apply makeup, all the while glancing at the clock by my bed. I pull my hair into a loose ponytail and rush to the kitchen to make a cup of coffee. I will need at least one to get me on my toes for meeting with the florists today.

I had emailed Trey before I left work yesterday to confirm our appointments with four of the local florists. I know who my preference is, and I hope that it's the one Trey selects, but it's important to give him options. He insisted on coming to the Elle E. Grant office to meet me, because he wasn't planning on going to his office today. Not wanting to push it, I agreed.

I finish my cup of coffee and grab another for the road. Yeah, it's going to be one of those days. When I get to my car, I realize that I have random articles of clothing, empty bags and trash scattered throughout. I rush to grab one of the bags and do a half-assed cleanup, tossing everything into my trunk to deal with later. Ryan would be beyond irritated to see what a mess it is, but he'll never see it this bad since I plan on cleaning it this afternoon. I sit behind the wheel and turn the ignition; the time reads seven fifteen, more than enough time to get to the office. I plug in my iPod and find a song to listen to on the way there. "Lucky" by Jason Mraz fills the car, and I start off for work.

chapter 12

Our wedding group at Elle E. Grant probably has the hardest job because, not only are they on a deadline, but they also have to work with bridezillas. I'm so happy that I get to handle the corporate events, even though I've helped with a few weddings since I started here.

Elle asked everyone to come in early today since there are three weddings on Saturday alone. She usually has three employees for each event. I would normally step in, but with Ryan's arrival tomorrow, it just won't work. I was more than happy to come in early, but I still won't be much help since I have an appointment with Trey. I emailed him yesterday to confirm the time, even though I don't feel it's necessary for him to be there. This event seems to be really important to him, and since he's the client, he calls the shots. If he wants to be there for every meeting, with every vendor, then so be it.

"Emogen." The sound of my name over the phone on my desks grabs my attention. "Trey Miller is here to see you."

"Thank you, Callie."

I look over to Cam, who is knee-deep in York-Slayde wedding details. "Cam? We still on for movie night tonight?"

"Yeah," she responds automatically, never looking up, "see you later."

I pause for a moment, wondering if I should make sure she heard me, but she's in the zone, and you don't mess with her when she's like this. "Alright, see you then."

I make my way to the front and notice Callie trying to gain Trey's attention. She's a cute, spunky girl, but he doesn't seem to notice. It's a shame, because she's smart and funny, a far cry from the clean-cut girls I imagine he dates. *Why am I thinking about the type of girl he dates?*

"Mr. Miller," I call out, earning a raised eyebrow. "I'm ready when you are."

He smirks and I know that he's annoyed by my use of formal titles. He leads the way and addresses me as he holds the door for me, "Ms. Kane." I can't help but feel somewhat awkward being with him. I mean, I just had a really nice dream about him. *Not Ryan.*

"If you don't mind, I'll be driving today," I inform him, mainly because I need the distraction of the road. "We have several stops to make, and I don't want you to have to rely on my directions. So if you wouldn't mind, I have the maps of our stops." He might know this town better than me, but *I* know *me*. If I let him drive, I'll probably be checking him out the entire time.

I hand him the paperwork for the locations and his fingers brush mine when he takes them from me. I shudder at the brief contact, loving it and hating it all at once, but I do my best to conceal it. When I look away I feel his eyes on me, so I chance a look in his direction, but he is looking over the list of places we will be visiting.

"I guess we better get moving," he says, flashing a flirtatious smile. "Which is your car?"

I point to my old Acura that still looks new, and as we make our way toward it, I make sure to keep a safe distance from him. As I make my way to the driver's side, I finally speak, "Hearts and Flowers is expecting us in about thirty minutes. We should have enough time to get there, right?"

He climbs into the passenger seat and shuts the door before looking at the address. "Yeah, that shouldn't be a problem. We'll just take a few side streets and avoid the construction on Mason."

I give him a tight smile and nod, acknowledging his instruction before turning the ignition. I begin driving out of the office parking lot knowing, at least to a point, where I need to go. The conversation is relegated to a 'turn here,' or a 'make a right at the next light,' which is fine with me. But I guess that's not enough for him because he eventually breaks the silence. "Is everything okay, Em?"

"Yeah," I answer innocently. "Did I miss a turn or something?"

"No. I mean, what's going on? You're acting a little strange."

"I'm fine." I try hard to sell it.

"If you say so." It's obvious that he's not convinced, but I'm glad he lets it go. It's not like I'm going to tell my client, *'Oh ya know, just started having a sex dream about you this morning, and now I can't stop thinking about it.'* I laugh at the absurdity and catch him looking at me bemused.

"Any big plans this weekend?" he asks as a genuine smile that answers for me spreads across my face. "Ah, the fiancé must be visiting."

"Yeah, he comes in tomorrow afternoon," I confirm, feeling like a kid on Christmas Eve. "I'm going to take a half-day off to be with him."

"So he's okay with us working together?"

I feel my smile fade and admit the truth. "Actually, he doesn't know it's you. It's not that I think that it's a big deal, I just don't want to cause any undue drama."

We arrive to the first flower shop and it comes at the perfect time.

I don't enjoy having my life on display, especially with Trey asking the questions. I pull into a parking spot and grab my files so we can meet with Katelyn. I gave her all of the information she needed for this meeting, but I'm less than enthused about this. She has been hard to get a hold of, and when I finally do, she conducts herself in a way I deem unprofessional. We walk into the small shop that is full of fragrant, beautiful flowers but no Katelyn in sight.

"Hello?" I call out, hoping someone is here.

"Just a minute," a low female voice calls out. She sees me and turns her nose. "Can I help you?"

"Hi, I'm looking for Katelyn," I say, knowing this is her but curious how she's going to play it off.

This woman has a huge chip on her shoulder, and I can't help but wonder if she greets all customers this way. But her attitude changes when Trey comes to stand next to me. Yes, he is a handsome man, but good grief, she acts as if he's God's gift to women. She drops her attitude and smiles right at him, ignoring my presence, and extends a well-manicured hand to him. "I'm Katelyn."

He shakes her hand as I make introductions and her smile never waivers. She starts on a hard sell about what she can do, and shows us an album of weddings and corporate dinners she has created arrangements for in the past. I'm not too impressed, but the arrangements on display in the shop *are* beautiful. I don't know what I expected from meeting her, but I feel less than wowed by her efforts. Trey and I leave, telling her we'll be in touch. I hope that he has no intention of using her. I put the information she provided in the file and give him the address of the next shop we're visiting, so he can navigate.

Fortunately, the drive to Flowers by Jaysen is only ten minutes, which is filled with discussion of his impression of Katelyn. I'm relieved to know that he thought her lack of preparation was pathetic, and her obvious interest in him laughable. He ended it with some squirrel reference that I didn't quite get, but he seemed to be amused by.

When we arrive to the shop, I purposely leave the 'information' we received from Katelyn in the car. *We won't need that.*

The flower shop is quaint, but trendy, and as I take the two steps to the entrance a thin, tall and handsome guy greets us at the door. "Emogen?" He cocks his head and squints when he says my name.

"Yes, and you're Jaysen." I extend my hand to shake his and he swats it away, in exchange for a hug. I don't hug, personal space and all.

"We've talked on the phone so many times, I feel as if we're already old friends," he says with a smile when he releases me.

I return his smile before introducing Trey. "This is Trey Miller, from T.M. Enterprises."

"Someone thinks highly of himself, *T.M.*," he comments on Trey's company name, emphasizing his initials. My eyes bug out, shocked by his brazen observation, but Trey just smiles.

"Great minds, huh?" Trey says with a self-confident shrug, pointing to Jaysen's sign, in reference the flower shop's name. I imagine no one has ever said that to his face before, but Trey smiles and shakes his head.

"Oh yeah, we're going to get along just fine," Jaysen says over his shoulder, as he leads us to his office.

"Emogen already told me that your colors are lilac and brown, so I took the liberty of creating a few centerpiece arrangements to show what I can do. She mentioned that you don't want oversized arrangements to get in the way of your guests chatting, and I totally agree."

"Great," Trey and I both say in unison, so I nod and he finishes, "let's have a look."

Jaysen gives me a crooked smile and raises his eyebrow in question, and I go wide-eyed. I give him a tight shake of my head, hoping he moves on, and to his credit, he completely reads me. Trey is already ahead of me, so he misses the entire exchange. I follow both of them and gasp when I see what Jaysen has put together. Not only did he work up an arrangement, but he also put together a table, complete with a brown tablecloth and dark lilac napkins. There is a white place setting, with a small name placard thanking the person for their business. And at the center of it all is an understated, yet beautiful flower arrangement. A small square vase contains an assortment of purple flowers, in varying shades, with splashes of cream and brown twigs woven in. It looks amazing, exactly what I envisioned when I told him the look I was going for. I can't believe he was able to do this based on just our conversations.

"This is perfect," I say in hushed tone, before realizing they heard me. I look at Trey apologetically, because he has the ultimate say. But he just nods his head, as if he reads my mind.

"I think you're right, Em." He looks away from me to Jaysen. "This will be great."

Jaysen gives us a confident nod, as if he knew it was in the bag, "So what are you going to tell those other florists you were supposed to meet? Because we know, I'm the best."

I can't argue it. In fact, I don't want to see the others, but we have meetings already scheduled. "We have two more to see, but I will let you know something by the end of the day." He smiles, and for a second, he appears unsure.

Trey leads the way toward the entrance but steps aside to let me pass. When I do, his hand accidently brushes mine, causing tingles to run down my spine. But when I look at him his deliberate smile tells me that he knows exactly what he's doing. There's nothing I can say about the gesture because he looks over at Jaysen who looks like his eyes are about to pop out. *I guess he saw that, too.*

"It was nice to meet you Jaysen. Emogen will call later today to make it official." And with that, he steps past me and continues walking out the door. I turn to Jaysen with a shock-filled look and he gives me a wide smile.

When I reach for his hand he pulls me close and whispers in my ear, "What was that all about?" I look at him and shrug, still stunned. "Well, figure it out and let me know. That man is hot."

* * *

We meet with the other two florists, and as suspected, they were ill-prepared, as well. Our meetings with each of them last no more than twenty minutes, one ending when Trey faked an urgent work situation he had to get back for. I am grateful for his white lie, and follow dutifully, since I need to get my client back to the office.

"Are you hungry?"

"I'm fine," I say driving toward the office. "I'll grab something at the office."

"Okay," he responds. "So what do you and Ryan have planned this weekend?"

I feel the smile creep onto my face. "We have some wedding details to take care of on Saturday, but other than that, I'm not sure. We'll probably end up at Wired Spirits, that's where a few of our friends like to go."

"How long has he been gone?"

"It's only been a month, but it's been a really hard month. Thankfully work and my friends have been my saving grace. It's hard being away from everything you know." I don't know why I just shared so much with him, but I don't feel weird about it.

"Having friends around is really important," he says, looking at me a little too intimately. "And working with me won't be a problem, right?"

I'm thrown off by his question, because I thought we already covered this, but if I have to say it again, I will. "He doesn't know that I'm working with you, but it won't be a issue. Ryan is a great guy, and he's proud of the work I do. He would never interfere. And he's not the jealous type, anyway."

"Could have fooled me, Em." The way his voice dips when he says my name causes something to stir inside me.

Thank God the girls are coming over. A movie and wine is the distraction I need.

chapter 13

My evening with the girls was a great time filler while I waited for Ryan to come home. Sitting with my two closest friends, watching *Top Gun* and eating pizza only got better when Joss decided to turn it into a drinking game. Every time a character in the movie named a call sign, we had to drink, so we were feeling no pain pretty quick. I might have to watch the movie again, you know, just to make sure I remember what happened. I can't believe my mom never played that one for Langley and me. Hot guys and volleyball, that's right up her alley.

I didn't mention my dream to Joss or Cam; it felt weird to talk about it when it was just that, a dream. And like Lang says, the dream means nothing. Even after spending part of the day with Trey scouting florists, I know that to be true.

Leaving work early today adds to my excitement that Ryan will be home tonight. I tried calling him this morning, but I missed him, much to my disappointment. He said that he was driving straight to his old office, because his boss wanted a report, so he would meet me at the apartment when he was finished. That works for me, because I didn't bother cleaning up the pizza boxes or the empty wine bottles from last night.

I don't have any of Ryan's favorite foods at home, so I decide to stop by the grocery store and grab a few things. Hell, maybe I'll cook lasagna; he's always liked my recipe. Now I'm on a mission. This is going to be the best weekend ever, no pressure or anything. I start to mentally time how long it will take to start dinner and straighten up the apartment before I should expect him, and I think I'm good to go.

As I make my way to my apartment door, I am doing my best to balance everything in my arms. Stupid me, wanted to make it in one trip, so my arms are loaded with everything from the store as well as my bag from work. My key is in my hand, and I'm about to slide it into the keyhole when the door opens.

"Hey, babe," Ryan says with a beaming smile.

The bags slip from my hands as I stand in shock before jumping at him and throwing my arms around his neck. I close my eyes and take him in. He's here with me, holding me, and my heart clenches, knowing I never want to lose this feeling.

"I guess you're happy I'm here early?" he asks, while I keep my grasp firm around him.

"You didn't answer this morning, I had no idea when you'd be home." My voice is muffled because my face is buried in his neck.

"I had a feeling I'd be done early, but I didn't want to get your hopes up, so I figured I'd wait and see how things ran."

I finally release him and he sets me down. I can't believe the tears welling in my eyes. I knew I was going to be happy to see him, but now, I'm not sure I can let him leave in two days. "I can't believe you're here," I say glancing around the messy apartment, and he follows my gaze.

"Yeah, I guess you girls had fun last night," he remarks with a wink.

"Wine, *Top Gun* and pizza," I count off on my fingers. "Not a bad night at all."

We walk back to the entry and grab the bags I so carelessly dropped and set everything on the counter. He starts emptying the bags and looks at me. "Were you planning on cooking for me tonight?"

"I thought about it," I say coyly, watching as he puts the eggs away in the refrigerator and faces me when he closes the door.

"What else did you think about?" His voice is low, daring me to play along.

I walk over to him and extend my hand, grazing his side, but I continue the movement right past him to the boxes sitting on the counter and smile. "That I was just going to take a shower and change."

I take the box I grabbed to the small cabinet across the way and stand on my toes, pushing it onto the top shelf. I smile to myself, knowing he's getting a good look at my ass while I do it. When I face him, he's still staring at me, with a readable look.

"Why do you need to change?" He raises his eyebrow in question.

I look down at my work outfit and point to an invisible spot on the hem. "Well, my dress is dirty," I say with an innocent shrug.

Ryan starts moving toward me with slow steps and pins me in the corner between him and the counter. "And the shower?"

"I don't really need one, yet."

I watch his eyes graze the length of my body, but he doesn't kiss me, he doesn't even touch me, there is only the silent, desire-filled look he's giving me. My stomach is swirling in anticipation, while I try to act unaffected. I try to steady my pulse, but I know he can tell he's getting to me, and why shouldn't he? It's been a month. I move to touch his face, but before my fingers reach him, he pushes off the counter and gives me space that I don't want at all. His grin is sexy and mischievous, and I want to smack it. Or maybe kiss it.

Two can play at this game.

He stands in the other corner across from me, leaning against the counter with his arms crossed over his broad chest, waiting for my move. I compose myself and take a deep breath, before finally moving. I walk to the sink and turn on the water to start washing the dishes from last night, and I can feel his eyes watching every move. I grab a glass and pull the sprayer from the holster to rinse it out, but just as I start to spray, I move out of the way and aim for him, drenching him in one swift move.

"What the hell, Em?" He stands there looking murderous, and I start laughing.

"Thought you could use a cold shower," I say with a shrug, trying to return the sprayer to its place. But he's behind me in an instant, grasping for my hand that holds it. When he frees the nozzle from my grip, he turns it in his hand and starts spraying, getting both of us wet. I'm screaming, and we're both laughing as I try to get away, but he holds me in place. I turn in his arms and look up at him, out of breath.

His face turns serious, the water dripping from his hair and running down his face. The movement of his chest matches mine, rising and falling rapidly. Before I can register the action, his lips are on mine, and he's pulling me so close, I'm not sure I can breathe, but I don't care. I return the kiss with equal fervor, throwing my arms around his neck and grasping at his hair that is damp and feels soft between my fingers. He removes a hand from my waist and it glides up, just over my breast, to undo the buttons on the front of my dress.

"I've missed you so much," he pants, between the kisses he plants on my neck.

"Me, too," are the only words I can manage, wishing this dress was easier to get off.

"Fuck it," he groans, dropping his hand from the buttons he's fumbling with and lifting me to sit on the counter next to the sink. Considering how much taller he is than me, I like this view; I can see every emotion and look in his eyes, and I know it's only for me. He pushes my hair out of my face and begins kissing me again.

Our hands are tugging and pulling at whatever they can, his pulling the hem of my dress from under me and grazing my thighs that are separated by his waist, mine tugging frantically at the buttons on his shirt. He places a firm hand at the small of my back, urging me closer, but I keep the space, if only for a moment, reaching between us to undo his belt. He trails kisses from my jaw, nipping at my neck, down to my collarbone, and I almost lose function of my hands when I try to pull his shirt over his head. Lucky for me, he helps, but only so he can remove my dress, the last piece of clothing that separates us.

I've missed him more than I would ever have thought, and when he lifts me, my legs wrap around his waist, as though by instinct. In one swift movement, my back is up against the cabinet behind Ryan, and even though it's not the most comfortable position, I don't care. His lips are on my neck one moment and nipping at my shoulder the next, desperate to get closer than we already are.

As we make love, we move in unison, rushed and needy, but it's what I have missed. I've missed him more than I ever thought possible.

I feel his fingers grip my waist tighter, and as his body stills, he continues to plant kisses at the base of my throat. I'm not sure how long we stand there, breathless and sweating, but he finally breaks the silence and kisses me. I drop my forehead to his as he whispers how much he's missed me, but all I'm able to do is nod in agreement.

"Now, you need a shower," he laughs as he kisses me one final time before setting me on my feet and pulling me toward our bedroom.

* * *

After our little private welcome home party last night, we decided dinner was a bust and perused the takeout menus I keep stashed in the end table in the living room. Ryan insisted we stay in for the rest of the night doing absolutely nothing but watching terrible movies and being together. Somewhere between Chinese food and the second movie, I fell asleep comfortably on his chest.

My alarm goes off at seven this morning, because we have some wedding plans to get out of the way before we go hang out with our friends tonight. Dean knew that Ryan would be in town and insists on going out, so Ryan has me call the girls to see if they want to go out, too. I am a little disappointed, since I had planned on keeping him all to myself this weekend, but I know we'll have a good time. Our first stop is to see Jaysen; my appointment with him the other day impressed me so much that I tell Ryan we have to use him for our own wedding.

"Well, I didn't expect to see you back so soon," he remarks when we walk through the door. "Another client for me?" he asks, looking at Ryan, who smiles at me.

"Yes," I say with a sassy tone. "Me - I mean, us," I stumble, pointing to Ryan and me.

"Damn girl." He eyes Ryan up and down. "Nice job." I laugh and nod in agreement before discussing what I am looking for in wedding flowers. He is amazing, and by the time we leave an hour later, I am finally able to check the first thing off our wedding list. Ryan appears to be quite impressed with what Jaysen can do, and even more so since he is going to cut us a deal, because I will be bringing more business to him.

Now, six hours later, I'm exhausted from all of the errands we ran, not to mention the lack of sleep from last night, and all I want to do is crawl back in bed. But everyone is expecting us at Wired Spirits, and the place doesn't look too crowded, yet. You wouldn't know from the exterior that this place is one of the more popular bars in the area.

It was an old pharmacy that someone renovated into a bar years ago, and it grew to be a local favorite. The lighting is awful, stench of stale beer is in the air and the place reeks of desperation. Men are standing at the bar hoping to pick up women while the ladies try hard to appear unavailable. Regardless, I love this place, if for no other reason than to people watch.

I walk to the booth in the far corner when I spot Cam and Joss, who are waving their arms as if we can't see them. Holding Ryan's hand, I pull him toward the booth and finally get to introduce him to my co-worker.

"Cam," I step aside and pull Ryan forward, "*this* is my fiancé."

"It's about damn time I meet you." She smiles. "This girl can't stop talking about you."

"That's good to know," he says, shaking her hand.

His body lurches forward and I turn to see Dean standing next to him, slapping him on the shoulder. "What's up, asshole?"

They start catching up, and rather than listen to guy talk, I take a seat next to Joss and catch the girls up on the day. I notice Cam keeps looking at Dean and when she realizes she's been caught, she scrunches her features in embarrassment. "He's single," I tell her, answering the question I think she might have.

"And obnoxious," Joss interjects, before I bump her shoulder.

"Only to you, because you're a bitch, but I love you," I remind her before turning to Dean. "Hey Dean, come meet my friend. You already know Joss, and this is Cam. We work together."

Dean nods at Joss who returns the gesture with equal disdain and then looks at Cam. His eyes grow slightly, before he becomes indifferent again. "Nice to meet you, Cam. So, where ya from?" he asks, taking a seat next to her. The two begin a conversation that Ryan,

Joss and I are left out of, so she nudges me to move out of the booth.

"Let's go dance," Joss inclines her head toward the dance floor.

"C'mon, Ryan." I grab his hand and drag him along. He's so great, because as much as he hates dancing, he'll do it for me. The three of us are on the dance floor, and Joss finds some random to entertain her for a while. I'm not sure how long we stay there moving to the music, but it's long enough that Ryan and I are hot, sweaty and if we don't leave the floor now, people might see part two of our reunion. *Or would it be four?*

"Let's get a drink," Ryan shouts in my ear over the music. I nod in agreement and tap Joss to let her know where we're going. We make our way to the bar, where Dean and Cam have moved to, still talking and seemingly getting along.

I lean against the bar, checking out the crowd in front of me. The room is packed, loud and oozing with drunks, and I'm having a great time. Ryan orders five shots and hands each of us one. We raise our shots to each other and down them in unison. As I lower my glass and open my scrunched eyes, my throat burning from the tequila I have taken in, I start coughing and Ryan is patting me on the back.

"Emogen?" Trey says, a smile playing in his eyes. "I thought that was you. What are you doing here?"

Holy crap! What in the hell is he doing here?

"Oh," I stammer, still coughing from the shot. "Mr. Miller, how are you?"

The look he gives me at the use of his title is one of amusement, but he covers it well. "Just enjoying a night out with Vivien," he says, wrapping his arm around the woman who appears at his side. She doesn't seem fazed by the gesture, perhaps even numb to it. She's about my height, thin and muscular, her dark black hair pulled into a tight ponytail. She reeks of superiority, and barely looks in our direction when he attempts an introduction.

"Nice to meet you Vivien." I try to meet her eyes, but she looks in every other direction. "I'm sorry," I add and step back next to Ryan, realizing that everyone is watching this exchange. "Mr. Miller, this is my fiancé, Ryan, and our friends, Dean, Joss, and you already know Cam."

"Please, call me Trey," he rushes, giving me a sideways glance. Everyone gives him a polite nod, except Ryan.

I begin to worry that he remembers Trey, but then he extends his hand to him. "Nice to meet you, Trey." His tone isn't as convincing as the words.

chapter 14

I'm still reeling from the realization that Trey is standing here in front of me. He asked what Ryan and I had planned for the weekend, and now I can't remember if I told him where we were going or not. Whether it is unintentional or not, my dream floods my memory and my neck is suddenly hot. I step back and wrap an arm around Ryan's waist, feeling exposed, but his arm at my waist protects me.

"Hey, babe," Ryan's voice breaks my thoughts, "You ready to head out? I think everyone's coming over for a bit, if that's okay with you."

"Yeah, that's great," I lie, anything to get me out of this situation.

Ryan holds me against him with one hand and reaches out to Trey with the other. "It was nice to you meet you, man. We're heading out, but y'all enjoy the rest of your night."

"Same to you," Trey answers and then looks at me. "See you next week, Em-Emogen." I give him a curt nod and allow Ryan to take my hand and lead me away. I don't bother looking over as I pass him, because I can feel Trey's eyes on me.

I hear his date snap at him, "What was that all about? You take me to a club and then flirt with some other girl?"

"She's a friend," he bites back.

"Looked like more to me." I hear her say, and it's the last thing before I'm out of earshot. I look up at Ryan to see if he heard their exchange, but he only looks down and smiles at me lovingly.

Standing out in the cool night air, our small group lingers in stale conversation. Cam and Dean decide to go get some coffee and talk some more. Joss looks at me with a raised brow. "I'm not going to be a third wheel. Love you guys, but I'm out." She walks over and gives me a quick hug. "Call me tomorrow when your man leaves." She walks over to Ryan and kisses his cheek. "Have a safe trip home - and, try to come home a little more often, this chick is crazy when you're gone."

I give her a playful 'I'm gonna kick your ass' glare, and she returns a similar look before heading off in the opposite direction.

Neither one of us drank too much, but we don't want to drive either, so we decide to walk the short distance to our apartment. Ryan's fingers are entwined with mine; our stride is slow and easy. The wind picks up, and an involuntary shudder escapes me. Without a word, Ryan lets go of my hand and wraps his arm around me, bringing me close to his side as we continue to walk.

"So that was your client, huh?"

"Yeah," I yawn, sounding bored with the topic trying to buy time. "That's him."

"He's younger than I thought," he admits, and I know there's a question in there. *Why didn't I tell him?*

"I was surprised to see him there," I offer, because it's true. "That doesn't seem like the type of place he'd go to."

"Too good for it?" he asks, trying to find a flaw in Trey.

"Not 'too good,' maybe," I pause, trying to find an accurate description. "Too uptight?"

"Seems like a nice guy, I guess. His girlfriend seemed a little pissed," he scoffs.

"I don't know anything about her, but yeah, he's pretty nice. Been an easy client to work with so far, but I don't want to talk about *my* work. Did you and Alex get that project completed?"

The arm that's around me tenses, and I know that work is stressing him out. He exhales a loud breath and groans, "We've busted our asses this last week, but we got an extension. It's only a couple of days, and that doesn't really help. I'll just be pulling more long hours this week."

"What's the issue with it?"

"There's a few key details missing, and our boss is insisting that we get those by Tuesday, or he will get involved. That's that last thing Alex and I want; this is ours," he adds, sounding as though it's personal if it ends up being taken from him.

"Is he easy to work with?"

"Mr. Jameson?" he asks with a shrug. "I guess he's alright."

"No," I correct, "Alex. Does he pull his own weight?"

He looks at me and cocks his head in confusion. "Yeah, pretty much."

He gives me a squeeze before letting me go to walk up the stairs to our apartment. He opens the door and closes it behind me, and the silence has become too much to bear. I turn around to say something, but Ryan is leaning back against the door, staring at me with sad eyes.

"I hate that I have to leave you tomorrow." He finally speaks up.

My eyes shut tight, willing the tears back, because I can save them for when he leaves. But when I open, they're still there, below the surface, waiting to erupt. I take a deep breath and walk over to him, stand on my toes and wrap my arms around his neck. He lifts me up and squeezes tight, and I feel all of his love in this embrace.

"I don't want to talk about you leaving, okay? Let's talk about what else we have coming up. I need good things to focus on, otherwise I might just spend the next twenty-four hours in tears."

He kisses my nose and winks before setting me on my feet. "What other wedding plans to we need to nail out?"

"Hammer, Ryan," I correct with a laugh, "the saying is hammer out."

"No, I meant nail," he says, lunging toward me, "as in nailing you, on our honeymoon."

I laugh and try to get away, but he reaches me too fast. He drags me to the couch and pulls me on top of him, and all I can do is gaze into his eyes. "I don't think we can afford a honeymoon, Ryan."

He narrows his eyes, no doubt trying to come up with an argument, but he knows it's the truth. It's already hard for us to afford the tickets to fly out to see each other.

"Vail," he says, making a decision.

"We can't go to Vail," I insist, because all of the resorts will cost an arm and a leg.

"I've already talked to Dean," he smirks at my confusion. "Remember that place we went to after graduation, before I started working? He's got a cousin who manages that resort. He said he could get us a deal. It's not free or anything, but this is our honeymoon, and trust me when I say I plan on taking one and getting all the advantages that come with it."

I lean down and kiss him, pouring every emotion into that single kiss. "Why wait for the honeymoon?" I get up and pull at his hand, leading him to our bedroom.

* * *

"Don't cry, Em," he says into my hair, holding me close. "We'll see each other in a few weeks, I promise."

"I know, it's just, this is the hard part - well, this and then the next few days," I admit.

His hands move to my shoulders and he pushes me back, dropping his head to look into my eyes. He lifts his hand to my chin, urging me to look at him, "You can handle this. Hell, you've already handled it, and I love you so much."

"I love you, too." The words escape past the tightness in my throat. "Have a safe flight."

He kisses me one more time and grabs his luggage and heads into the airport. I watch as he disappears through the sliding doors before getting into my car to head back home. I've barely moved before my phone buzzes a text from Ryan.

You're still the most beautiful girl I know. I love you.

That's all it takes and the tears spill from my eyes. I find Langley's contact information and call her cell. She answers on the first ring, "How you holdin' up, Emmy?"

"Not so good," I say through my tears. "I just left him at the airport."

"How was the visit?"

"We had a really great time." I smile, remembering our first night.

"Ew. Gross. Spare me the details," she gags, eliciting a laugh from me that I'm thankful for.

"Then don't ask questions you don't want answers to," I remind her.

"What'd y'all do?"

"We-" She interrupts and makes weird noises.

"Aside from the bedroom, what did y'all do?"

"We hired a florist for the wedding," I beam with excitement. "Then we went out to a bar with a few friends last night. That was- eventful."

"What happened last night?" she asks in a hurry.

"What do you mean?"

"You tell me," her tone turning nosey. "You're the one whose voice just sounded all down and mopey."

"Nothing happened, necessarily. We just, happened, to run into my client."

"At the bar?" she clarifies with shock.

"Yeah, it was weird, Lang. I don't think I told him I was going there, but he didn't seem shocked to see me. In fact, I think he liked watching me squirm. I dunno. But luckily, Ryan didn't seem to remember him from that night, so I guess that's good."

"Wait, what you do mean, he liked watching you *squirm*?" I can totally picture her using air quotes, even though no one is there to see them.

"Well, he knows who Ryan is from that night, he's the one who reminded me, but obviously Ryan doesn't remember him, and he seemed to be enjoying that little tidbit."

"Why don't you just tell Ryan, and get it over with? The longer you keep quiet, the more it looks like you did something wrong. *Did you do anything wrong?*"

"No, of course not!" I protest.

"Then stop acting guilty, dumbass!"

"Thanks, Lang. I needed this."

"Anytime, sis."

It's amazing how simple she can make everything appear. But Ryan is living in another city, I'm working with my first solo client, and we're planning our wedding, which is supposed to take place in less than a year. We don't need any more road bumps messing with us. And to say anything at this point would just be stupid.

The drive back to the apartment is quiet, and upon entering the empty home we shared this weekend, I feel tired and lonely, all at once. I still feel him here; our coffee mugs side by side on the counter from this morning, his towel hanging on the rack after our shower and a note? I see a folded piece of paper on my side of the bed that simply reads, 'Open when you go to bed.'

There's no way I can wait until tonight to read his words. I force it open to read the contents, laughing when I read the first line.

Em,

I knew you wouldn't wait to read this like I said, you never can. Guess that's why I love you so much. You can't wait for anything. (Kidding)

I know this is messed up. I don't like being away from you any more than you like being away from me. I still wish you'd pack up and come with me, but I know you have things to do there, and I'm proud of you for doing what you love. We'll get through all of this in the end, but this year assignment came at a bad time, and I'm sorry for that. I hope you know how much you mean to me and how much I love you.

When you go to sleep tonight, just imagine me next to you, holding you, because that is where I want to be. And if you need to, I'm always ready for a 'phone call.' Kidding. Unless you're up for it. Just kidding. I love you, Emogen Rae Tate. In case there was any question, you are taking that name, because you belong with me, forever.

I love you,

Ry

When I finish the reading his note, my heart swells with love, and my eyes fill with tears. Why does he do this to me? He knows that I'm going to be a mess until I hear from him tonight.

Nope, can't wait. I decide to call him right away and don't even wait for a greeting when he picks up. "I love you so much."

"You caught me just in time, we're about to board in a few minutes." Hearing his voice now feels like it's been years, not just hours since I last talked to him.

"Thank you for my note," I say through a tear.

"Impatient, aren't you?"

"You already know that about me, which is why you left it in plain sight." My giggle lightens the mood.

"It's one of the things I love most about you. We probably wouldn't be together if you were actually patient." A voice sounds over the intercom and Ryan stops talking to listen for a moment. "Hey, babe, that's me. I gotta go now, but I'll call when I land. I love you."

"Me, too."

chapter 15

"Morning, Cam." My voice is quiet in my greeting.

She wastes no time in joining me at my desk. She sits on the corner to face me, a huge smile covers her face. I don't think I have noticed how beautiful her smile is until now, but as soon as I notice it, it disappears. "How ya doin'?" Her look is sympathetic, and I feel bad that I'm bringing her down.

"I'm good," I lie, thankful I was able to make myself look presentable enough to back up my words. "It was hard saying goodbye, but we had so much fun. I'm good, I promise."

She looks at me and nods, which allows me to get away with the charade, for now. "What do you have going on today?"

"Oh no you don't." I shake my head, making sure I have her attention. "You don't get off that easy. You and Dean, huh? I don't know why I didn't think of it before. You two disappeared and I haven't heard anything from you," I tease, prompting a laugh from her. "Care to explain?"

Her smile is one of authentic happiness. "He's really funny," she gushes, which surprises me. Most people would probably comment on his eyes, or tall stature, but not Cam. It's all about what's on the inside with that girl.

"Funny, huh? Is that all he is?" She blushes. Cam actually blushes when I put her on the spot about Dean, so of course I continue. "What else is he?"

"He's kinda great," she admits with a shy smile.

"Ryan's a good judge of character, and he and Dean hit it off right away, so I think you're in good hands." I wink. "What did y'all do the rest of the night?"

"We were going to a coffee bar down the road, but there was some guy playing there. We wanted to talk, so we just ended up walking around for hours."

I look at the person who I've come to consider a good friend, and I love seeing her happy. She's been nice to me since day one, she's sobered me with unsolicited advice that I appreciate but I've been so self-involved that I didn't notice how things were going for her. I really hope that whatever this is between Dean and Cam works out. They are pretty opposite; sure, they're both good looking, but he comes off cocky and his loud inappropriate comments throw most people off. But then again, Cam isn't most people. She's a quiet observer and one of the most intuitive women I have met, so yeah, they make sense.

"I'm glad y'all had a good time. So- are you gonna see him again?"

The smile on her face is the only answer she gives as she gets up to walk back to her desk, so I push the button to power my computer on. My coffee mug sits at my desk, and I decide to fill it while I wait for everything to load on the screen. I haven't checked my email since I left work early Friday, so hopefully my inbox won't be too bad.

With hot coffee in hand, I sit down and open my email. The first one I spot is from Ryan.

      Ryan Tate
      September 16, 2013 6:04 AM

To: Kane, Emogen
Subject: Miss you

Hey baby,

I just wanted to let you know that I was thinking about you. I thought you might like to have a message from me when you get to work. I love you, and thank you for this weekend.

Love,
Ry
Ryan Tate
ARK Consulting

I consider a response, but stop when I see the next one is from Trey. The time stamp says that he sent it early yesterday morning, which I find odd. The only thing that makes it even stranger is the content of the email itself.

Trey Miller
September 15, 2013 1:32 AM
To: Kane, Emogen
Subject: (None)

Emogen,

I need to cancel our meeting this week. I apologize for the late notice, but I have some things I need to take care of out of town. If you have any questions, or if there is anything that needs to be done in the meantime, my new secretary, Hattie should be able to help you.

Regards,

Trey

Trey Miller

T.M. Enterprises

I'm not sure why, but this email has me confused. I wonder if I did something wrong. I'm not sure who Hattie is, maybe he finally found someone to replace Sandy, the woman I was originally working with. But still, I find the email perplexing, especially given the timing. I think back to the other night, aside from it being painfully awkward, nothing happened that sticks out as bad. I have no other emails or texts that would give me any indication as to what's going on, but I send a short response anyway.

Emogen Kane

September 16, 2013 8:13 AM

To: Miller, Trey

Re: (None)

Mr. Miller,

I will be sure to contact Hattie if there are any problems. Have a good week.

Regards,

Emogen Kane,

Event Planner

Elle E. Grant Events

I debate whether or not I should even hit the "send" button, because it seems pointless to respond, but business etiquette deems that I should at least acknowledge. Right?

"Emogen?" Callie calls through the intercom. "Mr. Miller is on hold for you."

"Thank you, Callie," I say; anxiety is filling me while I wait for her to send the call through.

He wastes no time in speaking when I answer the phone. "Emogen, it's Trey." His voice is hurried, and I can only assume he's running late somewhere.

"Good morning, Mr. Miller, is there something I can do for you?" I answer, bemused that he's calling, when his email already said everything, I would think, he needed to say.

"I know my email said I had to cancel the meeting this week, but can we meet today instead?"

"I'm sorry, but I'm not sure that's possible. The entertainers were set to meet with us on Thursday. I'm not sure how many, if any, we can get on such short notice."

"That's fine, we can reschedule that. I just need to discuss a few changes I'm thinking about making."

"If you'd like, you can send over a list, and then we can discuss them when you return," I offer, more for myself than for him.

"Em, please, I really would like to discuss this in person, if that's okay with you." It's not an invitation, but a request that is rushed. I feel like there is something distracting him, but I can't decline, even though I would like to.

I remain quiet, no doubt too long, and I can tell by his frustrated sigh that there's something he's not saying. Part of me is dying to know what's going on, and the other part feels like I'm walking into a trap that has nothing to do with work.

There is an obnoxious thump on his end of the phone that snaps me out of my trance and he clears his throat. "Emogen, are you still there?"

He can't see me, but I conduct a frantic search through my work calendar, trying to find any last minute reason that I can't go. Truth is, I don't have a good excuse why I can't and that leaves me feeling defeated. "Yes, sir. I can meet you at Chops at noon, will that work?"

"That's fine, I can pick you up on my way," he interjects.

"No," I answer, eager to get off that track. "That's okay, I have some clients to meet with this morning, so I'll meet you there when I'm done." If nothing else, I'll just help Cam out with whatever she's got going on since I'm undoubtedly free.

He's silent for a moment and offers a clipped goodbye. I can almost see the words flying from his tightly pressed lips and I know he doesn't like my plan to meet him there. The whole conversation leaves me dreading noon.

* * *

I arrive to the restaurant early to get settled and wait for Trey to show up. I go through a mental list of what changes he may want to make, or wonder if he wants someone else to handle his event. As much as I hate the idea of losing my first client, the thought does leave me feeling a bit lighter. I check my phone and scroll through emails, and when I look up, he's walking past the hostess desk, nodding to people as he passes. His confidence is evident, but his smile isn't until he spots me in a booth near the back. I keep my smile neutral.

"Thank you for meeting me," he says, taking a seat and reaching for his menu. He orders an iced tea and waits for the waitress to walk away before continuing. "First, I want to apologize for the other night."

"What about it?" I feign confusion at the mention of Saturday evening.

Trey's brow furrows, trying to gauge my question, but he presses on. "I didn't mean to put you on the spot."

I can't help but laugh at his arrogance. "You didn't."

Shock registers on his face at my words, but he gives it right back. "Clearly, because Ryan look thrilled to meet me."

"Mr. Miller?" I ask, giving him a pointed stare, prompting a raised brow from him at my use of his formal title. "You said you wanted to discuss some changes to your event, which is in less than three months." I pull out my pen and notepad to make sure I have everything covered. "What's first?"

His hand reaches for mine and I flinch, pulling away. "If you don't mind, I'd like to be able to write this down."

"I was just going to move your glass," he states with a calm voice, pointing to my paper that I didn't notice was absorbing the condensation from my glass. I feel my cheeks flame when he leans back in his chair, his eyes fixed on me, obviously entertained by my reaction to his innocent gesture. "The truth is, there are no changes; I wanted to speak with you in person."

Mr. Miller is a client, I repeat in my head over and over, until that isn't enough.

"Excuse me?" My voice rises to an annoying level. "Are you serious? This is completely inappropriate, *Mr.* Miller, so if that's all then I need to get back to work."

I begin to leave my seat, when he reaches out again, but as soon as my eyes grow wide, he drops his hand and his voice. "Please, just give me a second to explain."

Of all the awkward situations to be put in, this one has to be the worst. Trey is harmless, so I'm not worried about my safety. But I don't take kindly to someone taking advantage of their position. Then again, this is a client, and to walk away could cause problems for me with Elle. I ease myself back into the chair before responding. "Please make this fast."

"I had no intention of showing up at Wired Spirits the other night. I was on a date with Vivien, and I just needed a change; the night was dragging," he explains. "When she started complaining that she was bored, I remembered you mentioning that you might be there, so we headed that way."

"You wanted to run into me? I don't get it. Why would you do that?"

"I think you know the answer to that," he says, watching me as though he can read my every thought.

"Okay." Adrenaline is coursing through my veins, and my embarrassment is leaving me flustered. "I need to get back to work."

"This is why I asked you to meet me. Look, Em, I don't make it a habit of going after unavailable women, and you are clearly *unavailable*. From what I can tell, your fiancé is a good guy, but I'm attracted to you. I was ready to turn this entire event over to you to plan, but in all honesty, I enjoyed being with you that first day and the more time I spend with you, the more I think about you. I went the other night, because I *wanted* to run into you. Does that make me a jerk? Maybe. But it's the truth."

Thump.

Thump.

Thump.

All I can hear is the blood rushing through my ears, and all I can feel is my skin on fire. I reach for my glass and take a gulp of the ice cold water, trying to buy myself some time before I answer, because how do you respond to something like that. It wasn't a declaration of love or anything, but hell if it didn't just throw my world off balance. I set my glass down and clasp my hands together in my lap to steady my nerves.

"How, exactly, do you expect me to respond to that? As you've mentioned, I *am* unavailable and very much in love with Ryan. Aside from that, you are my client."

He shrugs his shoulders, with what I believe to be defeat, but his voice is assertive. "We're both adults here, alright? I figured it was best to address this and move on."

"Congratulations," I say in a calm tone, staring him down. "You have successfully unburdened yourself and have now placed me in the awkward position."

He returns my stare a sly smile appearing at my objection to his words. "Em, there's nothing to feel awkward about; I'm just stating something we're both already aware of."

"Whatever idea you have of me in your thoughts has got to be a far better version than the actual. You don't even know me, Trey."

"What I do know," he interjects, "is that you are an amazing woman and a friend. A really attractive, taken friend that I'm glad to know."

"Trey-"

"Friends, Emogen. I swear, that's all I would like from you," he says with conviction; and I believe him. "Well, that and to plan the best corporate event."

"No pressure there," I answer through gritted teeth.

"Which part? Friends or the event?"

"I'll let you know."

chapter 16

What do you do when your client tells you he has feelings for you? The same client that you interact with every day and invades your dreams at night. Well, if your name is Emogen Kane, you go home, eat a gallon of ice cream, get no sleep, go to work the next day and hope you hear nothing from him. Then, you call your big sister and hope she can calm your ass down. I could go to Joss, but she already thinks something is up with Trey. Langley always knows the best way to handle things.

I pull her number up in my phone and wait for the call to go through. As soon as she answers the phone, my voice rushes out, sounding urgent, "Lang, you got a sec?"

"Hey Emmy! Omigosh, I was just about to call you- I have some exciting news," she spills out before I can share my latest drama.

"Oh really? What's going on?"

"Reid asked me to marry him!" She screams so loud that I have to pull the phone away from my ear.

"Are you serious?" I have to ask, because it's not out of the realm of possibility for her to play a joke on me.

"Yes!"

"What? How? I mean..." *I'm at a loss.* "I had no idea you two were serious, I mean, you've been dating, what, two months?"

"And?" she retorts, hurt. "When you know, you know."

I'm an asshole; my sister shares her good news with me, and I'm raining on her parade. "That's amazing, Lang! I'm so happy for you. How did he do it? Does mom know? Do you have a date set, yet?" I rapid-fire the questions, hoping I sound as excited as she is.

"It wasn't as romantic as your proposal, but I loved it," she prefaces. Ryan's proposal was amazing and over the top; I'm not sure anyone could one-up it. "Last night, he took me to the restaurant where we had our first date, it wasn't anything out of the ordinary. He kept talking about the future, and I knew we had one, just not so soon. Anyway, after dinner we went to this courtyard and there were benches everywhere, so we sat down. We were talking and he said, 'this is the place where I saw you the first time, and I knew I had to meet you.' And then he dropped down on one knee, had a box in his hand, and he said, 'I know it seems sudden, but I need you in my life, forever. So, Langley, will you please marry me?' And I started screaming. I think people thought something bad was happening to me, because they came rushing over. But when they saw him on his knee with the ring, they started laughing and clapping. And I mean, of course I said yes."

Stunned into silence by her story, tears are burning my eyes, but I have the biggest smile plastered on my face. I wish I were there with her to hug her and celebrate, but I'm here.

"You still there?"

"Langley," I finally manage to croak through my constricting throat, "that's beautiful. Congratulations, sis."

"Thank you. And yes, mom knows, I just got off the phone with her when you called."

"What did she say?"

"Well, you know mom and marriage, she didn't seem thrilled. But she congratulated me. I'm getting a little worried about her. She's been drinking more lately and this Scott guy that she's seeing is an asshole. She seems to be morphing into someone I don't really know anymore. At least she was happy for you when you got engaged. She's met Reid, and I guess she likes him. She's just a little strange."

"I'm sorry, and then you tell me, and I'm no better. You're right, when you know you have to go with it, and Reid sounds like a great guy, I can't wait to meet him. Speaking of, when are you guys coming out to visit?"

"Well, I know you just had Ryan there, so I thought maybe you'd like some company next weekend? We could drive out Thursday after work. It would be really late, but at least we'd have Friday and Saturday there. Whatcha think?"

"Seven hours is a long drive, are you sure you're up for that?"

"Absolutely!"

"Then I can't wait," I tell her, happy that she's finally going to come see me.

"So wait, why were you calling me?"

I am not an asshole. I'm not going to lay this on her.

"It was nothing," I lie, not wanting for one second to take away from what is a wonderful day for my deserving sister.

We hang up and I bask in the awesomeness of her news. *Langley Jennifer Kane is getting married*. I never thought I'd see the day. She used to say she never wanted to get married, not after dad split when we were kids. It's a wonder either of us are in relationships, period, because mom instilled in us that men are ultimately single-minded, selfish creatures who will screw you over the second something better comes along.

Trey

His name floods my head again, and I decide to talk the next best thing to my sister, Joss.

Me: *I need you to come over, no questions asked, just meet me at my place.*

Joss: *What?*

Me: *No Questions. Get. Over. Here.*

Joss: *Fine*

That's the good thing about best friends; they really aren't in a position to argue, especially Joss. That's what she signed up for when she moved out here to be near me, and that's what she gets for being my best friend. We have had our girl's nights out, and nights in. We've laughed our asses off when one of us does something stupid and held each other when our worlds fell apart. I'm not sure what this situation falls under, but I'm pretty sure this is a girl's night in, where I vent, she listens, pretends that I'm making the right decisions, then snaps me back into reality.

I need reality.

There's a knock at my door, followed by her less than chipper voice. "Open the door, Emogen."

"One second," I yell, unlocking the deadbolt, followed by the chain.

She barely looks at me as she shoves past. "This better be good, because I had a date."

"Shit!" I slam the door shut and walk over to the back of the couch where she is glaring at me, "I'm sorry, I had no idea. Do I know him?"

"Well, I could have had a date, but you blew that one up."

"What do you mean?"

"What do you think? I was going to pick up some random guy tonight and 'date,' him for the evening," she says, turning to stare me down.

My jaw drops open, shocked at her revelation, "You were not!"

"No," she pouts, "but I could have. So what's the emergency?"

I shove her aside and take a seat on the couch, wondering if she would really do it. "You're such a bitch sometimes, you know that?"

Her face contorts to shock as she throws herself to sit on the other end of the couch. "Excuse me? I'm a bitch all the time."

I laugh, because it's expected, but it's not genuine. Now I have to tell her the reason I needed to see her so urgently.

"Something happened today." And for whatever reason, guilt fills my heart.

Her posture rights and she looks concerned. "Is everything okay?"

"I don't know. My head is all over the place. First off, Langley's getting married. But I just found that out. Second, it's about Trey."

"What about Mr. Intrusive?"

"Huh," I scoff, "funny you would call him that. I met him for lunch yesterday to talk about some changes he wanted to make. But the thing is-"

"There were no changes," she finishes for me. "What's the deal with this guy, Em?"

Here it comes. I fidget with the tassel on the corner of the pillow I'm holding, before looking her in the eyes. "He's 'attracted' to me," I cringe, repeating his words from yesterday with air quotes.

"He's what? Did he tell you that?" she asks, appalled.

"Yeah, he knows I'm with Ryan, he just thought it best to own up to it, I guess."

"What an asshole!"

"Yeah," I say half-heartedly.

On the one hand, I'm flattered that Trey told me what he did, but I feel like I'm not being true to Ryan. Ryan is the man I'm going to marry, and I love him with all my heart, so why is the unsolicited attention from Trey wreaking havoc on my head?

"Unless? He's not an asshole? What's going on? What are you not telling me?"

"Fuck, me!" I wail at the ceiling. I compose myself and finally look at Joss. "I've been having these dreams about him. Lang says it's because Ryan's been gone and I've had to spend so much time with Trey for work, that it's normal. But it's not. It doesn't feel normal."

She stares at me a little too long and I know what's coming. "Do you have feelings for him, too?"

This is the question I have tried to avoid completely, even with myself. *Do I have feelings for Trey?*

"Do I find him attractive? Yes. Do I enjoy working with him? Yeah, he makes me laugh. But do I have feelings for him? No."

The moment the words come out, I know it's a lie. Of course I have feelings for him, otherwise I wouldn't have been the slightest bit jealous that he had a date with him the other night and I wouldn't be trying to figure things out. My heart rate wouldn't sound in my ears when he compliments me.

Oh shit! I have a crush on Trey Miller.

"So what are you gonna do?" Joss asks, when she sees the look on my face.

"Nothing," I protest. "There is nothing I need to do. I'm in love with Ryan. We're getting married and that's it."

She looks at me and leans over to grab my hand before speaking. "Just because you have feelings for this guy, doesn't mean you don't love Ryan. But you better sort your feelings out before you do anything you might regret."

"I would never cheat on Ryan," I argue, wounded she would suggest anything of the sort.

"That's not what I'm talking about," she says, giving me a knowing look.

* * *

After our lunch, I do my best to avoid Trey as much as possible over the next week and a half, even going so far as to communicate only through Hattie. The first week is easy; he was out of town. But the Hattie-solution proved fruitless, because she's a few cards short of a deck. Every time I email her, she would email him to ask how to respond but keep me on the correspondence. At first, I thought it was funny, but every message is handled in this way, so finally Trey sends an email to only me, asking that I just send all questions to him. Now, when my inbox alerts me to a new message from him, I feel giddy. *Not what I was going for.*

Since he was out of town this week, I have found it much easier to think without the constant phone calls or meetings with him. Unfortunately, he will return by Friday and is already requesting two meetings for next week to select the caterer. He provides me with a list of items he would prefer for the dinner, so I narrow the companies down based on the ones I feel are the best option.

I visit with Lisa a few times, and even though she is giving us carte blanch, no doubt because she has a thing for hot younger guys, I still make sure to run things by her. Best decision I made, because Ivy Glen has certain "rules" about which vendors they let bring things in. When I mention we are using Everette's Catering for the evening, she seems less than thrilled with the choice. When I press for answers, she eyes me, prompting my hand to fly up to swear that I won't repeat anything.

"They overcharge by twenty percent," she admits in a hushed tone.

I am compelled to share this information with Trey. As my client, he needs to know the reason I feel we need to pass on the contract with Everette. He is happy to have the information, but again, insists we meet to go over the other choices once more before making a final decision.

"Can you meet on Friday?" he asks. "I get back in town late afternoon."

"I can't. I have other obligations," I admit, referring to Lang's visit. "Will Monday be okay?"

"Twenty minutes, thirty, tops. I just want to go over them one more time."

"I'm having dinner with my sister at six, so you can meet me at the office before then. Will that work?"

"I'll see you then," he answers, before hanging up.

chapter 17

"How was your visit with Lang and Reid? What did ya think of him?"

I haven't talked to Ryan since the middle of the week. When he has free time, I'm swamped. When I have a moment, I can't get him to answer the phone. We've exchanged a few 'I love you' texts here and there, but I have no idea what's going on in his life or work. In the two weeks since I've seen him, it feels like so much has changed.

"I really liked him, Ryan. I think you would, too."

"Have they set a date, yet?"

"Um, yeah, that's the thing, they're looking to do it in February."

"What's the rush?"

I roll my eyes, because I know he's asking if it's a shotgun wedding, which it's not. I mean, why wait? He and I have been engaged for almost a year and our wedding is still over ten months away. With all the planning that still needs to be done all we have to show for it is a lot of frustration.

"She's not pregnant," I finally tell him. "They just want to get married. They're doing something at my aunt's house."

"Aunt Gertie is letting her do it in that house?"

"It has charm, and it really suits those two, trust me. I just spent the whole weekend with them, and Aunt Gertie's place is perfect," I inform him.

The house is a large ranch house nestled on the back acre of her four-acre property. It's old and needs too many repairs to list, but my aunt is set in her ways and insists there is nothing wrong with it. She and my mom grew up in the house, and when my grandmother passed away last year, Gertie kept it. Langley always said she wanted to get married outside in the summer; it's obvious she's foregoing that idea to do it sooner.

"Did she ask you to be maid of honor?"

"No, but she will," I answer confidently.

"So, what did y'all do while they were there?"

Loaded question.

How do you tell your fiancé that your client met you at your office, as planned, but the meeting lasted longer than you expected? So your sister and the guy she's engaged to show up to get you and end up meeting said client. Oh yeah, and the client hit it off with Reid, and ended up joining us for dinner?

You downplay it.

"I had to meet with Mr. Miller Friday afternoon, but it didn't last too long. So I went to dinner with Reid and Lang and then showed them around the town on Saturday, since neither one has been here before. They said they want to come out next summer and try white water rafting."

"Sounds like y'all had a good time. I'm sorry I wasn't there."

"Me, too."

It seems like this is how more of our conversations go these days. One of us misses something and apologizes, and the other ignores it as no big deal. But it is a big deal. The talks are becoming shorter and shorter until it feels like there is nothing left to talk about.

"What are you thinking about?"

"What?" I ask, stunned out of my inner thoughts.

"You got quiet." His tone is hushed. "You always get really quiet when something is bothering you."

"Nothing," I lie, which seems to become easier for me every time I do it.

"I know you're lying." I can hear his crooked smile through the phone.

"I'm thinking things feel off with us, Ryan. Do you feel that way? I mean, we barely talk, and when we do, it seems like we have a hard time connecting."

"Yeah, I've noticed that, too. It's definitely easier when we're in the same place."

I exhale a breath before saying my next thought; "It scares me, Ryan."

He's quiet while he takes it in. Ryan is a thinker, not a reactor, so I know he's trying to make sure his next words are organized. "How did you feel when I was there?"

"I loved you being home. It felt right. Complete."

"So we just need to make sure we make the most of our time together when we have it, right?"

"Yeah, but-"

"No, 'buts' okay? Do you still want this?"

Shocked by his question, I answer with all of my heart. "Of course I do."

"Then it's just going to be hard for a while. But we can do it, right?" I hear doubt when he voices the question and it rattles me. He's my rock, and his doubt is pounding in my ears.

"Yes," I whisper.

* * *

Elle decides to have a staff meeting first thing this morning. In the time I've worked here, we have never had one, although it's my understanding it's something that used to take place once a week. The rumor is that she wants to start doing them again so the entire team is aware of what's going on.

"So, we've covered the weddings, and everyone knows what they need to do. Emogen, how is everything coming on the T.M. event?"

"We have secured the location, florist, caterer, and by the end of the week, we will have the entertainment lined up."

"What about the photographer?"

"He said that he doesn't want one, but I have told him that this would be a great thank you gift to his guests when it's over."

"Have the invitations been mailed?"

"We should get those out next week, he has a few more names to add."

"Great. So how many do you need for the night of?"

"I think we might just need two or three more, aside from myself?"

"Okay, I'll check the schedule and see who's available that night." She starts thumbing through her calendar and looks up at me again. "Why isn't it on the schedule?"

I rifle through my file, trying to find something to back me, but everything I have is in paper form. I thought I added it to the company calendar, but if she's not seeing it, then I have royally screwed up.

"Can you give me a second?" I ask, pushing my chair back.

"Wait…" She throws her hand up to halt my departure. "Is this it on December sixth, under TME?"

I lower myself back into my chair, relieved that it's there. "Yes, that's it."

"Alright." She starts writing something down. "Emogen, let's meet next week, after you've taken care of these items, to catch up and make sure things are on track. We're about nine weeks out, and this is when things will start getting a little haywire."

Once she dismisses the team, I head to my desk to see where things stand for the rest of the event. The photographer has been the toughest thing to sell him; he just doesn't see the need. But I keep reminding him that the women will love it, and that's what matters. I have a few in mind that I think he would like, so that's why I am meeting with him today.

>
> Trey Miller
> October 4, 2013 10:34 AM
> To: Kane, Emogen
> Subject: Photographer
>
> I still don't think we need this for the party. I've talked to several people that think it's not worth it. I'm still on the fence. You'll have to convince me.
>
> Trey
> T.M. Enterprises

Men are the last ones to appreciate the value of photography, assuming disposable cameras are the way to go. But being in this business, I know if you make the women happy, their partner will never hear the end of it.

Emogen Kane

October 4, 2013 10:42 AM

To: Miller, Trey

Re: Photographer

Would these "people" be men?

Emogen

Event Planner

Elle E. Grant Events

My cell phone buzzes and I assume that it's Ryan, until I see Trey's name with a text:

Trey: Guys don't like pictures

Me: Your point?

Trey: Unnecessary expense

Before I can respond, Elle comes by my desk. "Emogen, I wanted to talk to you for a second. Do you have time?"

"Yes, do we need to go to your office?"

"That's not necessary. I just wanted to get your opinion. Do you think you would be able to take on another event? I have one that is smaller than the TM one, but the budget is higher. I think you can handle it, but I know you are still taking care of this one, and I don't know how you feel about another, especially on the heels of it being you first client to handle alone."

Elle thinks I can handle it. She wouldn't be checking with me if she didn't have confidence in my abilities. Knowing that she wants to give me more gives way to a beaming smile. "Absolutely. And thank you."

"You've done great so far, and I appreciate all of your hard work. Mr. Miller has nothing but great things to say about everything you've done to this point."

She turns to leave and looks back over her shoulder, and her no nonsense tone catches me. "Keep it up."

I'm not sure how long I sit there, but Cam's voice breaks through my shock. "Congratulations, Em!"

"Did you hear that?"

"Uh, yeah," she says, giving me a strange look. "Why do you think I said *congratulations*?"

"I can't believe she's giving me more. I can't wait to tell Ryan."

"What time is your meeting with Miller?"

I glance at my watch, and start to grab my purse and files. I haven't seen him since he intruded on my dinner with Reid and Langley, and I have a few words for him about that, as well.

"I have to leave now if I want to beat the lunch rush," I say as I pass her. "Plans with Dean tonight?" She doesn't answer, so I know she does.

During the drive to the restaurant, I have a one-sided conversation with a fake Trey. The version in my head is contrite and quiet, only promising that it will never happen again. But the real Trey is not as easy to talk to. I pull into the parking lot and groan, because it's packed which means we'll be lucky to get a table. When I walk up, he's near the hostess stand, nodding and saying something. He spots me and waves me over. "Great timing, they just called my name."

The hostess ushers us to follow her, and Trey steps aside to let me pass, his hand briefly touching the small of my back. I don't know if it's him, or the fact that I haven't been with Ryan in weeks, but my body reacts in a way that leaves me unsettled. *I want more.*

We get to a table and I shake the thought from my head before I set my bags on the empty chair. I take a deep breath and compose myself, waiting to have his attention.

"That can't happen again, understand?"

"What can't happen?"

"You, being in my personal life. If I have to, I will refer to you as Mr. Miller, just so we are clear. Do I need to do that, Trey?"

"Em, it's not a big deal," he says easily. "You and I are friends, and I had dinner with you and your family."

"No, no that's not it. I'm lying to Ryan and I don't like it."

"I never told you to lie."

"That's not my point." I begin to explain, irritated that he's challenging me.

"Well, what is then?"

"Trey, you are a friend, but if it were the other way around, if Ryan had someone attractive that he was spending time with, I would be a jealous mess. And if I didn't know about it, it would hurt even worse."

"Attractive, huh?"

"Trey-"

"So tell him then. I've already told you, I have no intention of doing anything at all. And actually, being around you so much, you're starting to get on my nerves," he says making a face. "Kinda like your friend's little sister that won't go away."

"Shut up," I laugh, grateful he's trying.

"But in all honesty, you shouldn't keep anything from him. You are taken, and I respect that."

"Thanks."

"Aren't you supposed to go see him next weekend?"

"Yeah, but he's got a huge project, so I might have to wait a few weeks."

"How long has it been since you've seen each other?"

I give him a look, because he knows, maybe not the exact date, but the last time Ryan was in town. It was when Trey 'showed up' at the same place.

This conversation is getting us nowhere, so I try to change the subject. "So about the photographer, I think it your clients would really like it."

I take a sip of my water and raise my brow, challenging him to let the conversation move on. He gives me a lopsided grin and nods, lifting his glass to concede. "Alright, you win."

I return his smile because at least now we can finish our lunch by discussing things we actually need to take care of for his party.

chapter 18

Another weekend, another excuse why he can't come to town. Ryan has been so busy that it's been almost five weeks since I've seen him. I was supposed to fly out to California two weeks ago, but he said that he enjoyed being *home* last time. He wanted to wait and come back here; that melted my heart. But when it came time for him to fly out, he had to cancel for another big project; he needed to get a head start. I was disappointed, but he promised the next week he would be able to do it. That is, until he forgot to book his flight. That time, I was so pissed; there was no room for tears.

So this week, I was expecting it.

Ryan: Can't make it in this weekend. I'll make it up to you. Promise

Me: Okay

It wasn't okay, and it certainly wasn't okay that he did it over text. *Who does that?*

"Em?" Lang's voice calls to me through the phone. "Are you still there?"

"Yeah. I'm here."

"So that's it? A text and he's not coming out? Have you at least talked to him?"

"No." My answer is clipped. "I left a message. I'm so mad, I just don't care right now."

"Yeah you do, otherwise you wouldn't be pissed."

"Well, I can't make him answer the phone, so what do you suggest?"

Joss walks over to take the phone from my hands and starts talking to Langley; all I hear is her side of the call.

"I told her to get her ass on the first flight out and do something about it. If he can't come here, she needs to go there."

She nods in agreement with whatever my sister tells her and then looks at me with a smirk.

"You're right. That might have something to do with it."

"What are you two talking about? Give me the damn phone," I say, yanking the phone from her grasp.

"So you think she's falling for Trey?" Lang's voice filters through, not knowing I'm back on the phone.

"No," I yell, looking at Joss to make sure she hears as well. "*She is not falling for Trey.*"

"What are you gonna do then?" Langley asks, challenging me to make a move.

"I'm going out there," I declare, righting my posture and looking at Joss for support. "Y'all are right, I need to see him."

"Good. Hang up and call him to let him know," Lang commands me.

"No, I want to surprise him," I assert, causing Joss' eyebrows to raise in question.

"You just said he's working on a big project, give the man a head's up," Joss pleads, watching me debate my next move.

"Girls, it'll be fine. I'll book a flight and I have a key to his place, so I'll just wait for him there."

Neither of them says another word, and I'm grateful for that. I know showing up unannounced is absurd, but the last thing I want is to let him know, and there be yet another reason we have to reschedule. If I show up, he'll be forced to make time for me and we'll have to work through this awkwardness.

* * *

I talked to Ryan last night, and he had asked if I had plans for the weekend. I told him that I might go out with Joss, but it was a busy week and I just wanted to stay in. Joss dropped me off at the airport this morning, and after finally getting through security, all I had was time. Between Ryan's job and mine, we have no time for each other. But if we want this to work, we have to make time. And I want this to work. Buying a ticket last minute was expensive, but I'm willing to do anything to get to Ryan and get us back on track.

As much as I enjoy working with Trey, I don't like how he is always on my mind. When I'm at work, I can't stop thinking about him because it's my job. But at home, I can't stop thinking about how he makes me laugh or the way he looks at me, or how considerate he is. These are the things that Ryan is supposed to be doing, and the longer we go without seeing each other, the harder it is to ignore the distance between us. I'm not looking to replace him, but somehow, Trey is starting to fill the empty space, and I don't like that at all.

The flight was a nightmare, some kid was screaming in the back of the plane, and even my headphones didn't drown out the noise enough. The book I was planning to read didn't keep my attention, so I was left with nothing but my thoughts. Thoughts that consisted of Ryan, and how this weekend would play out. In my head, Ryan would spot me and give me a heart-stopping smile before grabbing me and kissing me like he's never kissed me before. He would lift me in his arms and sweep me off to the bedroom to make love to me; all would be right with the world.

But that isn't how it played out.

The plane landed at two o'clock, and I didn't want to be stuck waiting for hours with nothing to do, so I hailed a cab and had it drop me off at his office. The receptionist was an older woman, her nameplate reading, Virginia Hall. She was a petite woman with graying hair, and she made me feel relaxed. Ms. Hall handed me a clipboard to sign-in as a guest and when she finally spoke, a broad smile appeared and her voice was kind. "Ryan's told me so much about you."

I returned her smile. "I hope it was good."

She nodded as she directed me to the hall, noting his office was the third on the left. That was the last peaceful moment I had at his office. When I finally made my way to his door, I could hear him speaking to someone, so I waited outside until he was done.

"Listen, Alex," Ryan's voice was authoritative. "I know this is taking up a lot of time, but we have to get this done. I skipped out on going home for this."

When Alex responded, my stomach dropped. "No one told you to cancel. This could have waited until next week."

Alex is a woman?

I wrack my brain, trying to figure out if he had ever mentioned this detail. "Besides, I'd much rather go out tonight and deal with all this later." Her voice was low and seductive, and my stomach started to turn.

"Fine, do what you gotta do, and I'll get as much of this done this weekend as I can." When he said that, a wave of relief washed over me, right before disappointment.

"You can at least have one drink, right?" she purred, causing my blood to boil.

"Sorry, not this time-" he answered. I didn't stay to hear the rest of their exchange; I hurried out of the office, thanking Ms. Hall for her help. I didn't want Ryan to see me there; I felt like an intruder.

Joss called as I was getting into the cab. "Why didn't you call when you landed?"

"Hello to you, too."

"Hello," she answered, formality out of the way. "So are you there yet?"

"I went to his office," I admitted, running my hand through my hair in frustration.

"And?"

"And- Alex, the *guy* he works with- was there."

"So? Do you know the *guy* or something?" she asks, mimicking my tone.

"No," I answer curtly. "Alex is a woman."

Silence. Joss didn't have anything to say; I guess she was stunned into silence.

"I'm heading to his place as planned, I'll figure everything out then. Call you later, 'kay?"

"Yeah," she dragged out. "Later."

The cab dropped me off in front of his complex and fortunately I remembered where to go. My key opened the door to his place and it was just as nice as I recalled, but now it was lived in and he had it set up exactly how I imagined he would. The living room is so small that a sofa and chair make the space feel even smaller. A TV sits on a cheap particleboard shelf he probably picked up one weekend when he was bored; it looks like crap. The place screamed bachelor pad to me and made my heart sad. A pizza box sat on the counter; empty beer bottles looked stacked for recycle and bare walls confirmed my fears. I was forgotten.

I walked into his bedroom and I felt like I didn't belong; I was intruding on his private space. That was until I saw by the bed; a frame from home that I didn't even notice was missing, containing a picture of us from right after we got engaged. I picked up the picture and hugged it to my chest before walking back to the sofa with it. I laid down, and somewhere along the way, I fell asleep, only to wake up to Ryan's key rattling in the door.

"What the hell!" Ryan says as he pushes open the door, stunned by my presence. The greeting is a far cry from the romantic, dramatic version I created in my head.

"Hey," I manage, rubbing my eyes, trying to assess his mood. Ryan is clearly shocked as he stands there staring at me.

"What are you doing here, Em?" He asks as he walks over and pulls me into an awkward hug.

"Five weeks." That is my answer. *Five weeks*. He pushes me back to look at me, and when my eyes don't meet his, he bends down to see into mine. There is an unspoken conversation happening, but I need the words that only he can give me.

Instead of speaking, he grasps my face between his hands and kisses me softly, and I feel his apology. When I try to speak, he silences me with his mouth and I give up, allowing him to take control. He tugs my hand and leads me to the bedroom to show me how much he has missed me.

Now I'm laying here next to him with the ceiling fan blasting cool air on my face, my eyes concentrating on the circular movement. My mind won't shut off to let me bask in the lovemaking that took place. All I can think about is Alex, Trey, distance, and fleeting moments.

"Are you okay?" His voice filters through my thoughts and I turn my head to face him.

"So Alex is a girl, huh?" I'm not mad, I'm not accusing. I'm just questioning what I already know to be true.

He turns to face me, bearing his weight on his arm that propped under him before responding. "What are you talking about?"

"I went to your office earlier, I was going to surprise you there, but then I heard her. Why didn't you tell me?"

Ryan's look remains unfazed by my question, and I know I have nothing to be worried about. Until he speaks again. "Why didn't you tell me I know your client, Mr. Miller?"

I swear my heart just stopped, or at the very least, the planet ran out of air. "I-, I mean," I scramble to face him, trying to find the words, but nothing works. "It's not what it looks like."

"And what do you think it looks like to me?"

Shit! I backed myself into that one.

"I had no idea who he was. I was drunk that night at the bar; I didn't even remember him until the end of our first meeting. I went…" I'm unable to finish my explanation because I see it now. "Wait! You knew who he was? And you didn't say anything?"

"Yeah, as soon as he walked up to you when we went out last time, I knew. Still don't understand why you didn't just tell me."

"There was nothing to tell," I reply a bit too defensively.

"Was? As in there is now?"

"He remembered me, and asked about you," I tell him, recalling Trey's comments the first time I met him. "I told him we're engaged and that was the extent of the conversation. So, why didn't you tell me about Alex?" I ask, mimicking his tone.

He shrugs his shoulder and rolls onto his back, staring up at the ceiling. "I didn't want you to worry because there was nothing to worry about."

"I heard the way she talked to you, she's interested in you." And why wouldn't she be, he's young, handsome, and nice; what's not to like?

"And I saw the way he looked at you, Em. I'm not blind; he wants you." His voice is sardonic and perplexed all at once.

I groan and close my eyes, not liking where this conversation is heading. "I don't care what Alex wants or what Trey wants. What do you want, Ryan?"

"Honestly, I'm just not sure. I think we need to do some serious thinking about what we're about to do."

"What are you talking about?"

He rolls over and looks down at me with a sad face. "I'm talking about getting married."

chapter 19

My entire world stopped turning when Ryan said those words. I tried to argue with him, but he insisted that we needed time to think and figure out if getting married was what *we* still wanted. I left that night and waited at the airport, hoping to get a seat on a flight heading home. I had high hopes for our time together, but when it came down to it, the tension between us was heavy and I knew that nothing was going to be solved by the end of the weekend.

The entire plane ride, I alternated between sniffling and avoiding stares of concerned passengers, to sweating profusely from anger. I kept replaying the conversation over again, looking for any signs of what he was thinking, but he didn't hide anything, he said exactly what he meant.

"Do you not want to get married anymore?" I asked, willing my tears to stay away.

"It's not that, I just think that we didn't really know what we were getting into when we decided to get married," he explained. *"I know you don't want to talk about this, but we need to."*

"What are we supposed to talk about? The fact that you apparently regret asking me to marry you? You're the one who said we could make this work, and now you're giving up. Like that? You must want out," I argued, getting out of bed, angry that just ten minutes before we had made love.

All of my hopes and dreams were tied up in the *forever* I pictured for us. I guess that was my first mistake. Forever is something I want, but thinking that he was solely responsible for providing it was unfair to him. He insisted that we take the next week to think things out, and talk about it later, when we came to a decision. Needless to say, this week has been a blur, with me going through the motions at work, and collapsing when I get home.

We agreed to give it a full week until we talked again, but I can't wait until Friday. Tomorrow feels like a lifetime away and the ache in my heart grows heavier every day.

My sister has always been the one to pick me up when things have gone bad. Right now, things are terrible. I wish I could just let it go and pretend that everything is okay. But no matter how much I try to push the bad out of my head, it creeps back in. Since I don't want to burden Langley with my bad relationship crap, I call mom, because she is the only one who can help me right now. I hope this Scott character isn't around when I call.

It's times like these that I wish my mother lived in the same town so I could cry on her shoulder. I pick up the next best thing, my phone, from the counter and head outside to the balcony of our apartment. The fall air is getting crisp, so I grab a blanket to wrap around me. This is my favorite time of year because I get to cuddle with Ryan. Sitting on the patio, alone in one of the chairs, leaves me feeling lonelier than ever, so I dial my mom's number before I can stop myself, and of course she answers on the first ring.

"Emmy-girl," she says in a singsong tone. "I was just thinking about you."

"Hi, mom. You busy?"

"Not too busy to talk to you," she coos, annoyingly chipper. I assume boyfriend is gone and she's drunk because I haven't heard her this happy in a while. Ever since dad left, mom has refused to be alone. Luckily she never really brought men around until Langley and I were out of the house. But Lang says this new guy is trouble. The longer I remain quiet, the harder it is to find the words to tell her what's going on. I realize that I still haven't said anything when she speaks up. "Is everything okay?"

"No," I cry as a harsh sob escapes, "it's not." And just like that, I'm a blubbering mess. I tell her everything. I tell her about Trey and his feelings for me. I tell her about Ryan and the girl at work. I tell her about the secrets we've kept from each other and fall apart when I tell her that Ryan wants us to *think*. When I'm done, a silence settles across the phone line and I think, for a moment, that we were disconnected. "Mom?"

"Sweetie," she starts, and I know I'm not going to like what comes next. "What did you expect? Of course it's falling apart, you're keeping secrets from each other, why do you think your dad and I didn't work out?"

"Ryan is nothing like dad," I seethe, my voice is dangerously low. Ryan is a good man, and he loves me.

"No, he's not. But your father and I got married young, too young. We didn't get to experience life. But I wouldn't trade it for anything, because I have you and your sister."

"Wait, so are you saying I should walk away?" My nervous nail biting habit hits at this moment, and I refrain for only a moment, before remembering that she can't see me anyway.

"Not at all. You know I love Ryan." She's careful to choose her words, knowing the short fuse I'm on. "But you two have time."

"We're older than you were when you got married," I counter, "so maybe it isn't an age thing."

"Em, you didn't grow up witnessing a successful marriage. You were eight when the 'donor', as you so aptly refer to him, left. We fought all the time, he was a drunk and the day he walked out, I thanked God he was gone."

I shake my head at her words, calling *him* a drunk. I can hear the slur in her voice through the phone, and she thinks I don't know. She's always thought she hid things so well, but I know it killed her when dad left; she was in love with him, flaws and all. It was when he left that she began to drink.

"So what am I supposed to do?" I ask with sadness in my voice. "I don't like what's happening to us."

"I know you don't, but do what he's asking. Think about what you want, and listen to what he wants. If it's meant to be, it'll work out."

She's quiet, and I know she's thinking about him again. "Are you okay, mom?"

"Yeah," she mumbles as she clears her throat, removing all emotion from her tone with the sip of her drink. "I'm good."

I know she's lying, but I let it go for now. "Thanks for the talk. I love you."

"I love you, too."

When I hang up the phone, questions I have been unwilling to ask myself float to the surface. And in the quiet of night, I have nothing else to do but answer them. The night air is quickly cooling, so I head back in through the screen doors and take a seat on the beige cloth couch to warm up. The questions repeat in my head like a bad song that I can't shake.

Are we too young?

Is Ryan looking for a way out?

Do I have feelings for Trey?

Are we meant to be together?

I'm a problem solver. I fix and arrange things all day long. Why can't I fix this? Since the answers aren't coming to me easy, I blow out a harsh breath and walk to my, *our*, bedroom and notice how empty the place is without him. The dress that I wore to work is in a puddle on the floor where I slipped it off, but so are my clothes from the last few days. I release an exasperated sigh before deciding to ignore the growing mess.

All around our tiny apartment are snapshots of Ryan and me; every single one of them reminds me of how much I love him. I pull an album from the shelf in my closet to find the picture I'm looking for; the day Ryan proposed to me. It was the happiest day of my life.

Ryan arranged for my mom and Langley to surprise us in Las Vegas even though he told me that the two of us were going alone, as an early graduation present. I was excited because I'd never been to Vegas. We spent the first day gambling, but that evening we walked all over the strip. He stopped at several wedding chapels along the way, making jokes about getting married in a casino. I finally told him that if he didn't stop, I'd make him do it and then he'd be stuck with me.

We walked around, holding hands, until we stopped in front of a little white chapel that was busting at the seams with people waiting to get married. He turned to me and said, "Let's do it." It was like he was challenging me to object, but I never back down. So I played along, knowing he wouldn't go through with it. When they called his name, we walked to the altar and it became clear he was going to go through with it.

The minister started speaking and it all became a blur until Ryan waved his arm to stop the guy and looked right at me. "Emogen Rae deserves more. She deserves flowers and 'I love yous' and family." He looked past me, and I followed his gaze to see my mom and Langley, followed by his mom and dad. When I turned back to look at him, he was down on one knee with a ring in hand, looking at me like I was his world.

His eyes were glassy and his voice broke when he spoke. "Em, I wasn't expecting you when you found me, but you brought laughter and happiness back into my life. Every day since has been better than the last. I will spend the rest of my life, trying to make you as happy as you make me. Emogen Rae Kane, will you marry me?"

My body felt heavy and I could not stand any longer, falling to my knees in front of him. I was sobbing and laughing while he hugged me. When I said yes, his breathtaking smile was my reward, and I knew then and there that our forever would be amazing.

It wasn't the way he proposed that touched me, it was his words and the way he said them. I felt every ounce of love pour from those words and thinking about that day, I feel them now.

I love Ryan.

He's it, the only person in this world that I want and if I have find work in California to be with him, that's what I'll do for us. Our life *together* is what I want.

Tears fill my eyes, but only because I know in my soul that we are supposed to be together. With my newfound confidence intact, I pick up the phone and find Ryan's name before I lose my nerve. I may not surrender a fight, but this is one time I don't mind, because I will be a winner in the end. This realization solidifies my resolve to see this phone call through and tell Ryan how much I need him in my life.

On the third ring, I figure he's not going to answer and I drop the phone from my ear, only to hear his strained voice answer. I listen for a moment too long and he speaks up. "Em? Everything okay?"

"No, it's not, Ryan. I can't wait until tomorrow," I try to remain calm before continuing. "Since I left you, I have done everything I can think of to avoid thinking about our problems, but it was always there and all I've done is think. I don't need another day, I know what needs to be done."

"I was going to call you, too," he says softly.

"Okay, well, you go ahead, this was your idea," I offer, and wait for him to speak.

The silence stretches and with every second that passes, dread fills me, and it's confirmed when he speaks. "This isn't working, Em," he whispers so quiet, I think I must have imagined it.

This has to be a joke. I look around the apartment for something to tell me I'm losing my mind, because I did not just hear those words come from Ryan's mouth. "You there?"

A desperate sob escapes, and I don't care to stop it. "What? Are you serious?"

"Oh God," he sighs, and I know he expected me to come to the same conclusion. "Em, no. It's just, I've done a lot of thinking, and things have been a mess for a while," he starts, but I don't let him finish.

"So that's it? Just like that, you're done. Are you saying that you don't love me anymore? That you made a mistake?"

"No, that's not it at all. I do love you. Hell, if I didn't, this wouldn't hurt so much. But this, between us, isn't right. You're keeping things from me; I'm keeping things from you. This isn't what a relationship, let alone a marriage, is supposed to be. Can you honestly tell me that you're happy?"

"At this moment? No. But you make me happy Ryan. I love you and I did what you asked, I thought about it. And the only thing I keep coming back to is that I love you so damn much and we are supposed to be together. Yet here you are breaking my heart."

"I'm not trying to hurt you."

"But you *are* hurting me. You're walking away. You're quitting!"

That's what it is, he's quitting.

"I'm trying to do right by both of us," he argues, but I don't want to hear it. He's not doing this for us; he's doing it for him.

"Is there more to this? Did you already know that you wanted out when I was there this weekend?"

"What?" he gasps, trying to figure out what I'm accusing him of. "What in the hell are you talking about?"

"Alex, Ryan," I yell. "Is there more to this than you're admitting. I mean, clearly she wants you and I know you've gone out with her. You can try to play dumb all you want, but let's at least be honest. Do you want to know the *truth* about Trey? Truth is, he's my friend. He told me he has feelings for me, but you know what I told him? I told him that I love you and that *you* are my future. I just had no idea that I wasn't yours."

"Em-"

"No, you know what, thank you. Thank you for sparing me the pain that my mom went through and leaving before I give everything to you and you bail anyway."

"You don't know what you're saying." I hear the pain in his tone.

"Yes, Ryan," I bite out. "I do. My dad didn't love my mom or us enough, and he walked away, and look at the mess she is now. I don't want that for myself, so if you don't want me, I'm not going to beg you."

As if on instinct, my hand flies to cover my mouth and quiet my cry. Tears stream down my face because I know I am saying hateful things to Ryan. He's not like my dad, even through my agony and anger, I know that, but he knows how much I hate the man. I know he's drawing on the comparison and I hope it rips him apart like he is doing to me.

This is not how I thought this conversation would go. I thought Ryan felt for me what I felt for him.

"Em," he moans and his voice cracks. The tears never stop falling from my eyes. "You're trying to hurt me, and it's working. But you're going to see that I'm right. Maybe you won't hate me as much, maybe you will. But I'm letting you go, and I'll probably regret it for the rest of my life. You deserve more than someone who makes decisions without considering you. And I deserve more than someone who compares me to the dad I know she hates. You don't want me, Em. You want the idea of me."

"You don't know what I want, because you've never asked. You didn't give me a chance, because apparently you think you know what's best. I was planning to quit my job to be with you out there, because I wanted *you*, more than I wanted my career."

"Em-"

"Goodbye, Ryan."

I hang up the phone and drop to my bed in agony. He couldn't be more wrong about what I want, because since the moment I saw him, it's always only been him. Looking around this apartment, this home that Ryan and I created, I don't feel like I belong here. I swipe my hands under my eyes and gather myself up because I'm not going to be that girl. He made his choice and I have to live with it.

Who am I kidding? I can't turn it off like that, and I begin crying

mine to lose

for my aching soul that feels empty, in a way I have never known.

chapter 20

I have laid here, alone in my bed, every night for the last two weeks, trying to figure out where it all went wrong. Every morning, I come up empty. Was the writing on the wall all along and I just missed it, or worse, did I ignore it?

It's been twelve days since Ryan and I ended things, not that I'm counting, and the silence haunts my thoughts. This was a loneliness I wasn't prepared for. Langley has called every day to check on me, and every day, I tell her the same thing; *I'll be fine.* My mom has been no help, acting as if I should have seen it coming, but I'm not like her. I don't expect the worst.

"Em," Joss calls from the other side of my door. "Lemme in."

This has been the routine since the breakup. She comes by, and I ignore her. I go to work and do my job, but as soon as the day ends, I turn into a hermit. I don't want to talk about it. I don't want Joss to jump on my bandwagon, and if I have to see Cam look at me one more time with pity in her eyes, I might scream. I mean, honest to God, *scream.*

"I'm fine, Joss," I yell from the couch.

"Great, then let me in. We can talk or not talk, I don't care, I just want to see you," she says with no emotion in her voice. I'm not sure if she's talked to Langley, but knowing them, they've talked every day to figure out how to get me out of my mood.

I finally get up and unlock the door, but stop short of opening the door and let her open it herself. When she walks through, she gives me one of her stares, daring me to be a bitch. With a shake of my head, I turn away and wait for her to join me on the couch. The silence is annoying because she's waiting for me to say something about how I'm feeling, and I don't care to share that right now. I focus my attention on the television and turn up the volume to feign interest in whatever this show is.

There are two things about Joss I can count on; she hates the silence and will do whatever it takes to fill it and she likes to fix things, I'm about to become her pet project. The thing is, I don't need fixing, I just need time.

"You hungry?" she asks during a commercial and I shrug. Truth be told, I could probably eat because I haven't really taken care of myself lately. It's not that I don't want to eat; I have no appetite. "I'm ordering pizza and then you're gonna snap out of this, okay?"

What the fuck? Did she really just say that shit to me? I have to blink from the shock of her words as though she physically struck me. Yes, Joss is rough around the edges, but she's never spoken to me harshly unless I'm drunk. Her statement echoes in my ears and cuts a little deeper every time I hear it.

I finally look at her, my mouth agape. "*This* just happened, Joss," I remind her when she looks at me. "I'm allowed to be down about it, aren't I? A three-year relationship, a year engagement, the love of my life, gone. So excuse me if I can't just *snap* out of it."

"Good, so you are dealing with it then," she responds with a straight face, but I know she's happy she got me to admit what I'm thinking.

"Of course I am, I mean, what other choice do I have," I say in disbelief that she's being so hard on me. "It's over."

"So do you want to tell me what happened?"

I reveal the snippet of what I've been thinking about over and over. "Things between us were easy for so long, and I thought it would always be like that. It took years to build a good relationship, to get it just right. I mean, I'm not saying it was perfect, you know that. Hell we still fought and did stupid shit, but when those things don't break you, you know there's something special there. At least I thought it was special. I guess I'm just shocked at how quickly it all crumbled."

What I don't share is that all it takes is a little white lie, and it just starts to unravel. We both screwed up, I know that, but I didn't know it was beyond repair. I'm now left with the small apartment that feels too big, and memories of us everywhere I look.

"Have you talked to him at all?"

"He's called, but I have no reason answer; we said everything we needed to say," I shrug, trying to be interested in the television show.

"What are you gonna do now?"

"Not sure," I sigh and glance over at her, "I have work to keep me busy. Trey's client event is in a month, so it's crunch time now."

"Trey, huh?" Her question holds so many others that she's not voicing.

"Don't start, Joss." My hand flies up to stop her from pushing that any further. "It's work, and that's all. I've barely talked to him."

She acknowledges my words with a nod, but I know she still isn't convinced.

"But I'll tell you one thing; I can't stay here anymore," I state, looking around the living room.

"You can always come move in with me for a while, if you need to," she offers, as if it's not a big deal. What she doesn't realize is that it is exactly what I need. I have to get out of this place; I can't heal here, because I feel him everywhere. Work is a great distraction, but when I come back here, it's a graveyard for my failed relationship. "Just think about it, the offer's out there."

When I finally gather my nerve to look at her face, she smiles in understanding and reaches over to squeeze my hand. That simple gesture is my undoing, and the tears I have kept at bay since I stopped crying that night spill out again. She scoots over and gathers me into her arms while I mourn what I've lost, and I allow her to console me.

"It's really over, isn't it?" I ask, my sobs constricting my words.

"I can't answer that for you. What I can tell you is that you and Ryan were good together, but y'all let life and careers derail your path. And I know you probably don't want to hear this right now, Em," She waits for me to look at her and she grabs my left hand and points to my ring. "But as long as you keep this on, the mind-fuck that is this breakup will keep messing with you."

* * *

Moving out of the space I shared with Ryan for the last nine months causes so much pain. And moving in with Joss is certainly not ideal. Hell, we barely survived as roommates in college; but this time is different. She's helping me escape the memories this place holds and giving me what I need to move on. When she left my apartment that night, we had come up with a plan for me to move in with her when my lease was up. But she came to me a couple of days later and asked if I'd be willing to move in next week, because she found someone to sublet my place.

I have thought about Ryan so much, but unfortunately I have work, and now boxing up our place, to occupy my time. The nights are still sad, especially when I'm packing his things away to ship to him. Most of his clothes went with him to San Diego, but things like the guitar he never played, t-shirts he never wore, and his shot glass collection are still here.

I grab another box and scrawl his name along the side of it and begin loading it with his stuff. The t-shirts were already pulled out of the dresser, so I grab the first stack and place them in the bottom, not caring if they unfold. It's when I reach for the second stack that my favorite shirt of his comes to view. It's a soft worn-out shirt, the graphics barely readable, but what I love about this shirt is that he was wearing it the night we met. Against my better judgment, I pull the t-shirt over my head, covering the tank I'm wearing.

"No," I say aloud, yanking it back off, "you're not gonna do this." I ball the shirt up and toss it into the box with the others before getting up to get more of his things. Over the next hour, the box slowly fills with pictures, books, cups, and anything else that reminds me of Ryan. When it's all said and done, most of our relationship, or the parts I don't want, fit neatly into a large moving box.

Looking around the apartment, the only things that remain to be boxed are mine. Clothes, dishes, and albums were boxed days ago, and all that's left are trinkets and frames. The box I packed for him sits open and before taping it shut, I drag the t-shirt back out. I'm not ready to let it go just yet.

"Just do it," I tell myself as I grab my phone. I haven't talked to him or texted since the night we broke up, but it's time. I find his name in my phone to send him a text.

Me: Just wanted to let you know I subleased the apt. I'm moving.

Ryan: I've been calling you

I ignore his comment because I need to stay on track, and this isn't meant to be a conversation.

Me: You still have things here. I boxed them up. I'll send it out to you

Ryan: It's okay. I'll be out there for a meeting.

Me: I'll leave the box with Joss

I push send and exhale as I throw myself onto the couch. The hard part is over, right?

There doesn't seem to be a need to tell him that I will be living with Joss, although I'm sure he'll figure it out soon enough. He's called several times over the last two weeks. I deleted the voicemails, because I didn't think my heart could take it. I have a nice callous over it now that's hardening, and until it's unbreakable, I can't listen to his voice.

Ryan: Can I see you?

Toying with the idea of seeing him doesn't send warm and fuzzy feelings through my body. In fact, the only thing I feel is nauseous. I don't know if it's because I want to see him or I dread the moment when I have to. Needless to say, I have no plans to respond to his text.

"Em," Joss' voice filters through the door as she knocks. I let her in and stand next to her as she assesses the mounds of crap I've boxed, and the plethora of crap that still remains. "So, I see you've made some progress," she teases.

I point to *the* box. "I really have. And I let him know it'll be at your place when he comes to pick it up."

"Are you going to see him?"

"No. He asked, but it's too soon," I admit, knowing she understands.

She walks over to his box and riffles through some of the items. She pulls out a coffee mug that has our picture on it. Joss gave it to us a gag gift last year and it's been my favorite one to drink from. She raises a questioning brow and I answer with a shrug. She places the mug back into the box and spots the t-shirt that I pulled out.

"No, that's mine. He can't have it back," I say, grabbing the shirt possessively.

She scoffs and shakes her head, grinning like she knows something I don't. "None of my business."

I'm thankful she lets it go and sticks around to help me finish boxing everything up; it makes the task a little less sad. Looking at the apartment, boxes taped up and marked by room, it's hard to imagine that this was once a home. We hired a small moving company to load and deliver everything to her place tomorrow. All I have left to do is turn the keys over to the new tenant. She wraps her arm around my shoulder, knowing how hard this is for me, and gives me a squeeze.

"I'll meet you at home," she whispers before leaving me alone.

Our bedroom calls to me, and I give in, needing to say one last goodbye to what we were. Standing in the doorway, I see the ghosts of us laughing, fighting and making love, causing my body to react. A single tear rolls down my cheek, which I am quick to wipe away. My keys and purse are sitting on the top of a box near the door, so I pick them up and open the door one last time and shut off the lights.

"Always," I whisper my response to our imaginary *I love you*.

chapter 21

Joss has to be the best friend a girl can have, or at the very least, I'm grateful that she's mine. The movers dropped everything off at her, *our*, place by two o'clock, and we worked until dark to get it all put away. She had been using her second bedroom as an office space, but moved her desk into her room. I was touched by her kindness, but then again, that's how she's always been. It's strange how the entire contents of a life, or relationship, can fit into one small twelve by twelve room, yet somehow we did just that.

Last night, I was able to hang out with Joss without unpacking or moping. I was terribly hungry and I hadn't been eating since the breakup. So we ordered six different entrees from the Chinese takeout menu. We opened them all up and I devoured what amounted to two all on my own. She laughed, happy that I finally got my appetite back.

"Hell, no wedding dress to squeeze into, no boyfriend." I looked at the table covered in food. "This will be my new life. I will eat everything in sight."

When I went to bed, full and tired, I slept more sound than I had in a while. I was dreaming of Ryan and beaches that turned into Chinese takeout that was chasing me. I kept trying to get back to the good part of my dream when I sat upright and bolted to the toilet, vomiting every last bit of Chinese food I had inhaled. I threw up two more times before I was finally able to get to bed.

"Good morning sunshine," Joss coos over her shoulder from the kitchen. She does a double take. "You look terrible."

"You're such a charmer," I say with a glare.

"What? Did you cry yourself to sleep? Your eyes are puffy," she says as she walks over to get a better look at me.

"I think I got food poisoning last night."

"We ate the same thing, and I'm fine. Maybe you're pregnant," she says before walking away.

"Don't even joke about that," I warn her. "Besides, you didn't eat the sesame chicken because you said it's too sweet."

She wrinkles her nose and thinks about it. "Do you really think you got food poisoning?"

"It's more plausible than me being pregnant," I bite at her.

"Are you sure, because you're kinda bitchy right now? Is it that time of month?"

I roll my eyes and turn back to my bedroom. "Fuck me! I'm moving out!"

Joss' laughter behind me causes me to laugh in return as I shut the door to get ready for work. I'm not sure how she does it, but she's amazing at getting me out of my funk. I have dreaded going in to work today, mainly because I have less than two weeks before Trey's dinner party. There are still details to take care of, so I'll have to get those done this week.

I retrieve my favorite black skinny jeans and pair them with a vintage concert tee that I bought a while back. I haven't worn it yet, because I've been meeting with so many people. But there is nothing on the docket today, so this is perfect. I put my dark grey suede blazer on and spruce up the outfit with a few pieces of costume jewelry. When I check my reflection in the mirror, I realize that I look better than I have in a while.

My desk is still clean from Thursday afternoon, since I took Friday off to pack. The only thing I notice is the blinking red light on my phone, indicating that I have a message. The time stamp says it was left on Friday, so I rush to check it.

"Em, Emogen, this is Trey. When you have a moment I need to talk to you about some last minute details. I have a few concerns. Thanks."

I make myself a note to call him in a while, with the goal of checking up on all details so I can give him as much information as possible. Thumbing through the file, I find that everything is still going according to plan. I want to contact every vendor we've signed contracts with, just to ensure that they are on task and ready for next week.

I'm just finishing up the first of seven phone calls I have to make when a text from Trey buzzes through on my cell.

Trey: Call me. Issue with entertainment

Me: What's going on?

Trey: Urgent

I look over to Cam, who is knee deep in details for a wedding this weekend to see what she knows. "Cam, did something happen with the DJ for the T.M. event next weekend?"

"Not that I'm aware of, why?

"Not sure," I respond, getting worried that I dropped the ball somewhere along the way. "Trey just sent a vague text about it and said I need to call."

She looks as concerned as I do, but this is my client and my job on the line, so I have to do whatever it takes to make sure this goes off without a hitch. I pick up the office phone, dial his number and wait for him to pick up. "Trey, it's Emogen. I just got your text."

"All of them?"

"There was more than the one I you just sent?"

"No, that was all," he says with a laugh.

"So what's going on with the entertainment?"

"Nothing, they're great," he says as though it's any other conversation.

"Are you kidding me? You said it was urgent, I thought something fell through," I say with relief, but still confused as to the need for a call.

"I've had Hattie handling things here, and I know that Cam has been taking care of it on your end." He pauses for a moment before finishing. "I just want to make sure that everything's okay."

I read into that last statement, curious if he knows about the breakup. It's not something I plan to talk about with anyone, especially my client. I decide to ignore my gut and focus on the task at hand. "I was actually in the middle of making phone calls to reconfirm everything, so I'll email the details and a timeline later," I say, hoping to end the phone call.

"Great," he starts. "I have some things I want to go over, so let's meet for lunch."

"Today's not a good day," I tell him, while I look at my calendar. "I have a meeting set up from eleven thirty to one o'clock." I need to call Callie to see what this is about.

"Yeah, that's me."

"All it says is lunch at-"

"The Bistro," he finishes with a laugh while I gather my wits. "Pick you up at eleven."

I don't even have time to respond because he hangs up the phone. Dumbfounded, I hang up the receiver to pick it up again. "Callie, did you schedule this appointment on my calendar with Mr. Miller?"

"Yes," she replies timidly, like she's waiting for me to yell at her. "He called Friday morning, and I told him you wouldn't be in until today. He said that it was urgent that he meets with you. Is something wrong?"

Urgent. There's that word again. I don't think he knows the meaning of the word, because that is reserved for something that has to be taken care of now. Avoiding Trey for the rest of the week is what is *urgent* to me.

"No, Callie. Thank you," I say with defeat before hanging up the phone.

* * *

"Why didn't you tell me about this lunch date?" I ask as we take a seat at our table.

"Not a date. Besides, it's not like you've been easy to get a hold of," he reminds me as he slips his sunglasses off.

Ouch. Did I really just try to call this a date?

"I've been really busy. Cam's been handling some of the details." *Like calling you.* "But I've been keeping up with the schedule and working on the table layout."

He nods at my answer while studying the menu in his hand. I haven't really been around Trey since Langley and Reid were in town. Our meeting after that made things awkward and blurred the professional line. That's the reason I asked Cam to handle any face to face that might be needed. Had I known that he was going to give Hattie a shot at really taking care of everything on the T.M. side of things, I wouldn't have been so quick to step away.

He places his menu off to the side and takes a sip of his water. When he sets the drink down, I can feel his eyes on me. I stare a little harder at my menu, hoping to buy myself a little more time.

"You're looking at that thing like it can cure cancer." His statement elicits an uncomfortable laugh from me, but I can't help but look at him to acknowledge his observation.

"It does," I answer in my snarkiest tone.

"So what looks good?"

"Honestly?" I eye him and he nods. "Nothing. I got food poisoning last night, so I don't have much of an appetite." As if on cue, my stomach growls at an embarrassing level and he starts laughing.

"Either you're lying, or you're feeling better. Just order something, you can always finish it later," he instructs.

The waiter stops by and takes our orders before scurrying off, leaving us in silence once again. I pull out the file and begin going over the information that he needs for the evening. He knows that I'm going to send him an email, and I'll also be on hand to handle everything, but I get the feeling he's a bit of a control freak. But then again, this is his name, his company and his future clients that are being catered to. We discuss the table layout and he makes a few seating arrangement changes, but is happy with the setup overall. When Lisa told us about the caterer issue, we found another that she suggested. After sampling a couple of things on their menu and contacting a few of their references, I was sold, but Trey took a bit more coaxing because he wanted to use someone more established. I reminded him that he needed to take a chance on people, just like he expects potential clients to take a chance on him. He's still not completely convinced, but I appreciate that at least he trusts my judgment.

Our plates have been removed and the waiter brings me a box for my leftovers. The meeting has gone really well, and I'm glad that he insisted on seeing me. There is relief knowing that I have everything taken care of and Trey is happy with my work. Feeling our meeting is done, I remove my napkin from my lap to stand up, but he remains seated, so I do as well.

"How was your visit with Ryan?" he asks, making conversation.

"Trey, I'd really rather not discuss that, if you don't mind," I say as respectfully as I can, exhaling a breath.

"I'm sorry, I wasn't trying to pry, just making conversation," he says with a crooked smile.

"Yeah well, that's a dead conversation." My tone is clipped and I see concern in his eyes.

"What does that mean?"

"Nothing."

He leans toward me, assessing my short responses before slowly reaching for my hand. "We're friends, right?"

He's trying to comfort me, and while I appreciate it, his hand on mine clouds my judgment. Granted, we have become friends, but my heart is breaking over the loss of Ryan in my life. Trey's touch makes me feel guilty for craving this from him, and at the same time, it gives me peace. How can he read me and know that I need this?

"You're my client, first."

"No, right now, I'm your friend. What's going on?"

"Trey, I appreciate your concern, but really, I'm fine."

"Did you guys have a fight? I'm sorry," he adds in a rush, "that's none of my business."

"No." My eyes close and I shake my head. "It's really not, but I am fine. We broke up, it hurts and it sucks, and that's all I'll say about it. I don't want to talk about it. Okay?"

The sympathy I see in his eyes causes my heart to break a little more. I don't want sympathy or pity or anything else, but it seems that's what I'll be getting for a while. I suppose that's the reaction when people hear of a broken engagement. "I'm sorry to hear that, Em. If you need anything, I *am* your friend."

"Thanks." I smile, happy I've been able to keep the tears at bay. "And yes, we're friends."

chapter 22

"Hey Em." Langley's voice sounds through the phone. "You're still coming out next weekend, right?"

"Lang," I say with exasperation. "Can I please get through one big thing at a time? I haven't been feeling well and I have Trey's event tomorrow night. I need to focus on this."

"What're you gonna wear?"

"Black." Of course it's black. It's always black, that's Elle's signature. A knock at the door interrupts our conversation. "Hold on, someone's at the door."

"Maybe it's a serial killer," she says in a fake panicked tone. "Don't answer it!" she screams, causing me to laugh. I don't even look through the peephole before I answer the door and my world stops.

"Ryan?"

"Hey, Em." He looks unsure and as handsome as I remember. *Ha! Remember? I look at his picture every night.*

"What? What are you doing here?" I stumble over the words, confused by his presence.

"I called Joss earlier to see if I could pick up the box you left for me. She didn't tell you?"

"Uh, that would be a no," I say stepping aside to let him in.

"Lang?"

"Yeah, call me back," she says hanging up the phone.

I turn to face Ryan, stunned that this is even happening. Joss played me. She convinced me to try yoga with her, not that she exercises, but I figured I had nothing better to do. But this afternoon she called and canceled saying that she had a late meeting and couldn't make it.

"What are you doing here?" Ryan's voice interrupts my thoughts and I realize I've been standing silent like an idiot.

"I live here now," I inform him. My words are steady, and show no signs of breaking. I might just make it through this little surprise visit.

"She didn't mention that."

"There's a lot she didn't mention," I say more to myself than him.

"What's that?" He leans forward to listen.

"Nothing. Do you want something to drink?"

"I'm fine," he says as I walk to the couch, showing him a seat. "What did Joss do with her furniture?" He references our couch replacing hers.

"Donated it to a woman's shelter." When I tell him this, he seems to be mulling it over, or maybe he's reeling from seeing me.

When he finally speaks, it's as if we're mere acquaintants. "How have you been?"

"Good," I say, realizing that I am good. It's not a lie.

"You look good, Em."

"So do you. Work going okay?"

"It's going," he shrugs, clearly not wanting to elaborate.

"Where're you stayin'?"

"Dean's place," he admits, cocking his head to the side. "Cam didn't tell you I was in town?"

The eye rolling is involuntary, I swear. The knowledge that Cam knew, and didn't tell me, that Joss knew and didn't tell me. I don't know what game they're playing but it needs to stop. It's been over a month, I have to move on, and they need to let it go.

"Lemme get your box," I offer as I head to my bedroom. The box has been safely tucked out of my sight, keeping me from going through it over and over. It's heavy, but I manage to carry it out, only to have him meet me to help.

"What's in here?"

"Whatever you didn't take to San Diego. Mostly little things like shot glasses, some t-shirts and other junk."

"Junk, huh? What about that shirt you're wearing?" His eyes scan over my body and I fight the urge to hide, but I have no reason to slink away.

"I'm keeping this one." My tone lets him know I am not to be argued with.

"What if I want it?" He smiles like it's any other conversation, as though he didn't just rip my heart out weeks ago. I want to punch him or yell at him for being here right now. How can he stand here and flirt with me, as though no time has passed?

"Tough, it's mine." My hands fly to my hips and right then I see it in his eyes, he still loves me. "But this is yours."

I walk away, leaving him standing alone in the living room. There on my dresser rests the little box that holds what I treasured most. I pull out the ring and place it on my finger one last time and marvel how much it's been a part of me before slipping it off. When I come back, the box is on the floor in front of him and he's standing there waiting for me with a shy smile.

My smile is small, and filled with sorrow as I open my hand. "Here you go."

Ryan looks down and sees the ring, his eyebrows furrow as though he's in pain. "No. I gave that to you."

"And now I'm giving it back."

"I don't want it back," he argues, turning to walk away from me.

"Ryan, this was a promise that you made to me. A promise of love and a life of forever. I wore it with all the hope that it vowed, but that's over. I need you to take it back. Please?"

"But-"

"Please." My voice breaks and he shakes his head.

The sound of a key entering the lock outside the door snaps us back to the here and now. Joss walks in and spots Ryan and I standing apart, and not happy. I look to my friend and shake my head at her for the betrayal.

Ryan finally looks back at me and I walk over and wrap my arms around him one last time. When his arms embrace me, he pours so much into it, but I pull away. He still has his hands on my hips and I push to my toes and plant a chaste kiss to his lips. "I will always love you, Ryan Tate." My hand reaches down and I push the engagement ring into his front pocket before slipping out of his arms and out of the room.

With the door closed behind me, I try to steady my breathing in hopes that I won't cry, but it doesn't help. My emotions keep getting the best of me, but at least no one is around to witness them. *Score one for a brave face.* Their muffled voices are audible through the door, so I close my eyes to listen, pressing my ear against it.

"Why didn't you tell her I was coming in town?" I can hear the irritation in his tone and it's pretty clear he might be as angry with her as I am.

"I'm sorry, Ry, I guess I hoped that you would see each other and the old feelings would return." Joss's voice is sad, and somewhat shamed.

"The old feelings, which you're referring to, never left. At least not for me, things just got messed up." Hearing these words from him cut to my core. *He* ended it, and I felt like he didn't want to fight for me, or for us.

"Did you tell her that?"

"I hurt her, Joss. I don't blame her for hating me; you should have seen the way she looked at me when she gave me the ring back. What am I supposed to say to that? No, Em's moved on."

"If that's what you want to tell yourself." When I hear her begin to argue her point, I push away from the door to take a shower. Maybe the sting of scalding water will take away the pain my heart feels all over again just seeing him.

I don't know how long I was in the shower, but I couldn't tell my tears from the water, so I don't consider it true crying. I'm drying my hair when Joss slinks up, hiding to the side like a coward. My scowl gives my unhappiness with her away, but she moves into my space, ignoring my obvious disdain for her. The dryer is loud, but the thoughts in my head are louder, so I shut it off and turn to face her.

"What in the hell were you thinking, Joss? That was embarrassing, and shitty." My voice is raised as I glare at her.

"Look, we just thought-"

"We? Who was in on this?" My anger is boiling over as I discover this was a conspiracy.

"Cam and Dean-"

I no longer try to control the decibel of my voice, giving her the full brunt of my ire. "Are you kidding me? Were you trying to fuckin' *Parent Trap* us? Well, I got news for you, Joss, it didn't work. We are over. Ryan made his choice, he ended this, and I have to live with it. So I would appreciate it if you stopped interfering and let me move on. Can you do that?"

My eyes snap from her toward the living room, when I hear the door shut. She looks over her shoulder, and then back to me. "He was waiting to talk to you."

"Get out!"

* * *

Compartmentalizing has become an art form to me, one that I believe I've become quite good at. For example, today I am running all over town, ensuring that everything is ready for tonight. Elle has provided me with a team of people to help with Trey's event, and knowing I have support makes me feel better. Trey actually tried to get me to forego working the event and attend as his date. I had to tell him several times that it was not an option, but I would make sure to stop by and say hello. When I left the apartment this morning, I grabbed my dress for the evening, deciding I would get ready at the office. Joss was in the kitchen eating breakfast when I emerged from my room, but I was still giving her the silent treatment; I was not ready to talk to her yet. I took my actions a step further and called Elle to make sure that Cam was not on my team for the evening; I breathed a sigh of relief when I found out that she would have her own event to attend.

Ivy Glen is bustling with wait staff and vendors setting up tables and decorations. We adjusted the lighting to be dim, but bright enough that the guests will be able to see each other's faces when they talk. The table layout is exactly as I envisioned when I sent it to Lisa a week ago. Someone from her team passes by me so I ask where I can find her.

I haven't seen her yet, but when I ask her staff where she is, they inform me that Lisa's likely in her office. I walk down the hallway to find her sitting at her desk when I knock on the door. "C'mon in," she says without looking up.

"I just wanted to stop by and say hello before I get out there to help with setup."

"Well look at you! You look great. Did you do something different with your hair?" I can't help but laugh at her assessment, especially considering I spent the better part of last night in tears.

"You're a terrible liar, but thank you, I needed that." I wink as I turn to leave, but she stops me.

"No, something's up, but I can't put my finger on it." She rubs her finger along her lips in thought.

"The only thing different since the last time you saw me is that I find myself single these days."

I love this girl, because she doesn't give me *the* look. The one that says, *poor, Emogen*, the one that actually makes me want to vomit. "Well, the single life looks good on you."

Those words feel like a physical blow to my gut. Pangs of guilt, hurt and loss cause my stomach to roll, but I take a deep breath and try to accept her words for the compliment they were meant to be. My smile is small, but I offer what I can before making my way back to the hall to setup.

Four cups of coffee, a nervous stomach and three hours later, every table is adorned with brown colored linens and violet napkins. The centerpieces are exactly what Jaysen showed us months ago, a credit to his talent. Small square vases are overflowing with every variety of purple flowers I know, and even some that I am unfamiliar with. The work these people have put into this is impressive, and as much as I want to see it completed, I have a job to do, and if I don't look the part, it'll be my head.

I let Lisa know that I'm heading to the office to get ready, but she offers me use of her space, and I accept gratefully. I went shopping the other day, needing something to make me feel both different and special. After hours of looking, I finally chose a black satin dress with a sheer overlay that has beaded lace across the chest and arms. Slipping the dress on, I felt instantly confident, as if it had magic to make me feel better, which I know is ridiculous, but it works. In the middle of applying the finishing touches to my makeup, I hear voices outside in the hallway, so I rush to finish to make sure there are no problems.

When I emerge, I find Trey and Lisa in conversation only for him to stop talking altogether to gape at me. I feel exposed, but I'm completely dressed and ready to start work. "Is everything okay?"

Trey is still staring when Lisa gives his shoulder a shove. "Yeah. Yeah, fine. I was asking Lisa when you were expected."

"I've been here most of the day to oversee the setup. Have you seen it yet?"

"Yeah, it looks great."

"I was just going to check it out, when I left they were still working on setting the tables," I say over my shoulder, leaving them staring after.

Damn! He looks gorgeous. I know that he's an attractive man, and his confidence only makes him sexier. He is usually dressed in a button down shirt and casual slacks, but tonight, he's dressed in a black suit with a white shirt and a thin black tie is exposed through his open jacket. He seriously looks like he just stepped out of the pages of a men's clothing catalog. I keep walking to the main room, hoping to cool off and get my thoughts back on the work at hand, which is easy to do when I see everything in place.

The lights are set perfectly to provide the ambiance we were going for. The tables are ready, each decorated with tea light candles surrounding the floral arrangements and all place settings have been set. There is a small dance floor, although I doubt anyone will be dancing. Trey figured with an open bar, people might get crazy enough to head that way, so we asked Lisa to set one out anyway. The photographer must have arrived while I was getting ready because he has his camera placed to the left of the entrance, exactly where I wanted him. He spots me eyeing everything and mistakes me for a guest. "Would you like your picture taken?"

"Oh no." I shake my head and laugh. "I'm working this evening."

"Yes." I hear Trey's voice behind me. "She'll take one with me."

"Trey," I drag out in warning. "I need check in with my staff."

"I'm sure you have five seconds to take a picture with your friend," he reminds me, to which I roll my eyes and sigh in defeat.

The photographer poses us in a close embrace, which doesn't feel terribly uncomfortable. We are so close that I can smell his cologne that smells of musk mixed with something else I can't quite place. I fight closing my eyes to inhale because it's too perfect. I finally relax, allowing a smile to appear when he turns his mouth to my ear, causing me to take a sharp intake of air when he whispers, "You look beautiful."

My throat goes dry and my head spins from his words. This is not good. I have a job to do, and I need to stay focused. The photographer calls for our attention and we smile in unison before I politely thank Trey and excuse myself. Before I can rush off, his arm that is around my waist squeezes just slightly prodding me to look at him. He looks concerned, but I assure him that I'm okay.

"Well, since you can't be my date tonight, may I at least give you a ride home?"

"I have my car, but thanks for the offer," I reply. I step away from him because I need space from the things he's doing to my senses, but the disappointment is evident on his face. His hands are tucked in his pockets and he seems to be mulling over my response.

I start to walk away but look back once more. "Trey?" I wait until his eyes meet mine before finishing. "You look beautiful, too."

I rush off before I say anything else, leaving him standing openmouthed.

* * *

Elle certainly gave me the best of the bunch for the evening. They made sure that everything went according to my timeline and helped ensure that things flowed smoothly. Before dinner was served, Trey took a moment to thank his clients for attending and remarked that he hoped those who are not yet familiar with his work would be intrigued by the end of the night. I overheard several guests commenting on how great the room looked and raving about the food. There was no doubt, Trey was right in asking for a dance floor; as the night progressed and drinks were poured, the stuffy crowd let their guard down and started dancing like no one was watching. I couldn't help but laugh at the moves a few put on display. But when the music would slow, I would make myself scarce because the melancholy tunes would inevitably make me sad.

As guests were leaving, two impeccably dressed women approached me, inquiring about my name and wanting a business card, and I was only too happy to oblige. I gave them as much information as I could in the short time I had with them, but I knew that Elle would be pleased.

Returning to the main hall there are a few stragglers that remain and I stand there assessing how long the take down will last when I hear someone clearing their throat. I have to admit I'm not the least bit surprised to find Trey with his tie off and top button undone, appearing very pleased.

"So how do you think it went?" I ask him, even though I already know the answer.

He looks past me, at the almost empty room and looks deep in thought. He shrugs his shoulders seeming suddenly unimpressed. "It was okay." I give him a playful shove and he laughs. "I'm kidding. Damn. So sensitive."

I open my mouth to respond, but he grabs my hand before the words come out. "C'mon. You owe me a dance."

"Trey, I'm working," I complain while he tugs me along behind him anyway.

"Fine, then you're fired. Now dance with me," he demands with a mischievous grin.

"You can't fire me, I don't work for you," I remind him.

"See, you *can* dance with me then," he declares, proud that he tricked me. "Just one song."

"Do I have to?" I whine pointing to my feet. "I'm dying here, these shoes are killing me."

He bends down and reaches for my foot, causing me to grab hold of his shoulders for balance. He makes quick work of slipping my heels off before I can protest and stands up with a pleased grin. "Problem solved."

Deciding there's no way to talk him out of it, I let him lead me to the dance floor while a song I recognizes plays in the distance. "I love this song," I tell him, as he pulls me into his arms.

"I've never heard it. Who is it?" He has my hand, wrapped in his, and held close to his heart, his other on the small of my back. It's so easy to get lost in his arms, but I do my best to keep my head on straight.

"It's the Avett Brothers," I tell him, fighting the urge to close my eyes and disappear in the moment.

We move together easily in small movements, and he's careful not to step on my bare feet. My short stature is assisted with the four inch heels that I'm wearing, but now my head rests right at his chest, a little too intimate for my liking. I pull my head away to gain some space and look at the mess that is waiting for me. I can feel his eyes on me and I am timid when I finally make eye contact.

"Thanks for everything you did tonight." He smiles with appreciation.

I hate compliments, and tend to make jokes, why should now be different. "I was just doing my job."

"Well," he starts quietly, "you did great."

"Thanks," I respond with a smile, admiring his obvious good looks.

"If it's too soon, just let me know. Okay? But now that I'm no longer your client, and you are single, how 'bout letting me take you out?"

"Trey-"

"Just a date, Em. Let me take you out tomorrow night and treat you to a fun time."

I close my eyes and remember everything that happened last night. Ryan and I are done. He's the one who ended it, and even though I know there is still something between us, because I felt it, it's over. When I open my eyes, Trey is waiting for my answer with a lopsided grin. I have no reason not to give it a shot. There is something between us, there has been for a while, even when I tried to deny it. Ryan and I are over, his choice, not mine, and I suppose it's time for me to move on.

"Alright. Sounds great."

Before I can register the movement, he kisses me and tightens his hold on me while we finish the dance. The gesture feels familiar; as though it's something he's done to me for years. It feels intrusive and comfortable at the same time, and once again, my head is spinning.

chapter 23

Last night was exhilarating, the hustle and bustle of running an event all on my own was only surpassed by the accolades I received on my voicemail a few minutes ago. I slept in until nine this morning; I don't know when the last time that happened. I guess I was so exhausted from everything that had happened over the last two days, my body just wanted rest. I got in late enough that I was able to avoid Joss and go straight to bed. When I peeked out to see if she was up this morning, I noticed that her keys were gone, so she must have slipped out while I was still sleeping. I'm not ready to deal with her and her attempt to reconcile Ryan and me, yet. I didn't even give her time to explain why he was waiting around to talk to me.

The loud grumbling of my stomach reminds me that I haven't eaten since before I got to Ivy Glen yesterday, so I make my way to the kitchen to get some cereal and coffee. While waiting for the coffee to finish brewing, I look at Joss' calendar that is plastered to the fridge and eye what she's got going on. I can't help but laugh at her star on Thursday, the mark that shows her period, it explains so much. Mid laugh, I stop abruptly and run to my bedroom to pull up my own calendar on my cell. I mark it every month.

When was my last period?

I start shuffling through the month on my calendar and realize I'm late.

"Shit!" I yell, just as I hear the front door open and shut.

"What's going on?" Joss asks, walking over to my room.

"Nothing." I shake my head dismissing her. "I've just got someplace I need to be." I pull on my yoga pants and a t-shirt, not even bothering to wash my face or brush my teeth because I have one thought in mind. *Get to the store.* Joss is watching me scramble around the apartment like a crazy person, and keeps trying to ask if I need help, even apologizing for the other night; I don't listen. I shove my boots on and throw on my coat before grabbing my keys and my purse. I hurry out of the apartment leaving my best friend home alone and stunned.

One of the perks of living in Joss' area of town is that there is a convenience store within walking distance. The December air is cold, and under any other circumstances, I'd probably be freezing my ass off, but right now, I'm so hopped up on adrenaline that I'm almost sweating as I hurry down the street. When I walk through the door, the cashier looks at me as though he's scared of me.

"Pregnancy test?"

"Second aisle toward the back," he says to my back as I head in that direction. I locate the box and get queasy at the thought of being pregnant and realize I can't go home with a test in hand for Joss to see. *We're doing this* Juno-*style*, I tell myself, locating a restroom in the back of the store. I'm sure the poor fella up front isn't thrilled, but if this turns out the way I think, I'll be buying more than a test before I walk out of here.

I rip open the box and read the instructions before sitting on the toilet. When women do this on television, it's much funnier, because all I can manage to do is piss on my hand while trying to get the stick in the stream for five seconds. This isn't rocket science, but I'm making a mess of it. I grab a square of toilet paper and set the test on top of it on the sink while I pull my pants up. Three minutes is all it will take for me to know if what I think is true. Three minutes, and I'm going to have to figure out how to tell my ex-fiancé that I'm pregnant with his kid. Three minutes is a long-ass time to wash your hands, look at your haggard reflection and think about how much everything is going to change when time's up.

I chance a look and see one line and exhale a huge sigh of relief. "I'm not pregnant," I whisper aloud, relieved. I pick up the stick to throw it in the trash when I see the faintest of a second line start to darken.

What?

I grab the instructions back out and look at the picture that reads, "Pregnant=Two lines."

Different things jump out at me, starting to make sense. Lisa commenting on how I look different; she never said *glowing*, but she was going on and on about it. My food poisoning incident from last week, maybe it was just morning sickness. I've felt queasy a few times, but I just chalked it up to nerves about last night; never in a million years would I guess I'm pregnant.

Holy Shit. "I'm pregnant," I admit to my reflection, fighting my emotions.

When I finally emerge from the bathroom, the cashier is doing his best to avoid eye contact because I'm pretty sure he knows what I was doing. I grab some junk food and soda, along with the empty box and drop it on the counter in front of him and he doesn't say a word about my disappearance in the back.

"Nineteen oh five," he says when he finishes ringing everything up. I hand him my credit card and try to keep from crying as I sign the receipt.

There's no rush to get back to the apartment, but the slow walk is painful and cold. A million thoughts run through my head. Why did this have to happen? What am I going to tell Ryan? Will he want to be in the baby's life? Do I even want a baby? I don't want Ryan to be with me because we have a kid together. The tears are making their way down my face, and I wipe my runny nose on my sleeve like I used to when I was a kid. My first instinct is to call Langley, but when I reach for my phone from my purse, I remember that I dropped it on my bed in a hurry when I was looking at the calendar.

The walk home feels like hours, but I look up from my dazed state, standing in front of my building. When I get to the door, I start to put my key in the hole when the door flies open.

"Will you please talk to me and tell me what's going on?" Joss demands with a worried look.

"Joss, I'm fine. I'm really tired and just want to go back to bed."

"Why did you run out of here in such a hurry?"

I'm not ready to tell her about the pregnancy yet, so I do what's become natural as of late; I lie. "I thought I forgot some things from work at Ivy Glen, but someone else got it." Apparently my lying has gotten better because she doesn't bat an eye when the words come out of my mouth.

"Can we talk about the other night?" she asks, following me to the couch.

"I'd rather not right now. I have a lot on my mind."

"Well, can we at least hang out tonight?"

Crap.

"Um, actually I have plans," I admit, not looking her in the eyes. In the middle of all this, I completely forgot about tonight. She watches, waiting for me to offer more so I throw myself against the back of the coach and groan, "I have a date with Trey, alright? I'd appreciate you keeping your mouth shut about it."

I can tell Joss is disappointed, hell, if she were excited about it, she'd be trying to dress me now. Instead, she leans back and exhales, fighting against saying something that she shouldn't. There's nothing to say really, because tonight will be my first and last date with Trey.

"Look," she finally says when she turns to face me, "I know you're pissed at me and you have every right to be-"

"Well, thank you for your permission," I respond humorlessly.

"That's not what I mean, all I'm going to say is that I did what I did, because I really thought all you two needed was to talk."

"I love you, but you need to back the hell off. Okay? Whatever is going on between Ryan and me, or rather not going on, is none of your business. I mean it. Can you just leave it alone now?"

"Yeah. Alright. I'll leave it alone. I'm gonna say one more thing, and you might get pissed, but whatever."

"Fine, hurry and say it before I stop speaking to you again."

"From what you've told me, Trey is a nice guy, but you've known him what, a few months? You just got out of this thing with Ryan, so take it slow. Okay?"

She has no idea how slow I'm going to take it, as in, we're never leaving the station. "I'm in no rush for anything. Trust me."

* * *

Trey called earlier today to let me know that he would pick me up at six thirty. I almost backed out by telling him that I didn't feel well, but something told me that I needed to enjoy one last night out before I start telling everyone what's going on. Besides, he promised me a night of fun, and I really need this. I just need to remember not to drink anything, and hope that nothing makes me nauseous. He said to dress comfortably, which is perfect because I can wear my favorite jeans with my cream colored off the shoulder sweater. I'm not sure if this is an indoor or outdoor thing, so I need to remember to bring my jacket with me.

My makeup is done but I keep running back to the mirror to figure out what I want to do with my hair. I pull it into a ponytail, only to remove it and tousle the ends because neither look is making me happy. I'm not nervous about this date; I'm looking forward to it, if only because I won't have another one for a very long time. I figure this is as good as it's going to get, so I grab my jacket and purse before walking into the living room.

Joss is heating something up in the microwave and looks over to see me dressed and ready to go. "You look good, Em. I mean, like, you look happy or something." There it is again; thank God no one can put their finger on it yet. "Where's he taking you?"

"I have no clue. He said dress casual," I inform her as I dab lip-gloss on.

"By the way," she says turning to me, "your sister called a bit ago, but I didn't get to the phone in time. I'm not sure if she left a message."

I pull my phone out to check for missed calls, and there's one from her, but no message. "Huh, I didn't even hear my phone ring." I toss my phone back into my purse. "I'll call her later. She wants me to go home to help with her wedding plans. I don't think she realizes that I'm not all excited about wedding plans at the moment."

"Why don't you just tell her that?"

"Because she's my sister and I really am happy for her, and Reid is a great guy. I'll be fine," I assure her, just as there's a knock at the door. I move to answer, but Joss puts her hand up, halting me.

"Don't be so eager; you act like you've never been on a date before," she teases.

"No one has *dated* as much as you," I remind her and she laughs as she throws the door open.

"You must be Trey, c'mon in." She steps aside to give him space. "I'm Joss," she says as she closes the door behind him.

"I've never seen this guy before, Joss." My eyes are wide with concern and she looks worried. "Just kidding. Have any problem finding the place?"

We both start laughing while Joss shoots daggers in my direction. She should know better than to just open the door to strangers like that; serves her right, and I still owe her for what she put me through the other night. Trey walks over to officially introduce himself to Joss, who turns to mush when he shakes her hand. The first time I laid eyes on the guy, even though I didn't know who he was, I knew he was her type. *Her type being male and alive.*

We talk for a few minutes before he announces that we have reservations at a restaurant and I find myself suddenly famished. Lucky for me, we get to a quaint Italian place, just outside of town, and our table is ready when we arrive. Every time I've been with Trey, it's been work related, but tonight the conversation is easy. We joke as though we've known each other forever and there's no mention of relationships, Ryan or work; it's a true get-to-know-you first date.

"Where do your parents live?" An innocent first date question, but for me, it's a nasty story.

"No clue where my father is, he left a long time ago. My mom lives in Provo, that's where I grew up."

"Your sister's really nice. How long have she and Reid been together?"

"You remembered his name?" I ask rhetorically. "They've only been together a few months, but she said they just knew they were meant to be. She's getting married in February."

"Wow, they're wasting no time."

"Yeah, my mom isn't a big marriage supporter. She and my dad had a rocky relationship, so now she thinks it doesn't work for anyone."

"She never wanted to remarry?"

"She'd say no, but the string of guys she's dated says otherwise. She throws herself completely into it on the first date, and is crushed when it ends. Then she drinks for a month solid before landing the next winner." I'm not sure why I just admitted all of that to him; I just seem to have word vomit right now. He nods his head, acknowledging my admission before he speaks.

"She dating anyone now?"

"Why? You interested?" I tease with a laugh, "Yeah, apparently some loser. Lang doesn't like him at all, and I haven't had the pleasure. I don't know what it is about him, but she thinks this guy is bad news."

I hear my phone buzz in my purse so I excuse myself to look at the screen and it's from Langley.

Langley: Call me

Trey is watching me closely with a concerned look on his face. "Everything okay?"

I tuck the phone back into my purse, "Yeah, just Lang checking up on me."

"Y'all are close, huh?"

"She's my rock, I don't know what I'd do without her. I love my mom, but when she was too messed up to take care of us, Lang stepped up and did it all. She's amazing, which is why I will do anything for her."

Our dinner comes out and looks amazing, but my feeling of hunger fades and I can only manage to eat a few bites. Trey ordered some wine, but I told him that I'm allergic to the sulfites, so I wouldn't have to drink. The waitress brings us our check and I assume the evening is over, but he's got more planned.

"Have you ever been to City Park?"

"I haven't," I inform him happily.

He looks at my converse and nods in approval. "Great, you've got on the perfect shoes for a walk."

It was beginning to snow when we left the restaurant, which isn't surprising in December. I love this time of year because it's perfect for huddling inside with a cup of coffee and a good book. I'm not one to sightsee when it's cold, but I'm enjoying Trey's company. It's picturesque with the streetlight illuminating the grounds; people are milling around, or sitting on benches, content in the silence. He leads us to a concrete wall to sit on facing the Denver skyline. "Beautiful, isn't it?"

How have I lived here for almost a year and never seen this before? I've been too afraid to leave the comfort of what I know, to explore one of the most amazing places here. "I love it out here," I finally say to him.

We remain in comfortable silence, sitting so close that our arms are touching and his body offers warmth on this cold night. The wind and the snow whip my hair around in every direction, so I close my eyes and turn into the wind to get it off my face. I gather my hair into a messy ponytail and once it's secured and there's no threat of stray hairs poking my eyes, I open them to find Trey staring at me. He reaches for my hand and I let him take it because it's freezing, and I like that he's being so considerate.

"Damn, your hands are like ice. Do you wanna head back?"

I shake my head, unable to answer through my chattering teeth. He laughs and pulls me close to his chest, rubbing his hand up and down my back. Being here with him like this feels easy, but I know deep down, it's anything but. He leans back to pull away from me and cocks his head to the side. He's still holding my hand and it's the only time I've seen him look nervous, and I know what's coming.

He leans in to kiss me but I pull away apologetically. He starts to say something, but stops short and I feel bad for the disappointment I see in his eyes. As someone I've grown to consider a friend, being here with him holds so much promise, but I can't give him what he wants.

"Em, there's no rush. I know that you're still coming to terms with what happened between you and Ryan. I'm sorry, I shouldn't have pushed."

"No," I shake my head, feeling too many things at once. "It's not that. I mean, it is, I love Ryan and this is all so sudden, but I don't think I can ever give you what you want. You have been such a good friend to me, and that's all I can offer in return."

He starts to loosen his grip on my hands, but I hold firm to his, wanting him to talk to me. "We're friends, right, Trey?" I ask, repeating the words he has said to me many times.

Shaking his head, a sardonic smile on his handsome face, he finally answers, "Yeah. We're friends, but it *has* felt like more. Shit, I wish it didn't, because I know you don't feel the same."

I free one of my hands from his grasp and reached out to his face and he looks upon me skeptically. "Trey, I'd be lying if I said I didn't feel something. But-"

Before I can finish my sentence, he cups my face in his hands and plants the softest, sweetest kiss to my lips. Butterflies that went away some time ago reappear, causing my pulse to accelerate. He stops kissing me and rests his forehead to mine, and my eyes remain closed. It was a beautiful, perfect kiss, and one that I have imagined before. Hell, it was better than the way he kissed me in my dreams all those nights. But I can't help but compare it to all of those I've shared with Ryan over the years.

Flashes of Ryan kissing me for the first time on our second date outside of his Jeep, when I aced my midterm, after he had tutored me all night, in front of his parent's house before I met them for the first time, flood my memory. Ryan is and will always be the love of my life, and even though we're not together, it's not fair to give Trey hope when there is none. When he opens his eyes he wipes away the tear that escaped while I was missing Ryan, and he smiles, assuming something else.

"Just give me a chance to make you happy," he pleads.

"Trey," I pause, because I haven't said these words to anyone else, but I have to. "I'm pregnant."

His back straightens and his eyes grow wide as my words sink in. "Does Ryan know?"

I open my mouth to answer but my phone vibrates in my purse, so I look at the screen and notice it's Ryan, but I've missed several texts and calls. I swipe my finger to answer the call, "Hello?"

"Em," I can tell his in his voice he is bracing me for something, "It's me- it's Ryan."

chapter 24

Seconds.

In mere seconds, everything in your life can change. One minute you're coming to terms with the knowledge that you're pregnant and having to share the news for the first time, to hearing something that literally makes you drop to your knees. My phone slipped from my hand to the grassy area below while I tried to catch my breath, feeling like someone just kicked me hard in the stomach.

"Em?" Ryan's voice calls out to me. "Are you there? Did you hear what I said?" Ryan asks in a rush.

I locate my phone inches from where my body is plastered to the ground and hold the device to my ear. "What happened? Where is she?"

"Em, you need to calm down. What's going on?" Trey whispers next to me, but I can't answer, I'm trying to gather as much information from Ryan as I can.

"Lang called me about thirty minutes ago. She's been trying to get a hold of you all night. She asked me to keep trying because her battery was going dead. I don't know everything, just that your mom was in some sort of accident and she's at the hospital right now."

"Was it Scott?" I ask, bile rising in my throat at having to ask the question.

"Your sister seems to think so. Listen, Em- " I can tell he's getting ready to warn me.

"I will kill the bastard," I inform him so low and even, that I believe I actually might have it in me.

"The cops are looking for him, but right now, we have to focus on your mom because she needs you." The anger slowly recedes and tears begin to form.

"Is it bad?" I ask through my tears. Before I can even register the action, Trey is guiding me back to his car, tucking me into the passenger seat.

I hear him let out a shaky breath and I know. "Yeah. It's really bad. You need to get there as soon as you can."

"Tell Langley I'm headed to the airport right now, I'll catch the first flight I can."

"Okay, Em. Be careful."

His words echo in my ears, but only faintly behind the others I'm still trying to process. *She's at the hospital.* I don't have time to decipher anything else because all I want to do is go home so I can be with my mom and my sister. "Yeah, I will," I whisper. "Hey, thanks for letting me know."

I hang up the phone and my hand starts shaking and sobs rack my body. Trey is the epitome of calm, driving me to the airport without uttering a word. When we arrive, he parks his car and walks me to the ticketing agent who sees my haggard appearance. Trey stands beside me, speaking to the agent requesting availability for the next flight out to Salt Lake City. I'll have to drive almost an hour to get to my mom, but it beats driving eight hours through the night. I'm sure this ticket is going to be expensive, but I don't care. The moment she says she has room on the nine thirty flight, I pull out my credit card so I can hurry up and get through security.

Trey is beside me when I meander through the line to be

screened. I throw my arms around his waist and sob into his chest. "Thank you so much for getting me here."

"Em, I know this is hard, but you need to try to calm down. You have a baby to think about now, you can't stress yourself out," he says as he rubs my back while he hugs me.

I've been so consumed with what's going on that I actually forgot that he's right. I wipe my eyes and nod at him, appreciating his concern. He takes my face in his hands and kisses my forehead as the TSA agent calls me forward. I give him one last hug and walk away from him, having no clue what awaits me when I get to the hospital.

Everything that's happened since Ryan called is a blur. I go from crying hysterically, to doing everything I can to control my rage. I'm mad at my mom for staying with this guy, even though she knows Lang hates him. I'm mad at myself for not being more involved to know how bad it really was. And more than anything, I want to face Scott and tell him exactly where he can go. I want to see him rot in jail with nothing and no one to save him.

I make it through security and take a seat at the gate, my body physically aching from my sobs and clenching muscles. I try to remember what Trey said, but every time I do my best to relax, I remember that this guy has hurt my mom time and again. It makes me sick. She makes me sick. And then I feel guilty for how angry I am with her, when I have no idea what condition she's in.

* * *

I made the drive to Provo in forty-five minutes flat, catching almost every stoplight when I got to town. The hospital emergency room is on the corner of a busy road, but since it's after midnight, there is nothing stopping me from getting where I need to be. I find the closest parking spot available and run through the automatic doors.

I feel lost standing at the entrance, not knowing where my sister is. I know she's here somewhere, most likely with my mom. I walk up to the nurse's station where several women are congregating; my disheveled appearance is not surprising to them.

"Can you tell me where I can find Nora Kane?"

The heavyset woman furrows her brow. "Are you family?"

Before I can answer someone taps my shoulder and I nearly collapse into his arms. Ryan is beside me, holding me up while I cry. "This is her daughter. I know where she is," he says to the woman, leading me away from the emergency room waiting area.

He walks me back through a set of double doors to the side of the waiting room that automatically close behind us. This is most likely the second longest walk of my life, the other taking place today. *Or was it yesterday?* Before we get to her room, he stops me and waits for me to look at him. When I finally do I see the worry and fear in his eyes, which only makes me feel worse.

"Em, you need to know a few things," he starts, so I wait for his words. "She's on a ventilator and her arm is in a cast. She also has a broken eye socket-"

My vision starts to go dark and Ryan's voice sounds like it's coming to me through a tunnel. All at once, I feel lightheaded and my body starts to go limp. Ryan holds me up until he sits me in a chair and kneels in front of me.

"Are you okay?" The concern is etched on his face while he checks me out, "Should I call a nurse over?"

He starts looking around to see who he call over, but I stop him, "Please, Ryan. I'm fine, I think it's just shock; I need to see her."

He helps me to my feet, wrapping his arm around my waist while he guides me into the room. "Lang's with your mom now."

The room is quiet and Reid is standing behind my sister who's sitting in a chair by my mom's side. He taps her shoulder and she looks at me, tears filling her eyes.

She pushes the chair back and runs into my arms and we both start crying again. "I'm so sorry, it's all my fault. I knew he was hurting her, and I didn't do anything," she sobs into my hair while we hold each other.

"There's nothing you could've done, she knew what a monster he was, and she chose to keep him around. She didn't deserve this, but it wasn't your fault."

We stand there in each other's arms, crying at the circumstances that brought us here tonight. I know only the few details that Ryan gave me over the phone and in the hallway; everything else has been left to my imagination. I hear the machine breathing for her and she looks so small and frail in the bed. Langley holds my hand and walks me to the chair she just left, prodding me to sit.

The last real talk that I had with my mom was when I asked her what I should do about Ryan. My conversations since have been drunken five-minute calls that I realize now were a cry for help. When I asked how she was, her voice would get sad and then she'd start talking about nonsensical things, so I would end the call in a hurry. *I'm the worst daughter ever.*

I look at the monitors, not knowing what any of them are for, but all look serious. I reach for her hand and it's cold, so I wrap my other over the top of hers. "Lang, what happened? Ryan said Scott did this. Is that true?"

"That's what I think, but the police can't find him to question him."

"Who found her? Where did this happen?"

"A neighbor saw him run out of the house in the morning and watched as he peeled out of the driveway. He said something just seemed wrong, so he went to check on her. When he knocked on the door, he could see her lying on the floor so he broke a porch window to get in. He tried to find her phone to call me, but he was worried because she was barely breathing, so he called 9-1-1. I was at work when he called, I don't think I even locked up the office when I left. By the time I got to the house, they were getting ready to load her into the ambulance."

She starts crying again and my heart aches for her. Seeing mom like this is awful, but Lang saw her when it happened. My sister is the strong one, and watching her tear herself apart and blame herself kills me.

"There was so much blood, Em," she sobs, reaching out to cover mom's hands and mine.

"They don't know where he is?"

She doesn't answer, because she doesn't have to. "Where'd Ryan go?" she asks and I realize he didn't come into the room with me.

I stand up to go find him, but Reid places a hand on my shoulder. "I got it; stay here with your mom." He kisses my sister on the forehead before exiting the room and I'm so glad that he was here with her.

Ryan's here. For me?

I was so upset when I walked into the hospital and grateful for his presence, but it just didn't register.

"What's Ryan doing here?"

"When I couldn't get a hold of you I called him. He happened to be in Salt Lake on business, so he said that he'd keep calling while he drove over. I was so relieved when he got here and told me he finally talked to you." She looks down at me from where she's perched. "Why didn't you answer my calls?"

I bite the side of my mouth, preparing to tell her, "I knew you called, but you never left a message, so I figured it wasn't urgent and that I'd call later- since I was on a date." The words come out as the door shuts and I turn to see Ryan and it's obvious that he heard everything I said. I close my eyes, not wanting to look at him, but needing him here at the same time. He doesn't know that I'm pregnant, and that his world is about to change.

He gives me a tight smile, and I know hearing those words hurt him, but he walks over to be near me, offering his support. This small gesture means so much to me and I want so badly to fall into his arms again and let him console me. Before the break up, I wouldn't have thought twice about doing just that, but that's not us. He's not my person anymore. I have to take care of myself now.

A petite nurse comes into the room to check mom's vitals, but barely says anything to us. Langley still hasn't told me the extent of the injuries, but looking at my mom, I can only assume it's worse than I was expecting. "The doctor should be in shortly," she tells us as she starts to leave the room, but he comes in before she fully exits. He walks over to mom's bedside and starts to examine her, but doesn't give anything away with his demeanor. He writes a few things down and then finally turns to look at us.

"Your mom has suffered severe injuries. She has multiple stab wounds and a collapsed lung, which is why she's on the ventilator."

"Where do we go from here?" I manage to ask him. I voice the only words that I can without asking the one I'm too scared to ask- *Is she going to die?*

"I know you're worried and this is a lot to take in, but your mom is lucky. I expect her to pull through, but we're going to have to monitor her closely for the next twenty-four hours. We have her sedated to make her a little more comfortable. If you want to talk to her, she can hear you, but she won't be able to respond. She's going to need extensive therapy when this is done, both physically and emotionally. This was a brutal attack, if someone hadn't found her when they did, I don't think I'd be as optimistic."

I can't listen to anymore.

I stand up and rush out of the room, feeling the bile rise in my stomach. The hospital doors don't open fast enough, and I throw my body weight into them, pushing them along. When I finally get outside the cold air hits my face, sobering me for a moment. *This must be what shock feels like.* My body starts shaking, from the cold, from what I've just heard. I have no idea. All I know is that I start retching and I hurry to the bushes and start throwing up, crying through it all.

Ryan is right behind me, his hand rubbing soothing circles on my back while I continue to dry heave. "Are you okay?" he asks with concern laced in his tone.

I honestly don't know if it's morning sickness or shock that has me puking right now. "Yeah," I exhale, wiping my mouth. "I'll be fine."

When I'm finally able to stand upright, Ryan grabs me and pulls me into his arms, holding me close, while I let go and sob uncontrollably. His arms are my home, the place I feel the safest, and I need that assurance so much right now. He rubs my back and whispers calming words until my breathing settles and my body relaxes. My eyes burn from the crying and I'm starting to get a headache.

Lang comes outside to find us and sees me in Ryan's arms. She walks toward me muttering something that I can't make out but freezes, staring toward the parking lot. A chill runs down my spine, unsure what's unfolding in front of me.

"You okay?" I ask, walking to stand next my sister to see what she's looking at.

"Go inside," she says in an eerie calm. "Tell them to call the cops. He's in the parking lot. I don't think he saw me, but if I walk back in, he's sure to recognize me."

"What? Where?" I ask looking around, trying to see what she sees.

She nods her head and whispers, "Over there. Now, hurry up, Em." I see a large, disheveled man slumped against a car, smoking a cigarette. He fits everything I imagined when Lang told me about him the first time. *It's Scott.*

I back away from her and start to head toward the doors as she instructed, but before I reach them, I stop and look in his direction, catching his eye. He knows who I am, even though we've never met; I can tell by his cocky demeanor and the way he smirks at me. He puts the cigarette to his lips and takes a long drag; his eyes remain locked on me. When he exhales he rolls his neck and resumes his stance, challenging me to move. I don't know how long I've looked at him, but all it takes is his feigned innocent shrug that he follows up with a sneer to set me off. I start to move toward him and take off running full speed at the disgusting excuse for a man that seems too pleased with himself.

I can hear muffled yelling behind me, but barely over the blood rushing in my ears, adrenaline my encouragement. He just got away with destroying my mom and he thinks he's untouchable. Scott's eyes grow wider with every step closer I get to him and when I get close enough, I lunge at the asshole, knocking the cigarette from his hand while I scream and kick anywhere my foot will land.

"You bastard! What the fuck is wrong with you? How could you do this to her? I will kill you, you piece of shit!"

"Get off me you stupid bitch!" he yells, grabbing me by the shoulders and holding me out so his knee makes direct contact with my stomach. I fall to the ground clutching my abdomen in pain, tears streaming down my face, but adrenaline prodding me to my feet. I roll to my side and get to my knees when he plants three more kicks to my body while I gasp for air.

I hear wailing and screaming, but I realize these noises are coming from me and that freaks me out even more. Somehow, I manage to get to my knees and I claw my way out of his reach, before someone tackles him to the ground. Lang is by my side, helping me to my feet and I see Ryan standing over Scott, using his face as punching bag. My sister has her arms wrapped around me, guiding me back through the hospital door, as police arrive and pull Ryan off of him.

What have I done? What about the baby?

Hospital staff meets my sister and help get me to a gurney so they can wheel me away.

"Let's get you to a room so we can have a look," an older man says gently, as they begin to move me. I don't want Lang or anyone else with me, so I'm glad that they made her stay back. Hopefully she'll go back to be with mom while I get checked out. No one knows yet about my baby, and this isn't the time or the place.

My baby.

The nurse comes over to me and helps me remove my clothing and wraps me in a hospital gown. These simple movements cause shooting pain throughout my body; I just want something to make it go away.

The door opens and the doctor comes back into the room, "I'm Doctor Norman. I know you're in pain, but I need you to try to relax, okay? Can you do that?"

I nod and wince when he touches my ribs.

"What's your name?" he asks while he flashes a light in my right eye, and then my left.

"Emogen," I groan through gritted teeth. My body starts to curl protectively and I'm doing everything I can to listen to him. I have never known pain like this, "Please, will my baby be okay?"

He looks at me, concern evident on his face. The nurse leaves the room in a rush, only to return, rolling a machine in. She pulls out a device that looks like a pole or wand and places something over it before handing it to the doctor. He moves a stool next to the bed and scoots closer to me.

"Emogen." His voice is soothing, as though talking to a child. "We need to try and take a look at the baby. How far along are you?"

"I-" I start groaning in pain. "I just found out the other day. Maybe six weeks? Seven?"

He holds up the wand thing for me to see. "This is a transvaginal ultrasound so I can take a look at your baby. I'm going to place this inside of you so we can make sure everything is okay." The nurse holds my hand while he inserts the wand inside of me and the action causes my entire body to go rigid. "I know this is uncomfortable, but I need you to try and relax." He continues the examination, staring intently at the screen. The room is so quiet, you can hear a pin drop, and I do everything I can to keep my body relaxed while I am still in so much pain.

He moves the wand around and stares at the screen, keeping still. He repeats the movement a few more times, making a small noise under his breath, but keeping his eyes locked on the screen. Slowly, he removes the device from inside of me and pulls the gown over my knees. Doctor Norman stays seated next to me and before he can say anything, I know.

"I lost the baby," I whisper to myself as tears spill down my face. The pain my body is feeling right now is nothing compared to the pain my heart is feeling.

"I'm sorry, Emogen, but I couldn't find a heartbeat."

"Why?" I ask. I need answers; I need a reason why this happened.

"I wish I could tell you, but sometimes these things happen. It could have been the attack or any number of things. I know that doesn't give you any consolation, but it's all I have."

I wish my heart would stop beating.

Until this moment, I didn't realize how much I already loved and wanted this baby, with or without Ryan.

chapter 25

Dr. Norman continues to check me, but all I can think about is the baby I lost. If I had just done what Lang asked, this wouldn't have happened. Tears that haven't stopped falling run down my face and into my pillow as I lay down.

"You have some nasty bruises on your stomach and back that will heal. You have two bruised ribs that I'm sure hurt, so I'm going to give you a prescription to help you manage the pain."

"Thank you," I whisper. Too bad the pills won't heal the pain that I feel in my heart.

He looks at me waiting for me to give him my attention. "I know you don't want to hear this right now, but over the next few days, you may experience some vaginal bleeding and cramping related to the miscarriage."

I can't say anything in response because the word miscarriage feels like a scab being ripped off again. I want to leave this place. I want to go back in time to yesterday when the test showed positive and be happy about it. I want to go back to before that asshole almost killed my mom. I want to go back to an hour ago, when I decided to be stupid and put my life and my baby's in jeopardy. But I can't. All I can do is try to come to terms with the loss of my sweet little baby that I will never know.

"Would you like for me to get your sister?" he asks, interrupting my thoughts.

"No," I rush out before he can send the nurse. "No one knew I was pregnant."

"I don't think you should be alone right now," Dr. Norman reminds me. "There are a couple of people waiting outside that want to see you."

"Can I have a few minutes alone, please?"

"Of course." He places a sympathetic hand to my forearm and squeezes as he stands up. "Take as much time as you need. Just let the nurse know when you are ready for them to come in."

I wait until they have left the room and I roll to my side as my body convulses with sobs. I don't understand the loss that I feel, because I just found out this little person even existed, but I miss it already. The last piece of Ryan and me, the only part that remained from the love we shared, is gone. My angel just died, the precious little miracle that I didn't know I loved is no longer here, and my world shatters a little more.

I hear the door creak open and I wipe my eyes, and any evidence of my loss before looking to see whom it is. When I glance over my shoulder, Ryan is walking toward me with a concerned look on his face. *How is it that he always knows when I need him most?* I try to hide the tears, but figure he thinks I'm in pain, which I am, so I let them flow waving him in closer. He sits behind me on the edge of my bed and places his bruised and bloody hand to my arm. I reach my hand that is tucked under my head to touch his knuckles, acknowledging his wounds.

"Doesn't hurt," he whispers, answering my silent question.

He has no idea what's going on, and I can't tell him, at least not right now. But I can mourn our loss *for the both of us*, with him by my side, letting him take care of me. He doesn't ask if I'm okay, because he knows me; I'm far from it. He takes my tears for worry over my mom.

"Mom?" I ask, suddenly alarmed that I have pushed aside what's happened to her.

"No change," he says quietly. "I know you're worried, but you need to rest. What were you thinking going after him like that, Em?" He's not mad when he asks; I think he's curious because it's so out of character for me.

I wince when I try to face him, my ribs screaming in pain. I try to stifle the cry that wants to escape, a small moan replacing it. "I wasn't thinking," I remind myself aloud. "He was standing there so smug and all I could see is that he almost took her away." The moment the words escape I realize he succeeded. He might not have taken away my mom, but he did manage to take away the one thing I didn't know I wanted. I turn away and give in to the pain, both physical and emotional.

Without another word, Ryan crawls onto the bed with me and wraps his arm over me, cradling me as I let go. He runs his hand over my arm trying to soothe my pain, whispering over and over, "Everything will be okay."

I'm not sure it will ever be.

* * *

Dr. Norman came in to check on me, and asked Ryan to give us a few minutes. I was grateful that he remembered my earlier plea. Once he was gone, the doctor gave me the prescription for the pain, and said that I should check in with my local doctor when I get home. Langley came to check on me after both had gone and helped me get dressed. She confirmed what Ryan said; there was still no change with mom. She wanted me to go home with her to get some rest, but I insisted on staying. I tell her that someone should be here if mom wakes up. My sister had already been here for so long and she looked like a mess.

Mostly, I just wanted to be alone with mom and talk to her.

I waited until everyone took off for the night and settled into an uncomfortable hospital chair next to her bed. Reid left his phone charger for me; so I plugged in my phone and powered it on to see I had several missed calls from the girls, as well as text messages from Trey.

11:56 p.m. - Did you make it in?

12:22 a.m. - Just checking on you

12:46 a.m. - Getting worried

1:13 a.m. - Going to bed, but call anyway

I hug my phone to my chest as tears well in my eyes. I'm about to tell only person who knew I was pregnant that I miscarried. Considering his last message came through about an hour ago, I work up a simple text to rip the Band-Aid off.

Me: I lost it

Trey: What are you talking about?

Me: The baby

I wait for his response, but when it doesn't come, I tuck my phone away. What does one say when someone tells you they just lost their baby? There are no words, no condolences that make a difference. I'm not mad that he doesn't respond, I'm not even hurt, because I think I would be at a loss as well, because any sentiment I could formulate would be trite.

But Trey isn't trite.

My phone vibrates in my purse that's on the floor beside me. When I dig it out, I see Trey's name on the screen, but I don't even have to say anything when I answer, because I know he isn't looking for details.

"Hey. I didn't want to text. I know you're not okay, but I just wanted to let you know that if you need anything, I'm here for you."

I hold the phone away from my face as I exhale before responding. "Thanks, Trey. I appreciate it."

"Did you get a chance to tell Ryan?"

"No, he doesn't know anything," I admit with sadness. *Would he have even been happy?*

"Do you want to talk about it?"

I shake my head, knowing he can't see me. Tears threaten again below the surface, but my silence answers for me.

"How's your mom?"

My hand reaches out to touch hers. "Not good. I'm here with her right now, and I can't help but be scared."

"What do the doctors say?"

"They really haven't said anything that makes me feel any better, so it's pretty much a waiting game right now."

"Like I said, I'm here if you need anything."

We say our goodbyes and I promise to keep him posted. He offers to meet me at the airport, but I tell him one of the girls will probably pick me up. I figure I need to let Joss or Cam know what's going on because both have called, but I haven't returned their calls. I'm not trying to be a bitch; I've had too much other stuff going on to deal with them. I send them each a text briefing them on the news about my mom and promise to let them know when I'm coming home. All of the small details have been taken care of, and I'm left in the hospital room with my mom and nothing but time.

The room isn't quiet. In fact, the machine noises sing louder and louder while I try to hear my own thoughts. I get out of my chair and sit on mom's bed to be closer to her.

"So," I start, feeling a bit idiotic. "The doctors say you can hear us, but I'm not sure if that's true. Seeing as I can't sleep anyway, I figured I'd give it a try. Do you even know what happened?"

I lift her hand to cradle it in mine, careful not to touch her IV line. Her finger nail polish is chipped and scratched; her hands dry and wrinkled. Before my dad left us, she always took great pride in her appearance, but after, the rundown look has become her norm. She's only forty-three, but she looks so much older with all of the drinking and smoking over the years.

"Why did you stay with this guy, mom? He almost killed you." A tear runs down my cheek and I push it away with the back of my hand. "How many times will he have to hurt you until you realize he's bad news? Your asshole boyfriend killed my baby." Saying those words aloud hurt more than the bruises all over my body. "When I got here today, I was pregnant; you were going to be a grandma. I didn't know how I was going to tell you, or Ryan, for that matter. But your awesome boyfriend took care of that."

Anger wells deep within me, not at him for killing my baby, but at her for bringing him into our lives.

"I love you so much, but I hate you." I feel a sharp pain in my chest when those words exit my mouth. "I don't mean it, mom. I love you, I promise I do! I just don't understand why you stay with him, or half the losers you continue to date. Is this really the life you want for yourself? This jerk almost killed you, and from what Lang says, it sounds like he throws you around on a regular basis."

"I don't know anything about my baby, other than I should have protected it, but instead I was fighting for you. But that's *your* job, mom. You're supposed to fight for us, you're supposed to be the parent, but it's a role you easily relinquished years ago. Sure, you gave us advice, and scolded us from time to time, but then you just stopped altogether, and chose you. I've always hated that about you. Your choices have been whatever served Nora best. Shit, mom, Lang never had a childhood because you were too messed up to do the job right. She's more of a mom than you are, but I'm still waiting for my mom to grow up and choose me; choose us. Hell, maybe I'm more like you than I thought, because I wasn't even thinking about *my* baby when I went after Scott."

I brush my free hand through my hair in frustration. How did this become my life? Ryan no longer a part of it, mom in a hospital bed and me without the baby I wasn't even planning on.

"Would you have been happy to be a grandma?"

I laugh because I know she would have insisted she's too young to be a grandmother. She would have been thrilled, but mortified, and I naively wonder if she would have changed at all.

"When you make it through this," I squeeze her hand, "because I know you will, you have to make some changes. You have to take better care of yourself and stop dating jerks. I'm serious mom, if this is what you want, then I can't come around anymore. I'm pretty sure Lang's with me on this one, so you have to straighten up because I know you don't want to miss her wedding and she needs you there. We need you *here*, and you need to get some help. So no more bullshit, mom."

I try to lean to kiss her, but the action causes pain to my ribs, so I kiss her hand.

When I move back to the chair next to her bed, I try to get comfortable in any position, but it doesn't seem possible. Laying on my side, my eyes grow heavy and my silent tears fall once again.

chapter 26

My body aches.

I keep trying to move and get comfortable, but every movement causes greater pain. The same machine noises, which were so loud last night, lulled me to sleep after my "talk" with mom. But the scratching sound I keep hearing is a new one. The room is freezing and I do my best to keep my eyes shut because I'm sure I've only slept for a couple of hours. I keep having strange dreams that I can't remember, I just know they wake me briefly and then I manage to get back to sleep.

What in the world is that scratching noise?

It can't be normal. I roll over to see my mom's hand grasping at the blankets that are covering her body. I sit up as fast as my body will allow and get to her bedside. I take her hand in mine and look at her face; her good eye is barely open.

"Mom," I squeeze her hand. "It's Emmy. Can you hear me?"

She squeezes my hand back. "I'm going to get a nurse. I'll be right back."

I rush into the hallway to grab someone so they can check on mom. They send me out of the room while they examine her so I end up walking around the hospital, somehow ending up in the maternity ward. It's still early, so there aren't many visitors or even people standing to look at babies behind the glass. There are only a few that remain in the nursery, the rest are probably with their mothers. I stand there and look at them sleeping peacefully, so tiny and innocent.

Maybe it just wasn't the right time, I try to rationalize, but it doesn't make it hurt any less. *Would I have been a good mom?* I like to think I would be, but I've never really been around any kids. Hell, I never really considered having any of my own anytime soon. Even when Ryan and I were engaged, we never talked about it. I think we both wanted them, *someday*, but our careers were our top priority at the time. He would have been the most amazing dad. I've seen little girls look at him and he would smile widely at them and give them a wink. They would hide behind their parent's legs and peek their head back out and smile at him. Those times where he acknowledged kids would make me smile and excited for the day we would have our own.

I make my way back to my mom's room and knock on the door before opening it. She's still on the ventilator, but she seems slightly more alert. A nurse is there with her checking something when she sees me.

"You're her daughter, right?"

"Yes ma'am. How is she?"

"The doctor just left but he told her that he wants to keep her on the ventilator for a little longer. I've given her a pad and pencil to communicate. It's probably going to be frustrating for her, but I told her that it's just for a little while. Hopefully she'll get the tube taken out this afternoon."

"Thank you," I say to her as she leaves the room.

Mom waves me in closer and her one good eye is open more than it was before. She taps the pad that's on her chest, so I reach for it and hand it to her, assuming she has something to say. She shakes her head and points to me, so I take it and read her words.

"I'm sorry."

"Mom, you didn't do anything wrong," I answer, hoping to ease her guilt.

She shakes her head and points to the pad again, but this time she wants it back. She scribbles something down and hands it back to me as a tear runs down her cheek.

"About the baby."

"You heard me?" I start to cry reading her words.

She tries to nod her head and set the pad down on the table next to the bed. She waves me closer and I place my hand in hers. She squeezes weakly, putting as much love into the movement as she can.

"It hurts so much, Mom. I didn't know I could feel such pain."

She reaches out to touch my face and her brow furrows. She points to the pad again so I hand it to her. "What are you going to tell Ryan?"

"Nothing. He doesn't even know I was pregnant. I don't want him to go through what I'm going through. To say anything would kill him, and it's bad enough that I have to deal with it. I love him too much to hurt him like that."

She shakes her head and writes again. "He has the right to know."

"I know you're right. But what is it going to solve, is it going to make him feel better? No. I'm trying to spare him."

We look at each other and she silently disapproves of my decision, but she nods in understanding. I send Lang a text letting her know that mom is alert, but unable to communicate right now. She is on her way, so I only have a few more moments alone with Mom.

"So you heard what I said. What about everything else? What about Scott?"

She writes something down and shows it to me. "It's never been this bad."

She looks ashamed that I have to see her like this, and it gives me hope. Maybe she's going to do what's necessary to make sure it never happens again.

"He's in jail right now. They need your statement as soon as you're ready. Please promise me you're going to press charges," I plead with tears in my eyes.

She closes her good eye in defeat and nods her agreement before jotting something else down. She hands me the pad and I read her question. "Trey?"

I laugh, for the first time since early yesterday and shake my head, "Friends. We're just very good friends. He was worried because he's the only one who knows I'm pregnant." I pause to correct myself, "*Was* pregnant."

For the first time in a long time, being with her is a good thing. The sympathy she feels for me is visible through her bruised and swollen features. I wish my body didn't ache as much as it does, because I want so much to crawl into her arms and let her console me. The door opens to reveal Lang and Reid holding hands, Ryan trailing in behind them. I didn't know he was still around, I figured he would have headed to Salt Lake to get back to work. I remember the messages mom scribbled, so I take the pad and rip the pages free and toss them into the trash, leaving it ready for her next conversation.

I look down and shrug when she gives me that look, the one that says she knows exactly what I was up to. I wink at her and move aside so my sister can talk to her, and hopefully reiterate what I've already said.

* * *

By the afternoon, Mom's ventilator was removed and she was a bit more comfortable. She was in a lot of pain, but at least she was able to move more freely. Langley kept trying to tell me it was okay for me to head home and she would keep me posted, but there was no way I was leaving until I knew that Mom did the one thing I asked of her.

I was in the room when the police came by early Monday morning to get her statement about the attack. It was somewhat hard for her to talk because her throat was sore, presumably from the breathing tube. The officer was patient as he listened to her recount the events of the day, but I couldn't help but cry, hearing the story for the first time.

"Scott came over around three in the morning. He was still drunk from the night before, so I let him in and fixed him a place on the couch. I went back to sleep, but when my alarm went off for me to get up for work; he was in bed beside me. I didn't even hear him come in. I tried to get out of the bed without disturbing him, but he woke up anyway. He started yelling crazy things, he sounded paranoid. Accused me of cheating, and then saying that I don't make any time for him. I knew he was still drunk, so I tried to calm him down, but that pissed him off more."

She looked over at Lang and me before continuing, but we both nodded for her to resume and tell them everything.

"I told him that I was going to call in sick to work and I would spend the day with him, and that's when he snapped. He started screaming that he's not a child and doesn't need someone to babysit him. He started throwing crap all over the place and telling me that I'm worthless and lucky that he's even with me. I tried to defend myself but he backhanded me and said it was no wonder my husband left me. I was holding my face and crying, but he didn't care. I knew he was wrong, my husband left because he had issues, not me."

It was the first time I'd ever heard mom acknowledge that my father was the problem, not her. I grabbed Lang's hand and she squeezed as she heard the same thing. I felt hope; hope that maybe

Mom was going to come out of this stronger.

"I fought back. For the first time since I met him, I yelled back and that set him off. He grabbed me by my throat and threw me against the wall. I was trying to pull his fingers off of me, but he was too strong. He head butted me in my eye and dropped me to the floor. I put my hand to my eye and there was blood, so I tried to get up and run, but he pushed me into another wall and that's the last thing I remember."

Listening to her find the strength to file charges against him made me both proud and hopeful that things were going to change. It was hard hearing the details of what happened, but I was also thankful she couldn't remember the most brutal part of the attack. She knows she was stabbed in her stomach and her arm was broken, but she had already blacked out by that point.

I was convinced that things were taking a turn for the better, so I listened to my sister and decided to head home. Lang swore she would call me if anything changed, but she was taking Mom home with her once she was released from the hospital. Since I didn't have anything to pack, I said my goodbyes and told Mom that I would call her to check in when I got back to my place.

Ryan followed me out to say goodbye, or so I thought. He insisted he could drop me off at the airport in Salt Lake, since he was heading back too. I argued that I had a rental car, but he said it made sense to leave it at the nearest drop off spot and drive to the city together. Somehow, being with him was exactly what I needed, so I agreed and here I am, ten minutes later regretting the decision.

"Can I ask you something?" I ask him, as though we are mere acquaintances.

"Yeah," he nods, never taking his eyes off the road.

"Why did you drive all the way out here? I mean, I appreciate it, it's just, we're not together anymore, and well, I guess I'm just curious. You got me Langley's message, you could have stopped there. But you didn't, why?" I use the chance to stare at him while I wait for his answer. I haven't been able to really look at him with everything that's going on. He looks thinner than he did the last time I saw him. He's still so beautiful, but something about him looks worn, but then again, the last two days have been pure hell.

He shrugs and looks over at me before returning his eyes to the road. "You're my family, Em. I love your family and I knew that you would be scared. I really didn't even think about it, I just knew I needed to get to the hospital. For you."

"About the date-" I start to explain, but he shakes his head and interrupts me.

"You don't need to say anything, Em. It's none of my business, I mean, I don't like it, but what can I say about it?" He sounds hurt when says this.

"Agreed, I don't have to explain." I glance at him and see the faintest of a smile appear. "But, just to let you know, I haven't moved on. There are things that- I mean, work has me really busy."

He reaches out to my hand that rests on my lap, but pulls away, until I flip my hand over, welcoming the gesture. His fingers entwine with mine and he squeezes gently. "I'm sorry for the circumstances, but I am happy I got to see you again."

"Why did you leave the apartment the other night? I didn't even know you were still there until I heard the door shut."

He pulls his hand away, pain in his eyes. "You said it was over."

"As I recall, I only repeated your words, Ryan; you ended things between us and I've been doing what I have to do to be alright with your decision. It's been harder than you know," I admit, thinking about the baby we just lost.

I decide that now is not the time to talk about the failings of our relationship or what could have been. I'm still trying to wrap my head around the happenings of the last four days, and I'm exhausted and emotionally drained.

"How's work going?" I ask him, sticking to a safe, superficial subject.

"It's been okay, things have been pretty busy. We're supposed to talk to a potential client on Wednesday."

"Are you ready for it?" I'm curious how he could be; he's been at the hospital for the last three days with me.

"I told Alex she needed to handle it, I had family business to take care of," he states without any hint of sarcasm. "What about you? How'd your event go?"

I smile and give myself a mental pat on the back. "It went really well. I even gave out my card to a couple of interested ladies. I was supposed to meet with Elle this morning to brief her on everything, but obviously that didn't happen."

We talk the rest of the drive like old friends, but the air is heavy, and I can't help the sadness that hides beneath the surface. He pulls into the drop off area at the airport and reaches for my hand again. To him, everything going on with me right now is related to my mom, because he doesn't know that anything else has gone on.

"Nora's going to be fine," he says squeezing him hand.

"I know." I look him in the eyes, because I believe it with all my heart. "It's a lot to take in."

I open my car door to get out and he meets me on the curb. He pulls me into his arms and I hug him back, because even though he doesn't know what he lost, I do, and I'm sorry for that.

"Thanks for dropping me off, Ryan. I enjoyed being with you."

"Me, too." He kisses the top of my head before pulling away. "Call or text me when you get in?"

I nod before walking away to enter the airport.

The last time we were in an airport together, I was dropping him off, saying a temporary goodbye. This time, the goodbye is final, in more ways than one. The tears aren't for me and the separation I feel, it's for each of us, and what I know we lost, and the hurt I'm sparing him.

chapter 27

How long does it take to get over a loss?

I've asked myself that question almost every day for the last three weeks. And every time, I come up with the same answer: Not today. It hurts a little less, but it's still there. I haven't talked to Ryan since that day at the airport. I sent him a text when I landed, but that was it.

Joss was waiting for me when I landed and despite how angry I was with her before, I'm happy she was there. I didn't tell her anything about the baby, and like everyone else, she perceived my silence for concern about my mom. I let them all believe that; it was easier than admitting the truth. The thing is, Mom is better than she has been in a long time. She put her house up for sale, and she is going to move in with Aunt Gertie. Originally that sounded like a nightmare in the making, but hell, it beats being worried that something could happen to her again. I think the two of them are getting along, or as close to it as they can get.

She doesn't have as much pain, and was weaned off the pain meds rather quickly. Lang called me last week and told me that mom started attending meetings for alcohol dependency. I'm not sure if she'll stick with it, but I'm hopeful. When I talk to her now, I feel like I have the mom I lost years ago, and it's nice. Scott is supposed to be going to trial at some point, but all I care about is that Mom is safe, and she's doing better.

Trey has been an amazing friend; somehow, filling the void that

Ryan left. Since he's the only one besides my mom who knows about the baby, when I'm around him, I get to be myself. I don't have to hide what I'm going through, not that we even talk about it. It's nice to know that someone knows why I am the way I am. We've been spending more time together, going out for lunch a couple of times a week, and grabbing dinner after work. He's done his best to distract me from my sadness, but he also understands that there is only so much he can do.

I don't think Joss likes the time I'm spending with him, but she's kept her mouth shut. She seems to think there is more going on between us, but I also haven't done anything to make her think otherwise.

When he asked me to come over tonight for dinner and a movie, I was happy for the chance to get out from under Joss' watchful eye. I haven't been to his place before and under any other circumstances, this would be considered a date, but this is just me hanging out my friend. But I can't deny that it's always there when we're together, I'd be a fool not to feel *something* for him. But it's nothing compared to what I feel for Ryan. And maybe someday, when I get past that, there could be a chance for Trey and me, but I'm not about to ask him to wait.

"Ok, I have something to admit," he says from his kitchen.

"O-kay, shoot," I say, despite the strange feeling I have in the pit of my stomach.

He walks into the living carrying two plates, handing me one, "I don't cook. So I hope you like turkey sandwiches."

I can't help but laugh as I take my plate and set it on the coffee table in front of me. "Lucky for you, I'm not fancy."

He sits next to me on the floor and we start eating while watching the movie. I don't know why I let him pick, it's some artsy movie that

I heard about but had never grabbed my interest enough to want to watch, and now I know why. It's boring. I keep yawning and saying crude remarks, teasing him about his movie choice, but he laughs it off.

"I can't sit on the floor anymore, want something to drink while I'm up? Wine? Beer?"

I lift myself to sit on the couch; the floor is killing my back. "Wine sounds good."

When he returns, he hands me a glass and sits next to me, but it's not uncomfortable. The movie is quite boring and my eyes are getting heavy. I can't even drink the wine, because I know it will only make me even more tired.

I have no idea how long the movie was, or what happened, all I know is that the credits are rolling and I'm practically drooling on Trey's shoulder. Despite my best efforts, I guess I couldn't hack it. He looks down at me and laughs, wrapping his arms around my shoulder to make me feel more comfortable. If someone had told me months ago when I met Trey, that he would be one of my closest friends, I would have thought they were crazy. Yet here we are.

"You can stay here tonight if you want," he says as he rubs my arm.

"Nah, I should get home. But thanks for the nap," I tease as I sit up.

"You missed a good movie," he argues with a laugh.

"Trey?" I look and wait until I have his attention. "If it was so good, why did you fall asleep?"

"What? No I didn't," he protests as he gets to his feet.

I remain seated, watching him with a raised brow. "Are you sure about that? Because you were asleep before me."

He lets out a yawn and stretches his arms over his head, his t-shirt lifting to reveal a glimpse of his abs. I turn my head away, embarrassed that I even looked. He reaches his hands out to pull me up from my seat.

"You sure you don't want to stay? You can sleep in my bed," he offers as he walks me to the door.

"I'm sure. I'd hate for you to sleep on the couch." I nudge his arm with mine.

"Who said I was sleeping on the couch?" he asks with a smirk.

"Thanks for dinner and the lame-ass movie," I joke when he opens the door. Without even thinking, I turn and give him a hug, because the move has become something we do often.

"Anytime," he responds before catching me off-guard with a small kiss to my lips, as if that's something we do all the time, too.

I start to lift my hand to my lips, finding the unfamiliar gesture too much, too soon, but drop it, unsure how to react.

"So, Lang's wedding is next weekend. If you don't have any plans, do you want go with me? I'm sure there'll be some available ladies there." I smile, effectively ignoring his kiss.

"There's only one I'm interested in, but she's not really available, yet." His lopsided grin disappears with a wink. "But I'd be happy to be her date anyway."

"Trey-" I start, but he doesn't let me finish.

"You have a lot going on in your life. I know that. I'll be whatever you need me to be right now, no pressure," he says like he's thought about it before. How could someone *not* fall for him? But he's right, I do have a lot going on, and taking care of myself is what I need to do.

When I am safe in my car, I rest my head against the seat back and close my eyes, steadying my breathing. Trey was someone I never counted on coming into my life, and now that he's here, he's become an important part. But the only future I see for us is that of friends, and until I finally give up on the idea of an ever after with Ryan, that's all it can be. I hope when Trey realizes this; he'll still be okay with our friend status.

* * *

"How was the movie?" Joss asks when I walk in.

"I don't know, I fell asleep," I remark in a bland tone, because that's what the movie was. *Bland.*

"Ah, so you 'fell asleep,' huh? Did Trey 'fall asleep' on you?" she asks with air quotes.

I toss a kitchen rag at her and laugh. "Damn, Joss. Unlike you, falling asleep isn't a euphemism. I really did fall asleep. The movie was awful."

"Damn," she scoffs taking a seat on the couch. "You need to hit that already, or let someone else put a dent in it."

"Okay!" I shout, heading to my room. "Conversation over. Good night."

I close the door before she responds and start laughing. She's right, someone should hit that, it's just not going to be me. The first time I saw Trey, I thought he was Joss' type. But then again, if it moves, he's her type.

I love living with Joss, but at some point, I need to get my own place. We are opposite in personality, but we make up for it in loyalty. However, if I stay here too much longer, we might kill each other. Someday, I'll tell her what happened last month, and I'll share my sadness over my loss, but that won't be today. I grab a t-shirt and shorts from my dresser and change my clothes. I didn't wear much makeup to Trey's but if I don't take what little I do have off, I'll have that whole raccoon eyed thing happening in the morning.

My phone starts playing a familiar ring tone that I designated for Langley months ago, "In the Meantime" by Spacehog. I haven't talked to her in a couple of days and I know she's swamped with all of her wedding plans. Had they waited until February, like they planned, everything would be fine, but Mom's hospital stay put a rush on the nuptials. My sister will be saying her "I do's" in just over a week, so I talk to her when she has time, and help out as much as I can from here.

"What's up?" I ask, answering the phone.

"You alone?" she asks as though I'm in constant company.

"Always, sis. Thanks for the reminder," I respond in monotone before I laugh.

"Okay, I've been waiting for you to bring this up, but you haven't so I guess I'm going to." Her mothering tone makes me smile.

"Shoot!"

"Last month when mom was in the hospital you were the first one to talk to her, right?"

"Yeah, what's your point?"

"After you left, I was talking to her and she pointed to the trash can next to the bed," she pauses, no doubt waiting for my mind to catch up. "I thought she was telling me to throw something away, but she wrote down, 'look,' and I still didn't know what she was talking about. So-"

"You know," I finish for her, my nose starts to burn and I know the tears aren't far behind.

"Yeah, Em. I know." Her voice is defeated, and I know she's not mad at me for not telling her, she's sad for what I experienced.

"No one knows, besides Mom and Trey," I admit, fighting my emotions.

"Trey knows?" Her shocked tone gives everything away.

"It's not like that. Remember I told you I was on a date? I was out with Trey, and he was really understanding about what I was going through and he was putting himself out there, and I blurted it out. It was more of my way of letting him know why I couldn't give him more."

"What happened? Why didn't you want to tell me?"

"It wasn't that I didn't want to tell you, I didn't even know Mom could hear me. When she asked me about it the next day, I was shocked. I had just found out the day before, and I was scared."

Tears stream down my face and I wonder if they'll ever stop. "I took a test and I knew I was carrying Ryan and my baby. Part of me was so happy, and the bigger part was scared. When I told Trey, it was my way of putting the brakes on any feelings he might have for me. Ryan has been my world for three years."

"No, Em, he's been *part* of your world. You can't make him the center of your life," she reminds me in the way only she can.

"You're right. I know that. I was surprised that he was at the hospital, but at the same time, that's Ryan, even when things are jacked up, he's still where he feels he needs to be, and that day, it was there with me. I knew then that no matter what, I couldn't give my heart to anyone else because Ryan takes up the biggest part of it. When I saw him, he and the baby I was carrying were nestled in the most untouchable place in my heart, and even if Ryan and I were never together again, that piece will always belong to him. But then I saw Scott and all rational thinking went out of my head. I've replayed my actions over and over, and I can't help but wonder if I would have miscarried if I had just listened to you and called the cops instead of going after him like I did."

I hear her sob and it causes my own tears to fall. "You don't know what would have happened, and you can't think like that. It's not your fault."

"You don't know that." My guilt surfaces and I don't fight it. "Maybe I don't deserve to be a mom. I wasn't thinking about my baby when I went after that asshole."

"Stop it!" Her voice is stern and I know she means business. "Don't do that to yourself, you don't know what would have happened. You reacted, and regardless, you were protecting someone. You will be the most amazing mom; I have no doubt. I can't even begin to imagine what you've been going through; I wish you would have told me sooner, but I'm not sure what I could have said to make it better."

"Nothing," I admit. "Nothing is making it better, and I can only hope and pray that someday I'll wake up and it'll hurt a little less."

chapter 28

I told Langley that I would come out a few days before the wedding to help her get ready. Knowing that she knows everything, I don't feel so guarded, and I know that we have reached an even closer point in our relationship. My sister has been, and will always be, one of the most trusted people in my life, but sharing with her the darkest point in my life somehow made it more. We haven't talked about it again, but I know that if I need to, she and Mom are there, waiting for me.

My sister is one of the most unorganized people I know, hence why the wedding date moving up didn't seem to faze her, until two days before the wedding. I need everything in its place, and sometimes I wish I were a little more flexible like Lang. I knew she would start stressing out, so I had a binder, similar to what we use for work, ready to go with everything we needed to do. We ran through a checklist of things like the florist, DJ, minister and caterer, of which only the minister was not accounted for.

"You realize you can't get married without a minister, right? Didn't you line one up?" I ask.

"Of course I did," she snaps at me.

"What happened to him?"

"If I knew that, would I be getting a lecture right now?"

"Okay, give me his name, and I'll make some calls. I need you to go pick up your dress and make sure you try it on this time," I remind her, as she leaves. Last time Lang went in, she took the dress home and waited three days before trying it on. When she did, I was the one to get the frantic phone call that the dress what still too big.

"I'm not an idiot, Em," she says, turning into a true bridezilla. However, she is the only person in this world I would accept such behavior from.

The rest of the day, I was calling all over town, and contacting whatever connections I had to line someone up to marry my sister and Reid. I finally asked Aunt Gertie if she knew anyone and she smiled a wry smile and gave me the name of Reverend Jameson. He is a retired minister, but can still marry couples, and since we were in a jam, he agreed to perform the ceremony.

Coming out a few days early served two purposes: I was able to help Lang out with everything that I knew she didn't take care of, but I also got out of having to fly out with Trey. It's not that it would have been terrible, but there is still the question of whether he and I will get together. I do love Trey, but as a friend. He called today to say his flight is coming in early tomorrow morning, but he's getting a rental car, which gives me time to spend with my mom and Langley before she takes the walk down the aisle.

She didn't want a bachelorette party, she wants to spend time alone with mom and me, and that sounds great. We went to Aunt Gertie's and despite her surly personality, she disappeared for the night so we could be alone. Only Mom, Lang and I know what it's like to be us, and only we know what it's like to be there for each other. Things have turned into shit and have gotten better, only to go back, but in the end, I know these are the two women I can always count on. We share blood, but we share so much more and tomorrow, we open our lives up to a new person, and I know Reid is the perfect addition.

"I know I haven't always done right by you girls, but you have to know how much I love you. You are the two most important people in my life, and I'm so grateful God gave you to me. I will do everything in my power to be what you need, and I'm sorry I lost my way for a while."

"Mom," Lang interjects, "you are our mom and we love you." I nod in agreement as she continues, "It's never been easy being us, but I think we've always been there for each other. I'm so proud of what you've done for yourself, you are so much stronger than you've given yourself credit for."

Mom's eyes well with tears as she reaches her hands to each of our faces, "You girls are my world and if I've ever given you a reason to believe otherwise, I'm so sorry."

We spend the rest of the night recalling happier times and laughing at our more entertaining moments growing up. But mostly, it's being together in a way that we haven't in a long time.

* * *

"C'mon, Em," Langley fusses as she adjusts my dress for the tenth time. "Everything is about to start." She kisses my cheek and rubs the spot where her lips touched to remove any trace of lipstick. "I love you, sis."

"Love you, too." I smile at her, because she is the epitome of beauty today. "You need to stop all this fussing over me. It is *your* day!" I remind her.

Her wedding dress is a cream-colored sleeveless gown that flows from the waist. A beautiful, elaborate lace overlay exposes the small of her back, a small bow, flowing into the spills of the gown. She is wearing a set of pearls that belonged to our grandmother, probably nothing more than costume jewelry, but we never cared enough to find out. All we knew is that they were beautiful. Her hair is pulled into a low bun to the left of her neck and I've never seen Lang look more elegant.

She walks over to me to make a final adjustment to my coral-colored bridesmaid dress. This is not my color, and if it weren't Lang's wedding day, there's no way I'd be wearing this dress. The gown is an off the shoulder dress that is fitted at the top with a navy sash. Under any other circumstances, I would not be caught dead in this dress, but I guess that's how weddings are. I can't help but feel like I'm going to prom, all decked out, but there's no place I'd rather be. I had hoped that she would have picked another color for the dresses, but when Lang makes her mind up, she sticks with it.

She only has two bridesmaids and I begged her to let me wear my hair down. I was so grateful when she agreed, as long as I let her have it styled. When I look in the mirror and see my blonde locks curled and sprayed with so much stuff, I smile for my small victory. At this point, I'd be surprised if my hair moved at all.

"They're ready for you," a friend announces to Lang before shutting the door. She asked Mom to give her away, a gesture we didn't think she'd be capable of two months ago.

She walks over to me and we hug tightly before Mom joins us, "I'm so proud of you girls."

"Thanks, Mom," I say easily. "Are you sure you're up for giving her away?"

"I'll never give you away," she whispers to us as our foreheads are pressed together. "Are you ready for this?" she asks Lang, who smiles like she's won the prize.

Neither of us can say anything and Mom nudges me forward so I can follow Lang's friend. I look back to see the two of them, foreheads together and Mom touching Lang's face. It's a beautiful image that will be burned in my memory forever.

My big sister has always been my biggest champion, and today,

I'm hers. I know, in the brief time that I've been around Reid that he will be by her side and take care of her. I don't think I've ever been as sure of something as I am of that.

I step outside the doors of Aunt Gertie's guest room and collect myself before proceeding down the stairs where the ceremony will take place.

The door opens as I start to relax and Lang is looking at me. "Hey, I forgot to tell you, Ryan's coming today." And then she shuts the door before I can say anything in return. What am I supposed to do with that bit of knowledge?

My eyes are closed and I inhale a deep, steadying breath, calming my growing nerves. The door clicks shut and my eyes open, thankful that I'm alone. I hear the commotion downstairs, but the conversations are muffled. I turn to the small mirror in the hallway to face my reflection and try to push myself to get through this day.

I can't believe this is about to happen. In a few minutes, I will walk down the aisle and watch Langley, who never wanted to get married, become Langley Donovan. My stomach turns in anticipation, excited for my sister and waiting for the cue to make my way down the stairs.

As I walk down the steps, the living room is filled with the few family members we have, but mostly, it's friends that Langley has accumulated over the years. A violin plays the music near the stop where they will exchange vows and I look around and spot both Ryan and Trey, but only one of them makes my heart skip a beat.

A smile is plastered on my face as I take my place near where Lang will stand. Someone, who I can only assume is a friend of Reid, stands as his best man and smiles at one of the guests, who I assume is his date.

Ryan's eyes remain on me, I can feel them steady and affectionate, but I do my best to avoid them, as well as the gaze from Trey. The wedding march begins and I look at the center of the aisle to see Mom, escorting Langley, who can't hide her smile, down the aisle. I think my cheeks will hurt in the morning, because I'm so happy at this moment in time, and I never want to let it go.

Mom hands her over to Reid, and the two face the minister to exchange their vows. I can't stop smiling at the two of them, and I silently curse myself for doubting that my sister found someone who fits her so easily. They begin exchanging vows and I hold the ring that Lang will place on Reid's finger. Both of them barely look anywhere but at each other.

I'm not a jealous person, but I have to admit I'm envious at how easily this comes to the both of them. Then again, I'm not aware of their journey or their struggle, so who am I to judge?

My eyes wander and finally land on Ryan, despite my best efforts to avoid him.

"Do you promise to honor, love and obey, for as long as you both shall live?" the minister asks Lang.

"I do," she answers. But my eyes never leave Ryan.

"Reid, do you take Langley Jennifer Kane, to be your lawfully wedded wife? To love and protect, all the days of your life?" the minister finishes, looking up from his bible.

"I do," Reid responds dutifully.

Langley takes the ring from me and places it on Reid's finger, while he mimics the action. The two can't keep their eyes off each other, their grins replacing any other emotion they're experiencing.

"By the power vested in me by the state of Utah, I pronounce you husband and wife," he pauses and smiles. "You may now kiss the bride."

Applause and cheers fill the room and my hands join in, but all I can see is Ryan, who is beaming with pride for my sister. I swipe a tear away, as I look at Langley, who has never looked more beautiful.

chapter 29

"Ladies and gentlemen, for the first time as husband and wife, Mr. and Mrs. Reid Donovan," the DJ announces as they enter the tent outside. Their guests clap and cheer as they immediately start their first dance, staring into each other's eyes, carrying a conversation only the two of them are aware of.

I can't help but think of the wedding that Ryan and I would have had and wonder if things would have gone as smoothly for us. Regardless of our fate, my sister has found her perfect match, and I smile on with the rest of her guests as she dances in the arms of her husband, my new brother-in-law.

Trey is sitting at a table in the back corner when I finally walk over to greet him. The day has been a whirlwind, but he's there for me, and it's nice to see a familiar face.

"You look beautiful," he says with a smile as he stands up to kiss my cheek.

"Thanks," I answer with a wrinkle of my nose. "Coral isn't my color."

"I didn't know you didn't have a color," he offers as he pulls a chair out for me.

"You're biased," I tease, shoving his shoulder. We sit, side by side, admiring my sister and her new husband while they dance their first dance. Every once in a while, he nudges his arm to mine, but we remain still for the most part.

I don't know what, if anything, I would have done differently if I knew that Ryan would be here. I'm not surprised; he's been so close to my family since I introduced him years ago. It's a little strange seeing him across the room, and every once in a while when our eyes meet, I feel like it's just the two of us.

The reception continues, but I feel sad and out of place. I don't want to bring a damper on the festivities, so I slip out at the first opportunity and make use of one of Aunt Gertie's rooms. It still has floral wallpaper and an antique vanity that most would consider a find, but to me, it's just another piece of my childhood. I sit on the bed to collect my thoughts and have a moment to myself.

"I thought I'd find you in here," Mom declares as she shuts the door. "When you girls were little, this was your favorite room to hide in."

"Really?" I ask, not at all remembering.

"Yep," she nods and points to the closet. "I'd end up finding you in the closet asleep. You would get mad when I'd wake you up and you'd tell me this was your safe place. Nothing bad could get you in there."

I shake my head, unable to recall that memory, but I know in part it has to be true, because I feel that way right now. "Why aren't you out there?"

"I saw you walk off, and I wanted to make sure you're okay," she says, taking a seat on the bed next to me.

"I'm okay. I didn't know Ryan was going to be here, and I haven't really had a chance to talk to him," I admit, staring at my fingers.

"What would you say to him if you had the chance?"

I shrug my shoulders, because I'm not sure what I would say to him. "It's Lang's day. I'll be fine."

Mom wraps her arms around me and holds me like she hasn't done in years. I exhale and close my eyes, letting her do not only what she needs to do, but also what I've needed her to do. "It's okay to let it be about you, too." She kisses the top of my head and walks out of the room, leaving me to figure out what I'm going to do. But one thing is for sure, I need to get back downstairs before my sister starts to worry.

Music fills the tent and I move my hips to the music rhythmically. I stop when I see Ryan and Trey, standing side by side, watching the guests dance, and they seem to be getting along. I don't know whether to approach them or stay back and watch, but when they catch me looking at them, the choice is made for me. I plaster a bright smile on my face and walk to where the two men stand and both return my smile.

"What's up?" I ask, since I have nothing else to offer.

"Not much," Ryan says, nodding to Trey.

"So you two know each other now?"

"Well, we met once before," Trey reminds me. I look over at him and narrow my eyes at his brazen approach to the situation, but shake it off with a grin. I know Trey now, and he's not one to start trouble.

"It's good to see you, Ryan." I confess with a smile. "I thought you said you weren't going to make it."

"Yeah, well, you know Lang, she can be pretty persuasive," he reminds me; guilt has always been her means of motivation. I look over to see my sister look away in a hurry and I realize I'm being set up.

"I think Ryan was going to ask you to dance," Trey says, looking directly into my eyes with a smile. He's pushing me to engage Ryan in some way and it's becoming clear this whole thing is a conspiracy.

"Oh really?" I ask, looking at Ryan, who appears shocked by Trey's revelation, but recovers well.

"Yeah." He furrows his brow when he looks at Trey, who just nods his head in consent. "If you're up for it."

"Sure," I respond, offering my hand as he leads me to the dance floor. I look over my shoulder at Trey who nods his head with a tight smile, pushing me to do what I've needed to do for a while.

A familiar song plays as Ryan pulls me into his arms, but we keep a safe distance, which feels awkward. We move like teenagers being watched under a microscope, mostly because I know that I have at least three people watching every move I make. No matter what's happened between us, I can't fight it; Ryan's arms are my home.

He pulls my body closer to his, my head tucked safely under his chin. This is the one place where I have always known I belonged, until he said I didn't.

His hand grips my waist as we move to the music. I want to stay here forever, but everything has changed, and he has no idea how much. The longer I stay here with him; the innocence of our dance becomes less so, at least for me, because more than anything, I want to tell him everything. My arms are wrapped through his, holding him like it's the last time I ever will, and it rips my heart out. Every time I've been near him, it feels like the last time, and I don't think I can survive another last.

If I turn my face up, just a fraction, my lips will be within touching distance of his. Two months ago, I wouldn't have hesitated to plant a kiss to those lips, and despite the pull telling me to do it, I can't. Even when he drops his face closer to mine, the urge to make a move is hard to ignore. His left hand leaves its home on my waist and trails up to find my hand, and he pulls it to his chest and inhales so deep, it seems that it's a release.

My breathing is becoming rapid as I fight the forces that keep throwing us together. When I pull my head back to look at him, my forehead is near his when he whispers, "Don't."

"What?"

"Don't, Em. Whatever you're thinking right now, just let it go," he whispers as he pulls me close to him again.

"What are you trying to do to me?" I ask of him while we continue to move to the music. "You told me you didn't want to be with me anymore. I need you to let me go."

"I never said that. I've never stopped wanting you," he says before pulling me back to look at me.

"I'm sorry," I whisper, my eyes closed for fear that looking at him right now will destroy anything left of me. I take a deep breath. "I have to go."

"You can finish this song with me, Em." His voice is almost a whisper, as he pleads for me to stay with him.

"I really can't." My voice is desperate as I pull away.

"Open your eyes; look at me," he whispers directly into my ear.

Calming my nerves, I finally open my eyes at look directly into his. *Don't do it*, I tell myself. *Don't kiss him*. This would be the time, under different circumstances, to kiss the lips of the man I have loved so much. I blink back whatever tears were there and search his face for reasons why. Loving him was never the problem.

"Em," he says staring down at me, "I love you; that has *never* stopped."

I pull myself from his arms and walk away, unable to respond for fear of word vomit. I walk toward Trey and shake my head as I reach him to grab my coat. "I need a minute." I look at his concerned face and offer what I'm able. "I'll be back." He gives me a quick hug before I walk to the exit, but I'm stopped again.

Langley is standing near the entrance, "What's wrong? Where are you going?"

"It's too hard, Lang. I'm sorry, I need a few minutes alone." I reach for her hand to reassure her. "I'll be back, I promise."

chapter 30

I'm freezing out here, but I'd rather freeze alone than be warm and staring into Ryan's oblivious eyes. Aunt Gertie's property is huge, and any other night, I'd be scared to be out here alone, but the music and hundreds of people quell that. The property is lined with so many trees, I doubt she's identified all of them, but just beyond the place where lights reach, one of my favorite places in the world waits for me.

When I was a kid, this swing was my escape. Whether I was reading a book or hiding from my sister, the swing waited for me and was exactly what I was looking for. It provided the best view of the mountains in the distance, and the homestead where my mom and aunt grew up. Tonight, it offers a view of the darkness and a sky speckled with stars.

I push on the seat to check its ability to hold me, but the swing is as sturdy as it was when I was kid. I sit down and push my toes into the ground until the swing is at an angle before lifting my feet, setting in motion a rhythmic back and forth. The small jacket I brought with me for the evening isn't enough to keep the bone chilling cold away, but I'm not ready to go back yet.

I hear the rustling of something behind me, and I know I should be scared, but I'm not.

"You shouldn't have come out here," I say, keeping my gaze fixed on the nothing ahead.

"You shouldn't have walked off," Ryan's voice answers behind me. "Mind if I sit?"

I don't answer, instead scooting over to give him room. The swing stops its creaking noise when he sits, but resumes its song as we move our feet back and forth below. I'm a coward and I don't know where to begin, so I keep quiet.

"I asked Trey if you were okay, but he suggested that I find you. Told me that I don't deserve you because I let you go," he says, his voice giving nothing away. "What's that about?"

I scoff and shake my head. "No idea." I'm shocked that Trey would say something like that, but then again, he's full of surprises.

We sit in silence for a few minutes before he speaks again. "Is it me? Should I leave?"

"No," I say, before I can stop myself. "It's me."

"You used to be able to talk to me. But I guess that's before I screwed everything up," he says in defeat.

"Ryan." I close my eyes and realize now is the time. I never planned on telling him, but it's not fair to let him wonder. "I have to tell you something."

He stops moving his feet, causing the swings rhythm to unbalance. "What is it?"

"I'm so sorry," I say, closing my eyes and bracing myself to share my heartache all over again.

"What are you sorry about? You did nothing wrong. I should've never let you go. I just thought that our visits kept getting screwed up and when we saw each other last-"

"Stop," I say abruptly, tears welling in my eyes. "Just stop."

"What's going on?"

I exhale a long breath and prepare myself to say the words I never wanted to share with him. I don't know how he's going to take it, but I need to say something. "I was pregnant."

"What?" he says, his intake of air ragged. "What do you mean?"

"When I surprised you in San Diego, I was waiting in your apartment?" I wait for the pieces to come together before continuing. "I went back home to think, like you wanted, but then we broke up. Several weeks later, I realized I was pregnant, and I took a test to confirm. The night you called to tell me that Mom was in the hospital, I was on a date with Trey, and that night I told him. I knew that, no matter what, I was going to have our baby, I just didn't know how to tell you."

"Em-" he sounds confused, but I don't want him to speak until he hears everything.

"Please, I have to get through this." I wait before finishing the story. "When Scott showed up, I wasn't even thinking, you know that; I reacted. It wasn't until he kicked me in the stomach, I was clutching where he kicked and all of my thoughts were of our baby. Ryan," I choke back a sob, "I'm so sorry, I didn't protect our baby. When you came into the room, I had just found out and I was heartbroken."

He's quiet next to me, and I wonder if he wants to be alone or maybe he hates me.

I stand up to give him space and whisper again, "I'm sorry." I walk away, my head lowered, mourning all over again.

"Wait," he calls after me as he gets to his feet. I stop, feet away from him. "How did you do it?"

"What?" I ask, shocked by his accusatory tone.

He clears his throat before speaking. "I mean, alone? How did you go through all of that alone?"

"I wasn't alone, Ryan. You didn't know what was going on, but you were there with me, holding me and consoling me. Somehow being in your arms made the pain a little more bearable. You were with me, even when you weren't. When I took the test and it was positive, I was shocked and scared; I didn't know how you would take it, but I wanted that baby. It was a piece of us and I wanted it so bad."

"You should have told me," he offers, stepping forward and reaching out for me.

"There's nothing that you could have done. It hurt like hell. That bastard kicked me and bruised me, but it was nothing compared to the pain in my soul when the doctor couldn't find a heartbeat."

"You were pregnant. You had my baby inside you, Em. I had a right to know, even if you thought it would hurt me, I deserved to know."

"Don't you think I know that? But I thought I was doing what was best," I argue, finding myself feeling defensive at his words.

"That's not what I mean." He steps away and grunts, "Shit! None of this is coming out right. I'm just trying to say that I wanted to be there for you. I never wanted to let you go."

"Then why did-"

"Wait, let me finish, okay?"

"Fine," I say, crossing my arms over my chest, staring his silhouette down.

"I didn't want to end things, it just seemed like that was the direction we were heading. I figured if it was meant to be, we'd just find our way back. But as soon as you hung up the phone, I knew I was wrong. I kept calling, hoping you would return just one of my calls, because I needed to make it right. I needed to take it all back. My last hope was when I came to pick up my things. I had no idea you were living with Joss, I was just as surprised as you were. You broke my fuckin' heart when you gave my ring back, but I deserved it, after what I put you through. Joss begged me to wait and talk to you, but I heard what you said to her, and I knew I needed to let you go."

"Then why were you at the hospital?"

"Because it was where I belonged. I wasn't lying when I told Alex that I had family things to take care of." He reaches out his hand to me, waiting for me to give him mine. "You are my family. I needed to be with you, even if you just needed a friend."

My head drops in defeat, because that's what he's been for me. He wraps his arms around me and mine grasp the shirt on his back.

"I'm so sorry that you went through all of that alone. I don't know what I would have said, or how I could have made it better, but at least I would have been with you."

He walks me back to the swing and holds me on his lap as I cry into his neck. It's something that I didn't know I needed- to mourn with Ryan.

I'm not sure how long we've been sitting outside in the cold air, but time doesn't matter. We laugh, arguing about what our kid would have been like, Ryan insisting it would have been a boy who would have his looks and my drive. I insist our son, who I call Bean, would have been a slightly awkward kid that would have grown up to be the best version of both of us.

Somehow this conversation leads to us arguing about names, something we never talked about when we were together. We make fun of each other's choices, because he chooses stuffy family names, while I try to find unique ones.

When our laughter subsides, Ryan leads me to a tree beside the swing and touches it gently before looking at me. "We didn't get to meet our baby, Em, and I'm so sorry. I'm sorry you've gone through this and I wasn't there to help, but I want to be here now. If you'll let me."

He takes a labored breath and exhales before he speaks again, and I hear his voice strain. I reach for his hand to squeeze it because I know this is hard for him. He just found out he lost someone he never knew he had and I can tell he's hurting.

"I know it won't stop hurting right away, but I think we need to be able to say goodbye."

"I don't know how, Ryan," I admit through my tears.

"What if we say this is our baby's tree? This belongs to Bean. There was no baby to hold, no one to bury, but this tree can be the place we go to remember him."

I have no words, speechless by Ryan's proposal.

He continues, "I wish I could have met you little man, but I promise you, I'm going to take care of your mom, and I'll make sure that she knows every day how much I love her."

I look over at him, unsure of what he's trying to say. He kneels down and touches the base of the tree before muttering something else that I can't make out. It's a private moment between him and the baby we lost, so I don't pry. When he stands up, he walks behind me and wraps his arms around my waist giving me strength to say goodbye. I think the hardest part is letting go, something that up to this point, I haven't done.

I turn in his arms and bury my head in his chest, sobbing. "I can't, Ryan."

"I'm right here; you can do it."

I nod in his arms and slowly turn around, wiping my eyes. "Hey baby," I whisper through my tears. "I'm sorry I never got to meet you, but in the short time that I knew about you, I loved you more than I thought possible. I have to let you go now, but you will always-always, be in my heart."

We stand there, holding each other in front of our baby's tree until my tears fade, and when they do, Ryan takes my hand in his and walks me back to join my sister's wedding. As we near the entrance, I tug at his hand, prompting him to stop. He cocks his head to the side, questioning my action, but when I raise my brows, my unspoken concern is acknowledged.

I don't know what's going to happen with Ryan, if anything, but I have to talk to Trey. He's still seated at the table where I left him, and I feel guilty that I've been away so long. When I reach him, he stands up to check if I'm okay, but he sees it.

"He found you?"

"Yeah," I nod, "Why did you send him after me?"

"Because, I knew it's what you wanted." His smile is stoic as he looks down at me. His hand touches my cheek, causing my breathing to stutter and my eyes well with tears. In a short amount of time, he has come to mean more than I would have thought.

"You're kinda perfect, Trey," I say through my teary smile, unsure how no one else has snagged him.

He pulls me close and places an innocent kiss to my lips before hugging me. "Emogen Kane, you're everything I never knew I wanted, but you belong to someone else. But if he screws up, you call me."

He reaches over to retrieve his coat from his seat and kisses my cheek before walking off. I follow his path and watch as he passes Ryan, patting his shoulder and saying something. Ryan smiles at me and nods as Trey disappears.

chapter 31 ~ *Two Months Later*

I haven't heard much from Trey since my sister's wedding, not that I expected to. We've exchanged a few emails, but kept it pretty friendly. We've made plans to have lunch, but something comes up. We try to reschedule, but I'm not sure he really wants to see me. I miss our banter, but I guess this is the way it has to be. I still think that he and Joss would get along really well, but that would be weird. At least *I* think it would be.

When he cancelled today, I roped Joss into going shopping with me. Neither of us enjoys shopping, but we do love being together. You would think that living together, we'd be tired of each other, but our schedules keep us really busy.

"I'm hungry," she whines. "Let's scrap this shopping bullshit and eat."

"Well, when you put it that way, how can I resist?"

She grabs my basket that has a few random items, none of which I need, and pushes it aside. "What are you in the mood for? My treat."

"Whoa," I tease, "what's the occasion."

"I met someone," she beams.

"Italian," I say before she interrupts.

"I don't think so, but I could be wrong." I can tell she's thinking, but I'm not following at all.

"What are you talking about?" I ask, confused by her statement.

"Who knows, maybe he is Italian." She throws her hands up in defeat.

I stop walking and laugh so hard that it hurts my stomach. "Please tell me you're joking. I was talking about food."

She doesn't respond except with cheeks so red, she could give Santa a run for his money. We walk a short way to a tiny sandwich shop where she starts to tell me about the guy she met. Apparently they haven't even met, yet. Joss has no problems meeting guys wherever she goes; her outgoing personality and good looks have always opened doors, but she's never given herself enough credit.

"I signed up for one of those online dating sites," she admits embarrassed.

"Why?"

"I'm tired of the creeps I keep meeting, so I figured if I *want* something different, I need to *do* something different."

"What do you know about this guy?"

"His name is Rhen, he moved to the area about a year ago from Texas. He said he recently got out of a bad relationship and quit the family business. I guess he needed a change."

"So you've at least talked to him?"

"Yeah, we've actually talked on the phone for the last two weeks, but I'm nervous about meeting in person. I mean, what if his picture isn't really him?"

"What if it is?" I counter.

"Then I want to marry him right away and make lots of pretty babies."

I laugh at her answer. "So he's hot, huh?"

"If that picture is really him? Yeah. But why would someone that hot need to be on a dating site? I'm sure he has no problem meeting women in the real world."

I stare at her, waiting for her to find the irony in that statement, but she doesn't get it.

"He wants to meet me this weekend."

"Are you going?"

She looks at me and bites the side of her lip. "Look, I know Ryan is coming in town, and I know y'all need some alone time, but I would love you forever if you guys came with me."

"You want us to double with you?"

"No," she shakes her head, appalled at the suggestion. "I want y'all nearby, in case he's lying or scary. Just to be safe."

"We'll be there, but what if the picture is him? What kind of sign are you going to give me to let me know everything's okay?"

"When I start making out with him on the spot, you can leave," she laughs. "Or maybe I'll just subtly send you a text to scram."

"Sounds like a plan."

"I'll make myself scarce the rest of the weekend so you and Ry can have some alone time."

"You don't have to do that," I assure her with a smile. "I'd do anything for you, you know that."

When we finished lunch, I talked Joss into buying a new outfit for her date with Rhen. She found a cute low-cut purple top that fit her perfectly and she splurged on a pair of brown high heel boots to wear with her dark denim jeans. I don't think I've ever seen her so nervous about a date, and I hope this guy is everything he claims to be. And if he's not, Ryan and I will be right there to whisk her away.

I grab the bag containing the two shirts that I bought and head up the stairs to our apartment. I jump when I see a man sitting on the balcony outside the door, until I realize that it's Ryan.

"What are you doing here?" I ask when he looks up at me with *that* grin.

"Waiting for you," he answers, getting to his feet. When I'm sure he's ready, I leap into his arms, wrapping my legs around his waist. The long distance thing is still tough, but the times we're together make it worth it. I give him my key, kissing him senseless while he unlocks the door. He kicks the door shut behind us and returns my kiss until he sets me on the couch back and pulls away.

"I need to talk to you," he says as he nods to the couch so I follow. He's a little too serious for my liking, but he's here, so that's a good thing.

"It's Wednesday, I wasn't expecting you until Friday. Do I have you all to myself until then?"

"Well," he starts, and I get concerned.

"What's wrong?"

"Don't freak out, okay?"

"Of course I'm going to freak out. You just said *not* to, what the hell is going on?"

"I'm moving back to Denver," he says slow and easy.

"They transferred you back?"

He takes a deep breath and shakes his head. "I quit."

"You what? You're joking, right? You loved your job," I remind him.

"But I love you more."

"Ryan, that's a sweet sentiment, but you *need* a job to live. What are you gonna do?"

"That's why I'm here. I had a second interview today with another firm. Better pay, and I get to be here with you. I just figured it's time I put you first."

"Had?" I repeat. "So what does that mean?"

"I got the job," he says with a smile.

I let out a scream and climb onto his lap to kiss him, but I slap his arm instead. "You lead with that you ass!"

He laughs and cups my face in his hands. "Where's the fun in that?"

"You know, Ryan," I say as I get up from his lap and look right at him. "Payback's a bitch."

"But you love me anyway," he shouts over his shoulder when I pass by. "Hey, I have my stuff outside in my car, can you help me bring some of it in?"

"You don't think you're moving in here do you?"

"Just for tonight," he says.

It takes us three trips to get everything out of his Jeep, but he said the rest would be coming in a week. He's already lined up a new place to live, so he'll stay with me, for more than the one night he claimed. *I can't believe he's back.*

"Hey, we have to chaperone Joss' blind date Friday night," I shout to him from my bedroom. He's in the kitchen calling an order for takeout when she comes in with her bags from shopping.

"Ordering pizza, pepperoni alright?" he asks her as she passes.

"Perfect," she answers, distracted with her bags.

"Who's the lucky guy?"

"Sweet," she yells from her room. "So you already know."

"Know what?" he asks, confused by the lack of information.

"Oh hell, Em. You didn't tell him everything?" She stops in the middle of the room and sees the boxes of Ryan's crap. "What are you doing here? It's not Friday."

"Nope. Wednesday," he offers. "And before you ask, no, I'm not moving in, but I am moving back."

I walk out of my room and she looks over at me and smiles. "Welcome home, Ry! It's about damn time."

"Thanks." He smiles at her. "So what's the deal with this guy?"

I roll my eyes and laugh going back to my room so she can give him the details of her latest catch.

*　*　*

"Ryan," I whine, "I thought we got everything out last night."

"I had a few things at Dean's place, and since Cam's moving in with him, he needed me to get it out. Besides, you've been asleep all morning."

"You have to admit, you're exhausted, too." I don't think either of us went to sleep until after two when we heard Joss come in. Rhen was everything Joss hoped he was, and she shooed us away the first chance she got. I was still worried and waited up until I knew she got in safely, so sleeping until nine doesn't feel like *all morning* to me.

"C'mon, the sooner we do this, the sooner you can get back into bed."

I drag myself out from between the sheets and put my slippers on and grab a coat before following him outside. His Jeep is parked to the side of the building, and I silently curse him for leaving it as far away as possible. I don't know how much he had at Dean's but if it's anything like what he arrived with yesterday, there won't be much room left in the apartment.

"I left the passenger side unlocked, so we can grab stuff from both sides," he says, as he walks to the driver's side.

I get to the door and open it, and a folded piece of paper falls out and lands near my feet. I look at Ryan, but he doesn't see it, so I bend down to pick it up and open it up.

My heart skips a beat, and my body flutters in a strange way when I read the words.

> I'm the guy in the Jeep, standing behind you and I think you're the most beautiful woman I've ever seen. I don't think I can live without you.
>
> Marry me?

When I turn around, Ryan is down on one knee, holding my ring in his hand with a heartbreaking smile on his face. The last time he proposed, it was flashy and over the top, and as much as I loved it, it wasn't us.

This is us.

He pulls out his wallet and hands me a tiny piece of paper that's worn and folded. I'm careful when I open it, so as not to tear it, and in my hands is the note that started it all, the one I left on his Jeep years ago. I had no idea he even kept it, but the evidence is in my hands.

"You've had this all this time?" I ask, as a single tear rolls down my cheek.

"No one had ever done anything like that to me before, I thought it was pretty damn cool. I hoped you'd call, and when you didn't, I thought it was a fluke. But that night that you came up to me, all cocky and sexy, I knew I wanted to get to know you better. You're the best thing that ever happened to me, and I'll spend the rest of my life proving it."

"I love you so much," I say to him, handing back the note from his wallet.

"So is that a yes?"

I shake my head no, and his smile fades. He slowly drops his hand, reeling from my action and runs his hand through his hair.

"It's a hell yes!" I finally answer when I feel he's suffered enough.

"You could have just said that," he says, his smiling returning as he stands up and kisses me.

But I remind him between kisses, "Payback's a bitch."

THE END

epilogue

"When I tell you, I want you to push," the doctor instructs. We nod in unison, squeezing each other's hands.

"You can do it, baby," Mom encourages with excitement.

"Ok, Langley, push," he says.

Reid stays near her face, stroking her hair and kissing her cheeks. He doesn't know what to do, because she gripes if he does nothing, and gripes if he does it wrong. Poor guy can't tell whether he's coming or going, and I have to admit, it's entertaining.

"I love you," he says as she pushes. "I'm so proud of you."

"Shut up," she grunts through the contraction and I can't help the laugh that bursts out. "You, too." She glares at me. Reid and I exchange teasing glances, but we both fear the wrath of Lang if she catches us.

"You're doing great Langley. One more big push and your baby will be here. You ready?" the doctor asks, giving her motivation.

She's been at it for a while and she's exhausted, but if anyone can do it, my sister can. She made us swear not to let them pull the mirror out because she doesn't want to see her *business*, as she called it. All she wants is to hold her baby when she comes out. In a few minutes, my beautiful niece will make her entrance, and I can't wait to meet her.

"When you're ready Langley, I want you to give me one more big push, okay?"

Lang nods and prepares for it, grunting and pushing until she exhales, moaning in exhaustion. We're so consumed with encouraging her we didn't notice baby Theron made her grand entrance until we hear her sweet, deafening wail. We all look to see a goo-covered little angel screaming, her jaw chattering as they walk her to a table to clean her up.

"Is she okay?" Langley asks of no one in particular, but I walk over to look at her flailing arms and legs.

I look over at my sister and smile so big, my cheeks hurt. "Ten fingers and ten toes. She's perfect!"

Lang's head falls back and she starts crying while Reid and Mom fuss over her. I sneak out of the room, unnoticed, to find Ryan sitting in the waiting room. When he sees me, he gets to his feet and hugs me.

"You're an uncle," I say kissing him in excitement. "She's beautiful, Ryan. You have to see her."

"How's your sister?"

"She's great," I say as I flop into a seat and slump down, exhausted.

"Wanna take a walk?"

"Not really," I huff out with a laugh.

"C'mon," he says, pulling me up. "I've been sitting for hours now, I need to move."

As we walk, I tell him about Lang's delivery and how she kept snapping at Reid. Ryan's shocked that she didn't hit one of us, because it's in her nature to be demanding when she's uncomfortable. We end up in front of the nursery, the same place I stood a year ago when I lost our baby. Only this time, it doesn't hurt. We stand side by side looking at all of the sweet faces in front of us.

"You laugh at your sister, but I think you might actually be worse," he reminds me as he wraps his arm around me.

"No way," I argue. "She was pretty awful."

"How 'bout this, when the time comes, I'll just let your mom and your sister take care of you in there?" He nods back in the direction of the delivery room.

"Hell no. I fully expect you to be present and accounted for, whispering how awesome and beautiful I am."

"Anything else I should know?"

"Yeah." I face him and smile. "You have about seven months to get ready."

I turn away to go back and check on my sister, leaving Ryan frozen in place with his jaw wide open.

Totally worth the wait.

acknowledgments

There are so many people I want to thank for helping to make this a reality. First, a huge thanks to the bloggers and readers who have read *Being There* and *Mine to Lose* - without you, I'd have no one to share my stories with. Also, to the amazing writers who have bled before me and paved the way for others - thank you for showing a humble and kind spirit that sets an example for us to follow. Madeline Sheehan, Syreeta Jennings, Emmy Montes and Claribel Contreras - you ladies kept it classy and created a place where so many could learn and grow.

To the *Best Peeps Eva*, thank you for checking in and helping to keep me on track. Kim Greny, Toria Walker, David Broom, Donna Broom, Autumn Red, Erin Spencer of *Southern Belle Book Blog*, Lisa Karafa of *Reading My Way to Penned Con* and Jenn Beach of *Back Off My Books* - your suggestions, questions, edits and everything in between were exactly what I needed. I am beyond grateful to every single one of you.

Amy Queau, Claire Riley, Stacey Lynn - you three are rockstars. I *just* have to say thank you for your critiques and notes. I'm sorry I'm such a *bitch*, but it still makes me smile. Brittainy C. Cherry - you have an infectious enthusiasm for everything you do and I love it. Kelsie Leverich and A. Meredith Walters - the two of you make me fan-girl, but I also learn so much. Thank you for sharing with the class. I am so blessed to have all these amazing women because they are *Bad-Ass*.

To my *SIPs*, I love you and every acronym so much. Lisa - you started a dialog with me and it has grown into a friendship I value more than I can express. Jenn - I laugh everyday, because intentional or not, you do that to me and I love you for it. My wifey, Kim Stedronsky - we have Elvis, Viv and Top Gun. You are my Kimotherapy and I'm pretty sure you are the writing soul mate I didn't know existed.

Kari Gardner, the bestest bestie that ever bestied, I love you so much and I'm glad you came into my life all those years ago. (FYI, there are no squirrels in these parts.) To Naomi Ashwood - thank you for pushing me to do what I've always wanted. Had you not put a book in my hand two years ago, I might have just kept dreaming. And to the fellas at The Herb Café (Slim & Walt) - you made me blush, even when no one could see it. *(Gotta love the Rap-Special-Wednesday.)* To my editor, Jenny Sims, you can be my person. And to Rachel Wilson, what can I say, it was a happy day when I finally got to meet you!

To my family, the *T-10*, I love you all! Dea - I look forward to our dates, and FYI, you are my Lang. I have the most amazing and supportive parents, ever. I am blessed. Thank you, both, for reading my books and telling me what you think. Your opinion means the world to me.

To my precious angels, my daughters, you are *my dream* and I love you both so much. You are the reasons I was put on this earth and I'm happy God gave me the girls I always wanted.

And last, but never least, my husband Spence I love you more than words. You get me, quirks and all and I love growing old with you. I am the luckiest girl in the world. By the way, you are Ryan, Drew and all the others, rolled into one. I don't need a book boyfriend because I have you.

about the author

T.K. Rapp is a Texas girl born and raised. She earned a B.A. in Journalism from Texas A&M and it was there that she met the love of her life. He had a contract with the U.S. Navy that would take them across both coasts, and ultimately land them back home in Texas.

Upon finally settling in Texas, T.K. worked as a graphic designer and photographer for the family business that her mom started years earlier. She was able to infuse her creativity and passion, into something she enjoyed, but something was still missing. There was a voice in the back of her head that told her to write, so write, she did. And, somewhere on an external hard drive, are several stories she started and never finished.

Now at home, raising her two daughters, T.K. has more time to do the things she loves, which includes photography and writing. When she's not doing one of those, she can be found with her family, which keeps her busy. She enjoys watching her kids in their various sporting activities (i.e. doing the soccer mom thing), having Sunday breakfast at her parent's house, singing out loud and out of key or dancing like a fool. She loves raunchy humor, gossip blogs and a good book.

Made in United States
Orlando, FL
22 December 2023